“Dean Budnick really and truly lis
only to the band but also to the a
alogues/internal monologues of a
recognizable, so true: the languag
school rituals, the obsessions with and from being high. It all adds up to a brilliantly articulated, beautifully delineated portrait. Read *Might As Well* and you’ll have been there.”

—Dennis McNally, Grateful Dead publicist and author of *A Long Strange Trip*

“If anyone is qualified to teleport back in time to bring a reader to a Grateful Dead show in the eighties, it’s Dean Budnick. Dean grew up going to those shows and has been a fixture in the music scene that the Dead birthed for the past thirty years. Dean has the creativity and experience to capture the scene the way it actually was, the way it looked, the way it sounded.”

—Peter Shapiro, producer, Fare Thee Well Celebrating 50 Years of the Grateful Dead, owner, Brooklyn Bowl franchise, The Capitol Theatre

“I want to say this was a long, strange book but it's such a fun, quick read it doesn't feel long at all. But it is strange. Good strange.”

—Donick Cary, writer/producer, *The Simpsons*, *Parks and Recreation*, and *Silicon Valley*

“With an adventurous mind and a keen ear, Budnick has established himself as a top chronicler of improvisatory rock and jam bands.”

—Derek Trucks, Tedeschi Trucks Band

“A superb literary evocation of a seminal band and scene. Budnick brings a scholar’s insight and an artist’s touch to this colorful, compelling, and largely misunderstood wellspring of American culture.”

—Nicholas Meriwether, founding Grateful Dead Archivist, UC Santa Cruz, and series editor, Studies in the Grateful Dead, University of California Press

MIGHT AS WELL

DEAN BUD-NICK

MIGHT

WEL

DEAN

AS

L

BUDNICK

A RARE BIRD BOOK
LOS ANGELES, CALIF.

This is a Genuine Rare Bird Book

A Rare Bird Book | Rare Bird Books
453 South Spring Street, Suite 302
Los Angeles, CA 90013
rarebirdbooks.com

FIRST TRADE PAPERBACK ORIGINAL EDITION

Set in Minion
Printed in the United States

10 9 8 7 6 5 4 3 2 1

Design by Robert Schlofferman

Publisher's Cataloging-in-Publication data

Names: Budnick, Dean.

Title: Might as well / by Dean Budnick.

Description: A Rare Bird Book| First Trade Paperback Original Edition | Los Angeles [California], New York [New York] : Rare Bird Books, 2016.

Identifiers: ISBN 978-1-942600-76-3

Subjects: LCSH Grateful Dead (Musical group)—Fiction. | Deadheads (Music fans)—Fiction. | Concerts—Fiction. | Rock music—Fiction. | Murder—Fiction. | BISAC FICTION / General.

Classification: LCC PS3602.U336 M54 2016 | DDC 813.6—dc23

ZEB

I NEED A MIRACLE

That's what my sign says. And it's true because I'm

JONESING FOR JERRY.

That's what my sign said yesterday. And if I don't get in tonight then tomorrow I'll ask everyone to

PHIL MY HART WITH JOY.

Phil's the bassist. Crazy, crazy bassist. He plays the thing like he's playing lead. He stands by himself in the corner and sounds the thunder like he's the mighty Thor himself. The mighty Thor with glasses and a demon grin. Right on!

Hart's one of the drummers. Mickey Hart. They have two. Mickey and Billy. But names don't matter, what matters is the DRUMZ. And when those Rhythm Devils get going in their part of the show better warn your bones because they're gonna be shaking.

"Kind beers. Get your kind beers here. Ice cold domestics a buck, imports for two. Kind Bud-weiser, kind Beck's. Come on over and treat yourselves with kindness. Domestics a buck, imports a deuce… That's four dollars. Thank you very much, have a good show."

Gotta do this. Stand in front of the cooler holding my sign and throwing my pitch. It's crazy but it's the only way to stay on tour. When you never have the bread to mail order, this is the way to do it, day by day. Take 'em one at a time. And today

I NEED A MIRACLE.

BAGEL BOB

"Who's got your bagel? Who's got your bagel? Bob does, Bagel Bob. Who will accompany it with cream cheese? Who will accompany it with cream cheese? Bob will, Bagel Bob. Who needs a ticket? Who's looking for ONE? Bob is, Bagel Bob… Get your bagels, blueberry bagels, Stella Blueberry bagels right here from Bagel Bob. Sell your tickets, sell them here, sell them now, sell them to Bagel Bob."

Business is slow. Bagel Bob is tired. Still a couple hours until the show. Hopefully Bob will have a ticket by then. It—

(Captain Carbs!)

(Bagel Bob!)

"Kristen and Bradley, most fervid greetings to you. Bob hasn't seen you since Greensboro."

(We've been around. Touring. On tour. That second night Philly, hot! Ouch! When they pulled that 'Attics of My Life' I wigged. It was ki-ind. And the 'To Lay Me Down,' I called that didn't I Brad?)

(She called it Bob. Did you get in that night?)

"No, Bagel Bob spent that night in the parking lot enjoying macrobiotic falafels and chemically enhanced watermelon with Tennessee Jed the Pasta Head."

(Is he the tall guy who wraps his beard around his neck?)

"That is Jed."

(I like him. That beard reminds me of a barber pole. The way it circles around.)

(Or a candy cane.)

(And of course the next night, the 'Dark Star' night. Did you get in then?)

"No, alas. Bob shared that evening with the Crystal Wizard and his canasta fetish."

(Brad got in but I didn't. I couldn't believe it, a Tuesday night and I couldn't get a ticket. That's the only show I've missed. I've seen six of the seven. Brad almost saw them all but he had a counterfeit Friday night Greensboro. Anyhow, I can't believe that the one show I missed is the 'Dark Star' show.)

"Bagel Bob understands. Indeed Bagel Bob harbors a suspicion that he will never see another 'Dark Star.'"

(Oh, don't say that.)

"Bob has seen his share. If it is fated then Bagel Bob is satisfied."

(No, Bob, never be satisfied. Satisfied equals complacent. Never be complacent. They want you to be complacent but don't be.)

"At present time you need not fear such a mental state on the part of Bob."

(Right on!)

(Yeah! Right on, Bob!)

"Bob is not convinced that this revelation merits laudation."

(So you gots?)

"Bob does not."

(Neither do we yet but we're looking. Our friend Cosmic Charlie must have some good karma going for him, he made a ground score a few minutes ago. Floor seat too. But we're not giving up, we figure something'll happen.)

(Yeah, something will definitely happen. Hugs for the road, Bob?)

"Have a good show you two."

(Right back at you, Robert.)

Bagel Bob enjoys the company of Kristen and Brad. They remind Bob of the company he shared in days long past. Now, alas, the wheel has turned. Too many people without the right spirit. Bagel Bob accepts them but he worries about them, he worries for them.

Bagel Bob worries.

STEVEN

This is the day. A red letter day. A Grateful red letter day. My first show. I knew it would happen. I knew it would be here. I knew *I* would be here, even if here is still an hour away from here.

But hey, I'm cool about it. At least that's what everyone else must think. *If* they can think. They're all stoned. We're all stoned. So no one's all that interested in checking out my head.

And that head of mine is pumped and ready. I've practically lived with these guys for three years now… Wait, by these guys do I mean these guys the Grateful Dead or these guys in the car?… No, I mean the Dead. Well, it doesn't matter. Both. Willington Prep has the greatest Head per student ratio of any school on the East Coast and that's saying a lot.

I've been listening to the Dead ever since my freshman year. But I never made it to a show. I had to work my way into it. Nobody offered me a ticket back then. I was just starting to get into the scene—no actually I was starting to listen to the music, which is not the same as being into the scene. Besides, even if someone had a ticket it always went to a junior or a senior. Who wants to waste a ticket on a freshman? Anyhow, I probably wasn't ready for it back then. I mean I knew some of the music, the studio stuff, but I didn't appreciate the real stuff, the live stuff yet.

I was offered a ticket to one of the spring shows at the Civic Center last year but I couldn't handle it. It came too late and there was no way I could get out of school on that kind of notice. Okay, I didn't think I could, I probably could have. I could have made up an excuse or had someone call in and say they were my aunt or something but I don't know, maybe I didn't have the nerve to do it… Wait, by nerve to do it, do I mean the nerve to get out of school or the nerve to go to a show? I don't remember. Shit, I must be stoned…

Wait, what was I thinking about? Oh yeah, yeah…wait, no… Oh, yeah, yeah, nerve. No, back then I didn't have the nerve. The nerve to try to do it *and* the nerve to go to a show.

But that's behind me now. I am a certified Head. On spring tour with a carload of Willington spring Tourheads.

"This is gonna be cool, you guys."

Aaah, they're all baked. Nate got that primo herb from his brother at Swathmore and zowie! Bake down city!

And it can only get better. It's so cool that spring tour is the same time as our break this year. So there are six or seven Willington carloads somewhere on this highway grooving towards the arena. Six or seven cars of Willington kids, most of them high on Nate's herb getting psyched for the show.

There's this energy, I can feel it. We're probably an hour away but I can already hear the call and sense the music.

My first show.

They say that going to your first show is a lot like having sex for the first time. The thing is, who knows, maybe it's better. And besides, this tour could have some action on that other front too. Crashing at Emily's beach house after the show is gonna be out of hand. Shannon, Meg, Beth, Debbie and Steph, they're all gonna be there.

And who knows what'll happen. That's the thing about the Dead, you never can tell.

ROBIN

"Here tickie, tickie, tickie. Here tickie, tickie, tickie."

(Who's got my ticket? Who's got my ticket?)

"Tickie-tickie. Tickie-tickie."

(Who's got my ticket? Who's got my ticket to the show?)

"Here tickie, tickie, tickie. Here tickie, tickie, tickie."

(Someone's got it, someone's got it.)

"Here tickie. Here tickie, tickie, tickie."

(Someone's got my ticket to the show.)

"Here tickie, tickie, tickie. Here tickie, tickie, tickie."

(Who is unintentionally separating me from my ticket? Who is responsible for this tragedy? Please reunite us. Please sell me my ticket.)

"Tickie-tickie, tickie-tickie."

(We're star-crossed, my ticket and me. We're destined to be together. So please help us find each other.)

"Here tickie-tickie. Here tickie tickie tickie."

(Please reunite me with my ticket. Let us harmonically converge outside the show so that I can harmonically converge with Bobby and Jerry inside.)

"Tickie-tickie. Harmonically converge?"

(I don't know, it just came out. Come on, who's got my ticket, who's got my ticket?)

"Here tickie. Here tickie, tickie, tickie, tickie, tickie."

TAPER TED

(Okay, here's one for you. Second sets that opened with 'Morning Dew.' Gimme three.)

"Beauty question, beauty question. Although it's easier than you think. They've opened the second set with a 'Dew' about ten times or so."

(That's what it looks like here, I'm only asking for three. Get this right and once again you can prove to me that you're a freak.)

"I'm telling you, it's easy."

(Rez, tell him to do it.)

(Do it, dear.)

"Okay, okay. Right off the bat, Pembroke Pines, Florida… October twenty-fifth, nineteen-eighty-five… I taped that show. Hey Rez, what was the name of that place?"

(Wait, hold on, what's this teamwork thing? Because you're married you get to cheat? No way. If you're married you shouldn't cheat. Sacred vow and all. Okay, I'll let you cheat. But big bro, if you're gonna cheat don't do it with your wife.)

(The Sportatorium.)

"Right, the Sportatorium."

(Sportatorium? Now that is one of the truly dumb names in all of arenadom. I mean why'd they name it that? No, no, wait, it's flashing to me. After deep contemplation, I now strongly suspect they named it that because people play sports there. But then maybe the Grateful Dead shouldn't have—)

"And they opened the second set of a Greek show that same year with a 'Dew.'"

(They played in Greece? No wait, they sang in Greek? Wait, no, no, I guess that's appropriate. Isn't that a dead language? Ho-ho a Dead language, get it?)

"Got it. Thinking about dumping it."

(Hey, they can't all be gems, big bro.)

"The Greek Theatre. UCal Berkeley. June fifteenth, eighty-five."

(Right, right. Six-fifteen-eighty-five in your geeky, alpha-numeric Dead jargon… Unfortunately, Don Pardo must thank you for playing our game. However, you will take home a year's supply of Rice-A-Roni.)

(The San Francisco treat.)

(Fitting, no? You see unless I'm reading this wrong and let's be honest, I care so little about all of this that it could be the case, they opened their second set with 'Morning Dew' on the *fourteenth*. On the fifteenth they began the second set with 'China Cat' and then, no, wait, this is a serious question. Turn around and check this out. No, not you, Rez, you're driving. What does this sideways arrow symbol mean?)

"It means they played into the next song without taking a break. So they played 'China Cat Sunflower' into 'I Know You Rider' into 'Lost Sailor' into 'Saint of Circumstance' into 'Terrapin' and so on."

(Where'd you get this book anyhow?)

"I sent away for it. DeadBase, it's your standard Deadhead tool of the trade."

(Yeah well then I've got your tool in my hand, which seems more than a little inappropriate but—)

"So anyhow a third…"

(And you know what they say, a tool in the hand is worth two—)

"April twenty-ninth, nineteen-seventy-one. The last Fillmore East show. I just listened to that a couple nights ago. There you go, three."

(Not bad, although you only got one perfectly. So this book has all the songs the Dead ever played?)

"It has most of the setlists. The Base is a little shaky on the sixties stuff but after nineteen-sixty-nine it's pretty much complete."

(And who wasted their time doing this—I mean who compiled this fine tome?)

"Some guys in Hanover. I think they're connected with Dartmouth."

(Well I hope they're connected to something because they're not tethered to reality so well. And what's this in the back?)

"JerryBase. It's the same thing for the Jerry Garcia Band."

(And how about this?)

"That's where people voted for their favorite versions of certain songs. Here, give me the Base. Like here, see the best 'Morning Dew' according to these people was May eighth, nineteen-seventy-seven. The quintessence of 'Dew,' huh, Rez?"

(Tommy, your brother is trying to bait me. He knows I'm partial to October 18, 1974. But as they say, rational Heads can disagree…)

(And just what part of this is rational?)

STELLA BLUE

"Mommy, when are we going to get there?"

(When would you like us to get there?)

"Now."

(Why? Don't you like our company? You're hurting Aunt Jenny's feelings.)

(Alison!)

"Mommeeee!"

(Okay darling, soon.)

"How soon Mommy? I want to be there."

(You are there. Wherever you go, there you are.)

"Mommeeee!"

(Stella, honey, why don't you lie down, take a little rest, and by the time you wake up we'll be there.)

"Mommy, I don't want to lie down."

(Aunt Jenny will sing to you.)

"Well..."

(Your mother's right, honey. We'll be there soon. Lie down... that's it...now close your eyes.)

(Not just one, close them both... Fine. Now Jennifer, oh dearest and most ancient friend of mine. Habitual fellow traveler. Regale my daughter and myself with song.)

(Stella, tell your mom that twenty-five's not ancient.)

"Mommy, twenty-five's not—"

(I'm sorry honey, I was just kidding. How about 'Cassidy,' do you remember that one?)

"Uh-huh."

(Okay then, here we go, honey. lie back down. Okay now close your eyes. Close 'em. Okay, here we go...)

Pretty.

RANDY

"No freaking way."

(Sorry, Macho Man.)

"No freaking way."

(That's the best I can do for you, Macho.)

"Man, is that necessary?"

(The vehicle won't run without a clutch, Macho. You'll need a new one.)

"It's not my car but that Macho crap, consider my balls already busted by the broken-ass Chevette I can barely fit into that your guy towed here, which already cost me fifty bucks."

(I thought you said your name was Randy.)

"Yeah?"

(Well I figured you for a hero. You're big enough to be a hero. Macho Man Randy Savage all the way.)

"I don't know anything about that."

(You don't know if you're a hero? Who are you, King Kong Bundy?)

"I'm just a kid who's late for work. My coach pulled a few strings and if I don't make it on time, he's going to be pissed. I'll be cut during spring practice and never play next season."

(Where do you play?)

"Morristown Tech."

(So are you a hero or a villain?)

"Are *you* a hero or a villain?"

(It's impolite to answer a question with a question but I am clearly a hero. Not to brag but we're talking superhero. You see this Citgo logo on my shirt? I've got pyramid power. What do you got?)

"A dick friend who let me borrow his car."

(Well be a hero, Macho Man. Pony up the $500 for him.)

"I'm not ponying jack."

(I'm Sal, not Jack. Where are you headed anyhow?)

"I'm working in the lot over at the Grateful Dead show tonight."

(Security?)

"Yeah."

(Then you *are* the villain.)

"Nah, I'm just there to do whatever I'm told for a few days."

(Like keeping nitrous tanks out of the parking lot?)

"If that's what they ask me to do."

(Like I said, you *are* the villain. You know what my attitude is towards nitrous oxide? I follow Nancy Reagan's campaign leadership and I just say NO. Get it, I just say N-O.)

"I get it but NO is actually the chemical formula for nitric oxide. I believe you're thinking of N_20 which is the formula for nitrous oxide, laughing gas."

(Really?)

"Not up for debate. It's an oxide of nitrogen."

(No, do you really need to be such a prick? I was making a joke.)

"What do you want from me, I'm a chemistry major."

(Ahhh, a six foot two inch science nerd.)

"Six three. So you think nitrous tanks are heroic?"

(What can I tell you, I like to laugh. I once saw Nancy Reagan on an episode of *Different Strokes*, although that didn't make me laugh.)

"And what's all this with the heroes and villains?"

(Don't you watch the WWF? Everybody's a hero or a villain.)

"Nah. I'm just a kid on scholarship hoping to make his coach happy and earn a little scratch to take his girl out next weekend. I'm supposed to be there at five and the goddamn clock is ticking."

(I'll tell you want, if you promise to act like a hero, I'll give you a ride over there on my bike. I'm headed out in thirty minutes.)

"I don't have the five hundred dollars."

(Well make sure your buddy has it in the morning. And don't Iron Sheik me over there if you see me enjoying a balloon or having a puff.)

"Now why would I do that?"

ZEB

"Nice cold tasty imports two bucks, domestics a buck. That's right I've got kind Bud-weisers and kind Beck's."

And by the way:

I NEED A MIRACLE

But hey who doesn't? Friday night. All of New York is out here trying to score a ticket. Not an easy night. Uneasy. Very uneasy.

"Nice cold tasty imports two bucks, domestics a single. And speaking of singles please sell me your extra ticket. Someone please sell me an extra."

Gotta say that. SELL me your ticket. Especially when you're holding a miracle sign. Otherwise you scare 'em off. Some Heads think a miracle ticket is a free ticket—and don't get me wrong, a free ticket is always a miracle. But to me it's miracle enough just to get in and see the Boys. Even if I have to pay thirty bucks that's still a miracle to me. But that's where I draw the line. Nothing more than thirty. I'm willing to cover gas costs or whatever but anything more than thirty is not a miracle, it's a crock of shit.

It's crazy what I've seen people pay for a ticket. Second night Greensboro some Head bought a ticket off a guy for eighty bucks. And the dude who sold it didn't look so right on. He was standing there rolling a wooden egg back and forth in his hands. He might have been dosed or something but it was too obvious, like the dude was trying to pull something over on someone and he was using this freaked out look as a cover. So the Head forked over eighty bucks. And if it turned out to be counterfeit…

Shit, Friday night Landover I bought a countie. Highly unkind. Twenty bucks for the bunk. The guy seemed cool enough. He had longish hair, knew his shit. Wasn't wearing a dye. Nowadays that's a good sign. With all the undercover cops and posers, one clue not to trust someone is that they're wearing a dye. Crazy but true. People who want to pretend they're part of the scene figure they can put on a dye and they'll blend right in, which is sort of nuts if you really think about it. Narcs are pulling that crap too.

Or that Guatemalan stuff. People who want to show everyone that they're better than the Heads in the dyes wear those Guatemalan hoodies and caps. It's pretty much people who go to a few shows, like a run at a city or two who come in wearing this stuff thinking that they are THE HEADS. And they get all uptight about it. Like they're the perfect Heads because they've got the kindest Dead threads.

One thing I learned real quickly—during my first tour way back in the spring of '88—was that some of the biggest Heads, the ones who have been to the most shows, don't look like it. The short hair Heads. A lot of these dudes have been to 250 or 300 shows and they come to the arena wearing whatever they were wearing that day. They don't think about their clothes because the music is their Guatemalan hoodie.

At least that's how I see it.

My version differs from reality only in the details.

STEVEN

(Hey, Steven change the tape.)

"Hmmmm?"

(Change the tape.)

"Right, sorry. I was zoning."

(Well try not to zone so much when you're driving.)

"Nate man, I'm not driving."

(Yeah, right. Okay, you can zone then but not until after you change the tape.)

(And put it in the case or my brother will kill me.)

"Okay, okay. So what do you want to hear?"

(You're up there, whatever looks good to you.)

"Hey, Jason, what's this show like? It looks pretty cool."

(Come on, Steven, you know you can't tell a tape from the setlist.)

Oh yeah, right.

(No, that's not necessarily true. Have you ever heard a bad 'Dark Star?')

"Yeah, have you?"

(Well okay, you may be right there. But you can't tell with the other stuff. Besides, some of the 'Stars' are better than others.)

"But they're all basically good."

(None of them are basic, all of them are good.)

(And how is that show Steven has in his hand?)

(Hot.)

(Well then what are you yapping about?)

(I'm just keeping him on his toes.)

"Well I'm sitting down in here so it won't do me much good."

(Maybe I should direct my own foot to your ass and apply some force.)

(If that's what gets you off…)

"Yeah, Jason, just ask. I can be permissive."

(Nice vocab. But you know what I don't understand?)

"Fractions?"

(How to properly apply deodorant?)

"The particulars of the baby-making process?"

(What chicken tastes like?)

"*New Yorker* cartoons?"

(*New Yorker* cartoons, really? What is this, AP after-school strivers club?)

(Hey, man, let Steven be Steven.)

(Well that's my point. I'm happy to let Steven be Steven as long as you can do the same, Nate. Stevie's a big boy, you don't have to chime in for him.)

(I'm a lover, not a chimer. We're in this together. You're either on the bus or you're off the bus and all of here are on the bus.)

(Huh? What bus? This is a Volvo 240.)

(Never mind, Zack, just drive.)

TAPER TED

(All right, here we go. Into the parking lot. Now the real freak show begins. You're not going to buy a T-shirt out here, are you, big bro?)

"I don't think so. Why?"

(I remember a couple of years ago when all you wore were those bootleg Dead T-shirts. You were buying all your clothes in parking lots. My vicarious embarrassment induced a mild case of aphasia.)

"Well you'll be happy to know those shirts don't interest me much these days. Back then it meant something. Those shirts were made by kids trying to support their tours. Nowadays there are plenty of tie-dye corporations out here getting rich."

(If you say so.)

"Consider it said."

(And what do they call they call the area with the makeshift little flea market where everyone rolls out their ratty little tapestries and sells kind veggie burritos laced with bacteria and other pathogens? It's named after a song right? Shitstorm Street? Shitshow Street? I'm pretty sure the word shit is in there to reference the dysentery to follow.)

"Shakedown Street. How many shows have you been to?"

(I don't know. Nine? Ten? You should know. You were the one who took me to all of them. Come on, you can remember how many times the Dead played 'Hully Gully' but you can't recall how many times you've taken your only brother to see this band?)

"Well they only pulled the 'Hully Gully' once. Netherlands '81. Killer show. That night they also busted out 'Lovelight' and 'Gloria.' October sixteenth, nineteen-eighty-one. Bobby's birthday. That's the only reason I can think of why they broke out both of those. The tragic story of it all is that Rez and I had thought about hitting some of those Europe shows for a belated honeymoon but I lucked into a promotion and couldn't leave…"

(Right, right.)

"Shame on me. The Europeans understand work-life balance. When you ask an American what he does, he talks about his job, while a European will talk about his hobbies, his passions. I could have spent two perfectly lovely weeks mesmerizing strangers with a spirited challenge to the endemic mislabeling of the 'Mind Left Body Jam.' Perhaps I'd open up the discussion to include 'Spanish Jam' although that's a little on the nose for me… Tom? Tommy? You have nothing snide to say about any of that?"

(Sorry, Ted, but as surprising as this sounds, I just wasn't listening to you. I was distracted by this guy who was yelling 'How much would you pay for an exotic animal? How much would you pay for an exotic animal?' What the hell was that?)

"I don't know, he just does it."

(You know him?)

(Ted and I have heard him do that before. Not this tour but last summer, I think.)

(And what does he mean?)

"Mean?"

(Tommy, I don't think he means anything. He's just producing syllables, talking to hear himself talk.)

(Talking to hear himself talk? About the strike price for an exotic animal? Did you ever check it out?)

"Why should we?"

(Why should you? I don't know but if I were walking around a parking lot and someone asked me how much I'd pay for an exotic animal, at the very least I'd name my price. I'd do it right now it but I lost the guy. I had him in my sights and then he disappeared. I can't hear him anymore, either. With every single car blasting a different Grateful Dead tape, it's all cacophony."

"Cacophony?"

(Hey, I have a college degree. It came fully equipped with vocabulary. So did my medical degree for that matter. My competence might well surprise you.)

"That's a matter of contention. As for the exotic animal guy, I've run into him and plenty of others like him who are on their own trip or are just doing it to get attention. I prefer to stay in my own lane and let them pass. Your problem, little brother, is you need to get in some more shows."

(Get in some more shows? Do you even hear yourself? Get in some more shows? You make it sound like it's a chore or something. I mean, it is for me but you shouldn't talk like that. As if there's some intrinsic value to attending twenty or thirty more Grateful Dead concerts a year beyond just hanging a few more notches on your belt. Of course maybe that explains why you're here, you could use a few more notches on your belt. Speaking as your doctor, that expanding waistline of your is a matter of concern—)

"My *future* doctor."

(I wouldn't be your future doctor if you gave me the proper time of day for a consultation.)

"I'm not going to treat you as my doctor and I'm not going to refer to you my doctor until you complete your residency. In fact, I'm not going to call you doctor at all."

(That is a common faux pas. At this point in my medical career I have definitively earned the proper title of doctor.)

"Is that true? I'm asking the Bloch-head next time I see him."

(Justin Bloch. I'm never quite sure how to take it when I'm reminded that the chairman of our department is a Deadhead.)

"We are everywhere."

ROBIN

"Here, tickie, tickie, tickie."

(Who's got my ticket? Who's got my ticket?)

"Tickie-tickie, tickie-tickie."

(I know someone's got it, I can smell it. I know it's around here.)

(HEY! SMELL THIS!)

"Tickie-tockie, tockie-tickie. Tick-tick. Tock-tock."

(Come on, where is it? Who's got it? Who's got my ticket?)

(YO, I GOT YOUR TICKET RIGHT HERE ON MY FACE! BUT YOU'LL HAVE TO SIT DOWN AND PICK IT OFF! AND NO FAIR USING YOUR HANDS!)

"Here, tickie, tickie, tickie. Tickie-tickie. Tockie-tockie..."

(I'LL GIVE YOU SOME TICKIE-TOCKIE! COME OVER HERE AND RIDE THIS!"

(Who's got-hey, what is it with you? Why do you talk like that? What does that even mean?)

"Forget it Mara. Come on, let's keep moving. Some people are assholes."

(No, wait. What did I do to deserve this? Hey you, what did I do to make you say that?)

(YOU'RE HOT!)

(So what's it to you? I look how I look, I can't help it. I'm skipping along with my friend here trying to get a ticket and you—)

(SHE'S HOT TOO!)

(Yeah but what does that have to do with you? We're not leading you on. We're not prancing around in garter belts and high heels. We're not dressed up to get messed up. So don't give us that shit.)

"Yeah, we don't even shave."

(You're girls, you don't need to.)

"We're women. And check this out."

(Ahhh, fuck. That just fucking ruined it for me. Alright girlies, move the fuck along. No need to show off your freaking mulberry bush.)

(Her what? Stevie, did she just show you—)

(No, her nasty armpit hair, she showed me her nasty thatch of armpit hair.)

"Well we handled that with dignity."

(Yeah that shaving bit tends to get 'em. But I'm still pissed. I gave up that girly shit years ago. I don't need it.)

"No, stop. Listen, you're right. They're power tools. But there's nothing you can do to change it. It'd be nice if they were different but they're not and you're not going to make them change. Just let them do what they have to do. We're Deadheads, they're meatheads"

(Robin, you're too fucking kind.)

RANDY

Man, we're flying through the lanes. I gotta get me one of these bikes. That's what did me in yesterday, all the love caravan bullshit.

"So you're a Deadhead? I wouldn't figure you for a Deadhead."

(What's a Deadhead supposed to look like?)

"I don't know but you seem more like a metal maniac to me."

(I've run with the Old Bridge Metal Militia.)

"And you're also a Deadhead?"

(I'm no Deadhead but I've seen the Grateful Dead when they come around.)

"How many times have you seen them?"

(That's a rather personal question Macho Man, what's it to you? How many times have *you* seen the Grateful Dead?)

"Including last night? Nonce. Not a single note."

(Is that true? I thought I saw you at one of the stadium shows last summer. I'm pretty sure you were the guy in the upper balcony wearing the dayglo body paint and the tie-dyed Speedo. How long did it take you to get that green crap off your nipples?)

"What can I tell you, I'm a deviant."

(That's the spirit.)

"The thing I don't get is all the religious stuff though. All these people walking up and down the highway with their fingers pointed up to heaven. Like that guy right there on the roller blades with his 'I Need A Miracle' sign. I'm a good Catholic boy but I just don't get it. Are the Grateful Dead all Jehovah's Witnesses are something?)

"Wait, why are we slowing down?"

(You're shitting me, right?)

"Now why would I do that, seeing as how we're so close and all?"

(Point well taken, Macho Man. No that's not religion. Well, it's Dead religion. It's secular religion. Is there such a thing as secular religion?)

"I'm just a second semester sophomore. That's beyond my pay grade."

(They're not pointing to heaven and asking for miracles, they're pointing to the earth and asking for miracle tickets. It's a song. 'I Need A Miracle.')

"Well can you speed up, because I need one now."

(I don't have an extra ticket.)

"Well that's fine because I'm sure as shit not here to see the show. I just need some of that miracle action to get me there on time so I can do my job. The traffic out here is even worse than when they play next door at the football stadium. Cars are parked on the turnpike now and they're only playing at the hockey rink. That was my stumbling block last night. The road is packed worse than before a football game. How could I know that the hockey rink was gonna have more traffic than the football stadium. It's unnatural."

(Amen to that.)

STEVEN

Happy Heads. Carloads of 'em.

That goes two ways, I guess.

"Hey look, you guys, happy Heads."

(No shit, Sherlock.)

"Wipe me, Watson."

(What's that?)

(Forget it, Zack, just drive.)

"Get it? Happy Heads, happy Deadheads, happy heads, you know faces and skulls, Stealies, that sort of stuff.".

(Steven, my man, I think you're one toke over the line.)

Ahhh, they don't want to get it. Who cares. Happy Heads. With happy skulls. Yeah, skulls is exactly right because all the cars we pass are covered with Steal Your Face Grateful Dead skull stickers. And all sorts of other ones-like right there, the dancing turtles from the cover of *Terrapin Station*. And dancing bears, dancing skeletons. All sorts of dancing stuff. The stickers are sweet and they also identify you as a Head to the other Heads and to the world. They tell everyone that you're a Head and proud of it. They look festive and well, happy.

Which was my point. Everyone who passes us and everyone we pass who is wearing tie-dye or has a sticker on the back window is waving or giving the peace sign. And that's cool. No, it's more than cool. I bet this doesn't happen for any other concert. And that's why this isn't just a concert. There's music but it's more than the music. We're drawn here by the music but there's something here that's bigger than the music. At least it seems so to me. But then again, this is my first show, what do I know?

No, I know. It's more. Okay, I've never been to a show yet but I've been close. I've seen Max Creek plenty of times.

Besides I can feel it, I'm a part of it. And not all of it is right here and now. It's like at Willington, almost everyone's a Head. I bet seventy or eighty percent of the students at least like the music. But the biggest Heads, the ones who are really into it, we hang together and we work together to do stuff. A bunch of Heads organized a food co-op last year so that we could get soda and chips on campus. We all took turns working, we had the music cranking and everyone was grooving. It provided a service and none of us got paid. That's just one example of Heads working together to help each other and everyone else, too.

There was also that soup line thing. I wasn't into that but a number of Heads were. Faye organized it and they fed a bunch of the townies. It probably got her into Harvard. Shannon and Emily worked on it too. Stuff like that is real helpful to everyone and it looks good on your college applications. I bet that next year the two of them—

(Hey, you guys, check this out. On my side. That camper has a VW bus soldered into the roof. Man that's cool.)

(Yeah, I talked to those guys once. It was really easy for them to do it. They had this old van and they just cut off the top and added the VW.)

"You know those guys?"

(I've seen 'em at shows. Nate, you were there when I talked to them, right?)

(Last year at Buffalo. Yeah, it's primo dank inside. Plush. A thick rug perfect for sitting back and baking down. And the bus top's a skylight too.)

(Yeah, I remember that, it was after the show and I really wanted to sit back and get high.)

"So why didn't you?"

(It wasn't our van, it wouldn't have been cool. Besides, we had to find our car.)

(Yeah, the reason we talked to those guys in the first place was to ask them if we could stand on the roof of the van and look for our car.)

"And they let you?"

(Yeah.)

"And did you see your car?"

(No but we found it eventually. We were so stoned going in that we forgot to notice where we parked. It turned out we were looking on the wrong side of the building.)

(Yeah and check this out. I just remembered this. There were these other guys there, on the same side of the building as the van. They had this little campfire built and they heard us talking and they told us to sit down with them. They were pretty fucked up too. They were sitting there waiting for the lot to empty out because they couldn't find their cars either. So they decided to make a little fire to keep warm, pass around a bowl and wait for the other cars to leave so that theirs would be the only ones left.)

"Sounds like a plan."

(Yeah.)

"So did you sit down with them?"

(We took a couple hits off the bowl. Then Jason got antsy so we got moving. We should have hung there though. We pretty much didn't find the car until the lot emptied out anyhow and our legs were pretty fucking sore by then.)

Now that's a real Grateful Dead story. That's cool. That's something that only happens at a Grateful Dead show. And it's possible that—

"Hey, wait, do you think we'll have that problem tonight?"

(Not now we won't. We're putting you in charge. When we get in there, Steven, old pal, remember where we park. There's a number and a letter.)

"Okay, sure. But I wasn't just thinking about us. What about Emily and those guys? Do you think they'll remember to do that?"

(Probably. They're a lot smarter than we are.)

(No wait, Jas—hold on. Emily and those guys? You want to be more specific?)

"What do you mean?"

Shit.

(By those guys you wouldn't be referring to one Shannon Phelps, would you?)

(Dude, you got to set your sights a little lower.)

"Listen—"

(Actually, guy, I'm just busting your balls. Word on the street is that she thinks you're not altogether hane. So who knows, after the show—)

"Hey—"

(You could smoke a bone then slip her your bone.)

"Shit, come on, cork it."

I love this.

ZEB

(You got any smoke?)

"No, brother, I'm selling beer."

(I'm looking for the kind bud. Can you get me the kind bud?)

"I'm not holding."

(We've got an extra ticket. We'll trade you the ticket for the kind.)

"I'm not holding. But I'd be stoked to buy it off you."

(So would everyone else. We're looking for the kind.)

"Well if you don't find any would you consider selling me the ticket?"

(We'd consider it. We'd consider it a bit more if you can point us to someone who's holding the green.)

"Sorry, brother."

(Then what's with your shirt? It says 'Let It Grow' and it's decorated with pot leaves.)

"Sharon over there made it."

(Don't you think that's false advertising?)

"It's not advertising, it just keeps me warm. I'd be warmer inside the show though, if you're really concerned."

(We're not that concerned.)

(Sorry, man, apparently Kevbo isn't all that concerned.)

"Well we can all still work together to keep this a work free drug place."

(Funkin Gonuts!)

(Although you do seem to be sending mixed messages.)

"Nah, I'm just selling bumperstickers. Remember, hippies don't die, they go up in smoke."

Gotta be kind to the custies.

It can weird though. And not always the right kind of weird. Every night without fail. The dudes in the thirty-five dollar designer tie-dyes and hundred dollar sneakers come up to me, hoping to make the big score. And the harsh thing is they never look me in the eyes. They're always looking around, like they're totally afraid of cops but they really make an effort not to see me. I'm good enough to score them dope but they won't make eye contact.

There's fucked up people out here. There's fucked up people everywhere but there's a certain type of fucked up person out here that especially bums me out. Like those two dudes from New Hampshire I met last spring. I had thought they were pretty righteous. They picked me up in D.C. and drove me down to

Greensboro. They were on tour, had mail orders for the whole Greensboro run and they seemed right on. But we were eating at some diner and one of the dudes saw these two other guys eating and I didn't notice it, but the dude said that he saw one of the guys feeding the other guy some french fries in a sexy way. So these dudes from New Hampshire, I think they were going to college up there, started giving these two guys all sorts of shit and started throwing fries at them.

And I mean, no way. How can they be Heads? How can they listen to the music, feel it so much that they want to travel down to North Carolina to see the Boys and still have a problem with the french fry guys? A Head should be able to move beyond that and respect other people who aren't invading their space or anything. And these dudes had gone on about recycling and they were real careful about where they put their garbage, talking about mother earth and all that but how can you care about mother earth without being kind to her children?

Even I've figured that out, without a high school diploma.

ROBIN

"Wait, hold on. Emergency."

(What is it?)

"Doses."

(What about 'em?)

"We need 'em."

(No, we don't.)

"Okay, we don't *need* 'em but I do think they would contribute to our enjoyment of the show. Assuming that is we find some tickets. HERE TICKlE TICKlE TICKlE!"

(No, Rob, we don't need them because we already have them. I have a couple left over from Philly.)

"The unicorns? Oh, they were cute…"

(Yeah. I thought that guy gave us three but it turned out he gave us five.)

"Kind… But wait, those would've been our 'Dark Star' doses. It's sad."

(No, no, no. It's good luck. Those doses were there for us. They were good to go. It's our fault we couldn't find tickets, not the doses' fault. And I think these doses are ready to make it up to us if we can get into the show.)

"Well then, maybe it's time to pull out all the stops."

(You mean?)

"Singing. Let's do it, woman. Beatles style. Take my hand. All right, one…two…three…

"ALL WE NEED IS ONE!

"ALL WE NEED IS ONE!

"ALL WE NEED IS ONE!

"ONE!

"ONE IS ALL WE NEED!"

TAPER TED

(Okay, big bro, now I'll acknowledge this isn't a cult…)

"Generous of you."

(…Begrudgingly. But when you ask me to think back to my first show, I think Moonie. And not pie in the sky dreaminess here, I'm talking the Unification Church because everyone just seemed so fixated on my happiness.)

"Why that sounds horrific."

(I've never had so many strangers seem so concerned about whether or not I was having a good time.)

"I'm aghast."

(You're a ghast bag.)

(Ahh, bad puns, that must mean someone's brother is in line with us.)

(Hey, Reg. Dead greetings and all that.)

(What brings you out tonight, Dr. Tommy?)

(Who wouldn't jump on a chance to attend a Grateful Dead show and stand as quiet as possible with minimal physical movement to prevent any jostling of microphone stands?)

(Umm, me. And all of us in this line.)

(Hells yeah!)

(Speaking of *us* though, the last time you joined our ranks, you were with a dupe.)

(Yeah, I'd have to dupe anyone to suffer through an evening with this crew.)

(He means a duplicate, a plus one.)

"He wants to know what happened to Anna."

(Ahh, well, let's just say that I learned a valuable lesson. It turns out 'Why are you asking me that?' is a fine response to just about any question other than 'Do you love me?')

(And 'Why aren't you wearing pants?')

(And 'Does that grizzly bear seem agitated to you?')

(And 'Why did the angry officer just unholster his gun?')

(And 'Why did you just unholster your pants?')

(Enough with the pants.)

"And why is there a blinking Error 10 message on my TCD-D7?"

(How to bring it around, big bro. Yeah, it was a less than satisfying conclusion to a three year relationship. I suppose in the end my problem with Anna was that she made me stop believing in the power of redemption."

"And she stole your fancy coffee maker."

(That too.)

(Anyhow I'm on the prowl tonight and there's no better place to find a foxy, single woman than the tapers' section of a Grateful Dead show.)

(Come on now, no need to be sexist.)

(That's not sexism, that's the power of observation.)

(Well when you fall off that horse you've got to get right back on again.)

(Now, Reg, is that an appropriate thing to say to a recovering heroin addict?)

(I'm—)

(Just kidding.)

"You're quite a charmer. No wonder you're single."

STELLA BLUE

(Hey, Alison, do you hear that? They're playing our song.)

(What's that?)

(Listen.)

"What? I want to know."

(Oh yeah, I hear it. I thought we made that up.)

"Tell me!"

(I bet everyone thinks they made it up.)

"What? Mommmeee, I want to know!"

(Shhhh, Stella… Honey, I'm sorry. I didn't know what Aunt Jenny was talking about at first. I had to listen.)

"What is it?"

(Do you see those young women over there?)

"Which ones?"

(The ones who are skipping. Can you hear what they're singing?)

"Umm…"

(All we need is one, all we need is one.)

"Oh yeah, yeah. I can hear 'em now."

(Great. Now there's a song that you might have heard on one of Mommy's records or on the radio called 'All You Need Is Love.')

"Is it a Grateful Dead song?"

(No, honey, it's a Beatles song.)

"Are those the guys who sing about the octopus?"

(Exactly, hon. You're a smarty pants. Well those women are changing the words of the song from 'all we need is love' to 'all we need is one' so that people will know that they need one ticket.)

"But I can't hear them anymore."

(Jenny, why don't you sing a quick verse for Stella?)

(Oh sure, Aunt Jenny the walking jukebox.)

"You're my favorite walking jukebox."

(Why thank you, Stella. And you're my favorite walking giggle box.)

"I'm not a walkin"—*giggle*—"Hey! Tickling's no fair!"

(Okay, Jen, I'll join you. Let's do it.)

(ALL WE NEED IS ONE!
ALL WE NEED IS ONE! ALL WE NEED IS ONE!
ONE!
ONE IS ALL WE NEED!)

(Which of you needs a ticket? I have an extra I can sell you.)

(No, thank you. That was for instructional purposes only.)

(We still got it, Jen.)

(Maybe. Of course maybe that guy was a scalper and he goes up to everyone and offers to sell them a ninety-dollar ticket to the show.)

(Maybe. And maybe he was just someone who dug our act. So anyhow, Stell Belle, that's the song. Those two women just changed the words of a pretty song, 'All You Need Is Love,' to let people know that they need tickets to see the Grateful Dead. Isn't that silly?)

"Uh-huh, Mommy, it's silly."

STEVEN

So this is it.

This is the real deal.

This is THE SCENE.

I sort of had an idea what it would be like and I definitely feel like I'm a part of it but it's so cool to finally be here. I mean check out all the women in those hippie dresses, wearing bells and dancing or skipping. And those guys—like that guy right there with the robe and the long beard. He must be like forty-five years old. He could be one of the original people who listened to the Dead in the 1960s and he's still following them around, enjoying the ride. I mean that's cool. There's something about the people here, you can see it just walking past them, it's like they're wise. They understand shit. I mean Deadheads are not usually stupid people. Some of them are some of the smartest people I know. It's just they don't use their heads the way that everyone wants them to. They keep their heads sacred.

Sacred Heads with sacred heads.

That's what you have to do when you become a heavy-duty Deadhead. I mean I'm a Head but I'm not all that heavy-duty yet. Yet. This is my first show. This could be the one where I have that mystical magical Grateful Dead experience that changes my life forever.

"Hey, what do you guys say to some food? I've got the munchies in a big way."

(Yeah, what do you say to that?)

(In a little while. We have business to attend to first. We have to cover for Steven's bunk move.)

"What's that?"

(Doses. You said your cousin could hook you up, remember? That's how you ended up with my extra ticket. Remember?)

"I remember. I told you guys, she went back to college a few days early."

Not that I asked her.

(Yeah, we've heard your story.)

(Let it go. Stevie tried and now he's here with us at his first show. Let him enjoy it.)

"Nothing left to do but smile smile smile."

(Right on.)

(And score doses.)

"Well how are we supposed to get them?"

(We don't get them. They get us.)

"How?"

(Just keep your ears open, you'll know.)

(Hey, Jason, I've been meaning to ask you about that. I was talking to Meg last night in study hall and she says that she bought bum doses at her last show.)

(So she bought blank paper?)

(Not quite. There just wasn't enough acid on the paper to totally get her off.)

(Maybe it came off on her fingers when she was putting it on her tongue.)

(That would still get her high. She would absorb it through her skin.)

(No way. Impossible.)

(Way. That's what I've always been told. When you're handing out doses to other people only touch the corner of the paper or else you'll be taking someone else's hit as well as your own.)

(No, that's not how it works.)

(It is, you absorb it through your skin.)

(Steven, what do you say? You're the one who aced AP Chem.)

"Well, Meg is world-renowned for her really dirty hands."

(Ha!)

(Because she keeps stuffing them in Jason's underwear!)

(Maybe the question here should be what would happen if Jason rubbed a dose against his pecker.)

(Well, Zack, you two boys can conduct that experiment a bit later in the privacy of your room.)

(Hahhaa!)

"I learned something of my own last week in Bio II. Did you guys realize that semen is full of Vitamin C?"

(So?)

"Well I want to find myself a babe with scurvy and nurse her back to health."

(Haaaaaa!)

(Stevie, you're always on point with your eighteenth-century disease references. And your spunk talk.)

"I try… I do think Fletcher's right though. If you touch the corner of a dose, logic dictates that a little bit should be absorbed by your skin. Now if you're the one taking the hit, it shouldn't matter. Although I assume it would absorb through her skin at a much more gradual rate than if she touched it all to her tongue. Maybe that was the problem. Unless the person who sold it to her had his hands all over it and absorbed a bunch of it."

(I say this is worthy of additional research.)

(You just want to touch Jason's custard launcher.)

(Hey, I gotta be me.)

(Haaaaa!)

(Well you can do that by yourself.)

"Which is how the magic happens. Beating Bobby McGee."

(Haaaa! Haaaa!)

(Simmer down, Little Steven. Anyhow, someone told Meg that the best way to do it is just to go up to somebody in a microbus and ask them.)

(I bought dope that way once.)

(If we can't get any, it's worth a shot.)

"Speaking of which, aren't we supposed to meet Meg and the rest of them out here?"

(Listen to him. The rest of them.)

(Yeah, Stevie, like we don't know what's on your mind.)

"Okay, okay, Shannon."

(No, I told Meg we'd see 'em inside. They have seats behind the stage so they're going to meet us by the entrance to our section.)

(Are we going to stub them down?)

(I don't think we'll have to. It's not like we're down on the floor or anything. It should be no prob.)

(You think so? They were giving people shit last year. And have you ever been to a football game here?)

(Yeah but that's across the way at the stadium. This is the arena. Once we get inside they won't give a crap.)

(I hope you're right. Besides there's nothing we can do about it now, we have pressing concerns.)

(Thanks to Saint Steven.)

Okay, I didn't ask my cousin. I just didn't see her and it would have been too weird to call her. Maybe on some level I didn't do it on purpose. I mean ACID. It's a big thing. A scary thing. A fucking scary thing. When you say you're tripping that doesn't sound so bad but I still can't get it out of my head that the thing you're tripping over is acid.

I've taken mushrooms plenty of times before. At least two or three. And you never hear of anyone having bad mushroom trips. I think that's because when you take mushrooms you're not really going on a trip. It's because they're organic. Nate says that mushrooms just make your body secrete more of some substance that's already in there. But acid, I mean that shoots something into your body.

And I don't know. You hear about people who never come back. They say not to take it unless you're stable and if you take it six or seven times then the government classifies you as legally insane. So what happens if the acid eats away at my brain and takes control and I can't come back? Or what if I do come back but the acid does permanent damage and I become a vegetable? Or what if it messes with my head and I screw up my SATs? I'm supposed to take them in a couple of months. I mean what if all of a sudden because I put a piece of paper on my tongue I can't get into college. Alec and Marg would flip. I'd have to apologize and say 'I'm sorry, Mom and Dad. I'm sorry I couldn't get into college because I dropped acid at a Dead show and lost my vocabulary.'

They would bum big time.

RANDY

(Here you go Macho Man, I'll see you in there.)

"The hell you will."

(What do you have against the Grateful Dead?)

"One, I have nothing against the Grateful Dead, although their fans seem a bit like phonies to me and B, my job isn't inside, it's outside."

(So remind me, what is it you do here?)

"I do whatever the ornery crackpot tells me to do. He's my boss. Actually my real boss is my coach and the ornery crackpot reports to my coach."

(It sounds like you're good and cooked.)

"That's a Crock-Pot."

(Keep it mild, Julia Child.)

"What's with the Julia Child taunt? And do you really think that Julia Child uses a Crock-Pot?"

(Of course not, Macho Man. Just because I fix cars doesn't make me a Neanderthal. But if you'd give it any thought I think you'd recognize for the sake of argument—and that's what we're doing here, arguing—that the classic beef Bourguignon recipe can easily be adapted for a slow cooker. It's a little less high maintenance and you can even do some of the prep work the night before to make things easier in the morning. Then it can simmer all day while you head off to work at—let us say hypothetically—an auto repair shop. Now who's the brute?)

"Can we call throw fingers?"

(We can throw something. Why do you say the fans are phonies?)

"This will get me more riled up than I need to be but last night we caught a bunch of these guys with their tie-dyes and their peace symbols using wire cutters on the fence in the back of the arena. They were trying to figure out how to sneak in. They were still a long way from pay dirt but we shut them down. Then they were up in my face, working themselves into a lather, barking away and blaming me, like it was my fault they couldn't get in. One of them even took a swing at me. Not a good idea by the way."

(I'd give it a shot. Just for shits and giggles, mind you. I wouldn't coldcock you, that would be no fun. I'd let you know it was coming.)

"You're a gentleman and a scholar. Maybe when I pick up the car. If I pick up the car. That's Eddie's car and Eddie's business. My business is to put on my uni and report."

(Your uni? This ain't football.)

"Maybe not but there is some twisted form of gamesmanship happening out here though, as best I can tell. So it makes sense that I have a uni. I put on my yellow jacket and then—)

(You sting.)

"I stink? Well that's not very polite. First you offer to punch out my lights—I know, shits and giggles—but now you insult my odor. That's below the belt. The car broke down, I had to stand alongside an overheated highway for an hour waiting for a tow, while the clock was ticking away and I was literally sweating over the time as my job slipped away."

(You don't stink, you sting. Well, actually, since you mention it, your personal fragrance is something in the vicinity of reek. But also you sting. You put on your yellow jacket and then you sting. What you need to do is go inside and see some good ol' Grateful Dead, it'll mellow your harsh.)

(That will not happen.)

"Well have a good show."

(That I will not.)

ZEB

I'd never rip off a Head but it can be hard to tell.

Especially with tapers because sometimes they look like junior high school guidance counselors. Come to think of it, sometimes they *are* junior high school guidance counselors, like these dudes who gave me a lift last summer from Deer Creek to Alpine, with their golf shirts, Bermuda shorts and flip-flops. Turns out they hadn't missed a summer tour in over a decade.

I wouldn't sell them bogus anything. Not that I'm hawking bunk shit.

Okay, except for the occasional blank blotter. I have sold clean paper on rare occasion as a desperation measure but never to a Head, just to someone who didn't need it anyhow.

It's like last year down in Charlotte, this Head hears that I'm selling doses and asks me if they're good because he was driving ten hours straight to Miami right after the encore so he could be in town early for the next run of shows. He told me he needed something to keep him wired. Now that's not my stimmy of choice. For that kind of journey, I'd go with the truckers' pills, the mini-thins, but each to his own. So I told him I had some complaints and that my doses might be weak because they'd been out in the sun too much, whatever that's supposed to mean. They weren't weak, they were paper but I wasn't going to admit that, I'm not that wacked. So not only did I tell him no but I also set him up with some doses from this guy who wasn't even selling, he just had extras.

That's why it was so harsh when that dude sold me a bum ticket. He should have told me what it was. It looked right on and show time was at hand, so I might have bought it anyhow for less bread just to see if would get me into the show. If I had known I would have been a bit more strategic about picking the right line, so I'd end up with someone ripping my ticket who wasn't paying close attention and didn't feel the need to make a point of busting Heads with counties. I'd get behind some short hair Heads as well just to avoid any suspicious vibe. But that dude never warned me, he never gave me a chance.

We need to stop these Head to Head collisions.

BAGEL BOB

(Hey, Paulie, get over here, check this shit out.)

(What is it?)

(Go ahead man, tell him your name.)

"Bagel Bob."

(That's it? Nothing more?)

"Nothing more is required."

(Yes but Bagel Bob's so informal. What if you go to a formal dinner?)

(With the President.)

(With the President of the United States. Not the President of the Fairy Wing Guild.)

"Bagel Bob does not wish to meet the President of the United States at this time. Bob will acknowledge that he received his baccalaureate in tandem with the Chief Executive's eldest son. However, lest you believe Bob's avowed affection for skull and roses has weakened his resolve, he can offer no additional comment about Skull and Bones. However, this Fairy Wing Guild of which you speak—"

(Fuck the Fairy Wing Guild.)

"That seems an improper way to treat a mythical craft organization."

(Okay, screw the President…)

"You're quite the promiscuous private security detail."

(Which is precisely my point.)

(You have a point here?)

"That you are libidinous?"

(That I am working security. I am paid to enforce the rules here and there's a rule against vending—)

(No, screw the vending thing for now. Let's get back to the name. You're at a dinner party with what's his name, the main guy in the Grateful Dead…)

(Jerry Garcia.)

(Right, right. Jerry Garcia. You're eating with him. What does he call you?)

"He can call me anything he wants except late to dinner. Haaah-haaahh!"

Bob loves that one.

(You're a fucking comedic genius, Bob, but tell me this, when he asks you your name, what do you say?)

"Bagel Bob would suffice."

(Oh, it would? Not Robert, seeing how this is the Grateful Dead guy and all?)

"Robert also would be adequate."

(DO YOU HAVE A LAST NAME?)

"In what sense of the term?"

(Let me see your driver's license.)

"Bagel Bob does not wish to comply."

(I don't give a shit what Bagel Bob wants. AND STOP CALLING YOURSELF BAGEL BOB!)

(Just hand over your license, pal.)

(No, Bob, you don't have to do that. That's some bogus shit. These guys aren't cops. They're fucking security jerk-offs. These are the guys who weren't good enough to become cops. So they come out here to play make-believe. They put on their yellow jackets and fondle each other's walkie-talkies.)

"Please let Bob defuse this situation."

(Defuse? That's what you think you're doing?)

(When you come onto our property we *are* the cops. I imagine that even a low-life, high-stench excuse for a human being like yourself can understand that.)

(What are you saying? I don't understand you.)

(Yeah, yellow jacket, you're the ones with limited imaginations. This isn't your property. It's no more your property than it is ours.)

(We may not own it but these jackets mean that we rule it.)

(Fuck you! You can't rule your dick.)

(Oh yeah, well I'm about to kick the shit out of yours.)

(You're a fucking idiot! You don't even know that shit doesn't come out of my dick, it comes out of my ass which you can kiss!)

"Please do not involve yourself in this. Bagel Bob implores you."

(Too late, he's fucking involved. Empty your pockets you hippie freak.)

(Fuck you!)

(Empty 'em.)

(You got a warrant?)

(I fucking don't need one.)

(Then fuck off.)

(Did you hear me?)

(FUCK OFF!)

(Shit! Grab him!)

(You grab him, I'm busy with Robert.)

(Fuck Robert! Let him go, the other guy's taking off!)

(Okay! Okay! But we'll be back! Do you hear me Bob, we'll be back!)

Bagel Bob does not eagerly anticipate the reunion.

STEVEN

SHAKEDOWN STREET!

I've heard about this. I've seen the pictures in *Relix*. But I can't believe I'm really here. I am walking down SHAKEDOWN STREET!

Everyone's just sitting out in front of their cars selling stuff. It's like a giant Deadhead outdoor mall. There are even little food shops.

(Kind veggie burritos! We've got your kind veggie burritos!)

I could go for a kind veggie burrito.

And look: beads…crystals…T-shirts…I definitely could use a T-shirt. I have some Dead shirts, even ones that other people bought at shows but never one that I bought at a show myself. That would be cool. I could keep it and someday show it to my kids. Yeah, I could go for something with a Stealie and some dancing cartoon characters or something.

Nate's wearing a Calvin and Hobbes shirt that he bought on summer tour last year. Something like that would do the trick.

(Hey, Steven man, what are you doing?)

"Looking around. Nothing."

(Nothing is right. You're supposed to be paying attention, listening for the magic word. Instead you're slowing down in front of everyone who's selling something, which is everyone.)

(And none of them are selling what we want.)

"Alright, alright. But after we find some acid I wanna grab something to eat and get a T-shirt."

(Food is fine but you should wait until after the show to get a shirt.)

"Why?"

(Where are you gonna put it when you're inside?)

"Why can't I put it under my seat?"

(I cannot believe you're arguing with me on this. Have you ever been to a show?)

"No."

Cheap shot. He probably wants Shannon and he's pissed.

(Okay, then let me tell you. You don't know if you're gonna have a seat. You might be dancing in the aisles or something. Who can tell at a show?)

(Speaking of which, check it out, Alex Burns.)

(No shit. Hey Alex! Burner! The Burnster! What's shaking?)

(My bones in like an hour. What are you boys up to?)

He probably doesn't remember me. I never really hung out with him, never went to shows with his crew. Nate did though. Man, his hair is even longer than it was at Willington. I wish I could go for a ponytail. But there's no way. Alec and Margaret would disown me.

(We're just here to see Jerry.)

(What about you, is Bowdoin on break?)

(Nah, break ended last week. I'm just down for the shows. Wanted to make sure someone's keeping up the Willington tradition.)

"Yeah, there are a bunch of us down here. Six or seven cars worth. We're trying to make you proud."

That was cool.

(And that I am. Hey do any of you want this? I was going to throw it out.)

"Yeah, I'll take it. What is it?"

(I don't know. Some sort of kabob thing. I started eating it before I remembered that I've become a vegan. Anyhow the meat's all red and gross-it sort of made me sick.)

This is definitely sweet. I'm at the show finishing Alex Burns' kabob thing fresh from the lot, purchased right here on Shakedown Street.

(Some amigos and I came down from school last night and caught the show. Killer 'Uncle John's' > 'Playing.' Smoking 'Sugaree' too. Anyhow, we've been here pounding beers all day. Then I dropped about a half hour ago. Now I'm getting crinkly so I better head in while I still can figure out which way to head.)

(Do you have any extras?)

(Tickets?)

(Acid.)

(No, sorry, kids. But don't worry, it's all over the place. Just keep your ears open. Hey are you guys partying after the show?)

(Yeah.)

Oh no. Don't tell him, don't tell him.

(We're headed down to Emily Pratt's beach house.)

Shit.

(Sweet Emily. Yeah, I remember where that is, we partied down there after one of the shows last spring. Who else is gonna be there?)

(You know, her crowd. Melissa, Beth, Shannon—)

(That Shannon is tasty.)

Yeah she is. Wait, didn't he used to go out with her?

(I haven't seen her in some time. Yeah, she is primo.)

(They all are man. You should check out Debbie O'Neill. She really filled out this year.)

(No shit, I always knew she had potential. Alright, me and my buds'll put in an appearance. Have a good show boys!)

(Yeah, have a good show Burner! No shit, Alex Bums. He's someone I would've thought we'd see here if I'd thought about it.)

"He's The Man."

(He is, although he could be gunning for Shannon. Better stay on your game.)

No shit. I just hope he spends his time with the new and improved Debbie O'Neill.

(Come on, Stevie, don't sweat it. Let's get going. Hey, and give me one of those peppers on the kabob thing.)

"Sure. Want a hunk of meat?"

(Nah, maybe later.)

"Jason?"

(No, thanks. Let's just get a move on. No more rubbernecking.)

ROBIN

"ONE!

ONE IS ALL WE NEED!"

"Hold it, Mara."

(What?)

"I just realized. We don't need one ticket, we need two."

(Right. So?)

"I don't know. I mean we're skipping around all sweetness and light singing a lie. I think there's something wrong with that."

(No, not really. We're each singing that we need one. And there are two of us, so…)

"So together we're really asking for two. I thought of that but we're singing 'one is all WE need.' The we sort of tells people that together we only need one ticket. I don't know, I guess it's not that important, it's not why I stopped you. I stopped you because I think it's unicorn time."

(You sure?)

"I think so. It feels like unicorn time. There's like thirty minutes till the show starts. If we take them now we'll get the tickles when they come on and we'll be flying for the second set."

(We always have this discussion. You know I like to take them later. I don't like peaking, even if it's only semi-peaking during the set breaks. Too many people out in the hall.)

"Well I sort of do. I can walk around and smile at people and most of 'em smile back. And then it's really fun to get all excited for the second set, go inside and watch them climb up to the lights, then—"

(Okay, okay. We took 'em when I wanted last time, anyhow. Okay, let's do it. Right over here behind this van… Open up and say 'aahhh.')

"Ahhh…"

(Here you go. And one for me.)

"So do you think it's time to split up?"

(It worked in Philly.)

"But wait, not the 'Dark Star' night."

(We didn't split up the 'Dark Star' night.)

"Right, so maybe we shouldn't split up now or there won't be another 'Dark Star' night."

(But then even if there is another 'Dark Star' we'll never get to see it.)

"Yeah, but I wouldn't want to wreck it for everyone else."

(Well, everyone else wouldn't want you to wreck it for them. But luckily everyone else has forgotten about me. I'll wreck it for them. I'm a way huger bitch than you are, so it'll be cool.)

"Okay then. Hug time."

(I'll see you inside. And if I don't, have a good show.)

"You will. So when I do see you, have a good show."

(Well if you do see me then I *will* have a good show.)

"You sweet talker, Betty Crocker."

RANDY

(What's your problem, Ellis?)

Crap.

(I can't hear you, Ellis. What's that?)

"Well—"

(Forget I asked. I do not want to hear it. I do not want to hear it. The second goddamn night in a row. The second goddamn night in a row.)

The second goddamn echo in a row.

(How many days have you been working for me?)

"Two."

(And out of those goddamn two days how many goddamn days have you been late for work?)

Goddamn two?

(I do not want to hear it. I do not want to hear it. Save your excuses for your English teacher. I did your coach a favor by taking you on. And you are letting him down. Do you hear me, son? You are letting him down…I said, do you hear me?)

"Yes, I hear you."

(Fine. Now I can't remember, where did you work last night?)

"For a while you had me on the perimeter. Then I was escorting people away from the door who had counterfeit tickets."

(Too easy. That's a waste of muscle or whatever you have that passes for muscle. And the other job almost requires a brain, Scarecrow. I want you sweeping the lots. Report to Davis. You can sweep with his crew.)

"Sweeping?"

(Don't worry, you won't need a broom, although come to think of it, you won't need anything tomorrow. Report to Davis but this will be your last night with us. And don't worry about your paycheck, I'll make sure it goes to your coach. I'll explain it to him when I call him up and ask him to send me someone else, someone punctual. Not a punk, punctual.)

STELLA BLUE

"Mommy, I want this necklace."

(It is very pretty… How much?)

(Nine?… Eight?… No, no seven.)

(Apparently I'm driving a hard bargain.)

(Well, she's just so cute. All decked out in her little peasant dress and flip-flops. I want to see her in the beads. How old is she?)

(Tell the woman how old you are, Stella.)

"Four."

(Stella! Actually, she's three.)

"I'm threeandalmostfour."

(That's right, honey. Next month you'll be four. But until then you're three.)

(Stella? Did you say her name was Stella? Stella Blue?)

"Hey, how do you know my name?"

(Because it's the name of a song. A beautiful song. And you are a beautiful girl. I love your dress. It's very pretty.)

"I know it is."

(Hey, I do hair wraps too. For seven bucks how about the necklace and a hair wrap for Stella?"

"Mommy, what's a hair wrap?"

(It's a little like when I braid your hair except they take your hair and put it in a pretty…tube.)

"Like a tube of toothpaste?"

(Yeah, Stella, you'll be walking around with toothpaste in your hair. You'll love it!)

"Aunt Jenny! Mommy, what do you mean?"

(Look over there. See that woman with the pretty colors in her hair? It almost looks like she's wearing your anklet in her hair?)

"Mommy, you're silly."

(Yeah, I guess I am. But can you see the colors?)

"Uh-huh."

(What colors do you see?)

"Umm…red…and green…and yellow…and, that's it."

(Right. And that's a hair wrap.)

"I want one. Please, Mommy, please."

(I'll take care of it, Stella, hon. Your Aunt Jenny will treat you. Necklace and hair wrap on me. Well okay not on me, on you Stella Blue.)

"You're silly too, Aunt Jenny."

(And what do you say to your silly Aunt Jenny, Stella?)

"Thank you, silly Aunt Jenny."

ZEB

This one's going down to the wire again.

Friday night in New York is not an easy ticket.

It's not an easy ticket in New Jersey either, which is I suppose is where we are even though that big sign on the stadium over there makes it pretty clear that this is New York Giants territory.

It's New Jersey but it's the New York Giants' New Jersey. That I don't quite understand. It's like a cosmic prank that no one notices.

Gotta make a call soon, though. Do I want to move in a bit closer to the arena where I'll have better luck with beer sales for folks who want one more pop before the big bang or should I keep working the periphery and catch people coming in late who want to take a Shakedown lap or two before they even think about unloading their extras?

"Get your kind Beck's here, two bucks. Kind Buds a buck. Beck's two bucks, Buds a buck."

(Did you say the kind bud?)

Not this again.

"No, I'm selling beers not dope, bro."

(And you're looking for a ticket too, right?)

"Yeah."

(Well I'll trade you tonight for some kind bud.)

"I'm not holding. But listen, the show's going to start any minute now, why don't you sell me the ticket. You're not going to find any buds now."

(No, man, I want buds.)

(Hey, you want buds, come over here.)

(Yeah, man, I'll sell you buds. Thirty an eighth.)

(That's pretty steep.)

"No, wait, it's cool. I'll buy your extra off you for thirty and then you can pay him for the eighth. We can all groove on that."

(Cool by me.)

(Wait man, you've got an extra?)

(Yeah.)

(Hey Pam, come over here, this guy's got an extra. Okay, I'll trade you the buds for the ticket.)

(Okay, cool!)

(Alright.)

(Sorry, man.)

"That's harsh. New York's got the ways and means but just won't let me be… Even when New York is in New Jersey."

(Yeah, cry me a polluted river.)

TAPER TED

(Now that was a moment of beauty. You see that kid over there, with the Philsbury Doughboy shirt? He was talking to this grey-haired guy with a ponytail. And I can hear the kid say 'Really? I was a sociology major too!' Like it's a big thing. Like it was some amazing coincidence that the two of them are sociology majors. I've said this before and I'll say it again, this is where sociology majors come to die.)

(I'm personally affronted.)

"Well, speaking for myself, I'm drowned in your laughter and dead to the core."

(Good one, hon.)

(Good one, hon? That was a witty retort?)

"Well, I'm a humble man but—"

(I assume you were quoting lyrics and I suppose if I wanted to waste the brain power on it, I might even be able to figure which song it was but I am not expending that much mental energy on the project.)

(Well you only have so much to spare.)

(Face!)

"Alright, leave my little brother alone. He can say whatever he wants but I just did the math. This is his thirteenth show tonight. He's not just here for the goo balls and the hacky sack!"

(Agreed! Wait, then what is it I'm here for?)

"Because there's nothing like a Grateful Dead concert?"

(You mean other than every other Grateful Dead concert.)

(Booooo!!!)

(Turn on your lovelight, Tommy!)

(I know, I know. It's different every night. Sometimes there's drums then space, sometimes there's space then drums…)

(Actually there isn't. It's the same order every time.)

(You guys said it, not me.)

(Okay, classic Dead trivia: when was the last show in the DeadBase with two electric sets that doesn't identify a 'Drums' and 'Space?')

(Easy. Amsterdam October 16, 1981, Bobby's b-day show.)

"That doesn't count. It has to be a night with two full-on electric sets."

(Well what about December 12, 1981, Fiesta Hall in San Mateo?)

"Same issue. Only one electric set."

(Plus that was a Joan Baez and Friends show, they were backing her.)

"Which leaves us with Providence Civic Center, January eighteenth, nineteen-seventy-nine."

(Don't forget December 6, 1980.)

(No one's forgetting December 6, 1980 but that was a one set acoustic performance.)

(Yeah, I didn't say it answered the question, I just said don't forget it. Sometimes people do, for statistical purposes.)

"Again which brings us to January eighteenth, nineteen-seventy-nine."

(Taper Ted, quick on the draw! I take it that's not the first time someone has asked you that question.)

"I vaguely remember the show. It's dwarfed by the next night when they dropped the Buffalo 'Dark Star.' Maybe they dumped the 'Drums' and 'Space' in Providence because they were conserving energy for the 'Star.'"

(See, big bro, I'm learning. Just when I thought things were the same every time, I discover there was a slight variance eleven years ago. Just like the slight variances I observe out here in the parking lot. The last few times I came here I saw Deadheads so stoned out of their gourds that they were trying to use their keys to open the doors of other peoples' cars. But now that time has passed, different doped-up Deadheads are failing to open the doors of an altogether different series of wrong cars.)

(Come on Tommy, get your story straight. In some cases it was exactly the same doped-up Deadheads.)

(And some of the same cars, too. Who can afford new ones with all the shows we're seeing.)

(Hey, it only happened to me twice.)

(Yeah, and sometimes I picked the right car, it was just the wrong key.)

(Or the wrong objects in lieu of keys. But I've seen that happen at the supermarket, too.)

(With a kiwi?)

(A key lime pie?)

(Is this getting too abstract and conceptual for anybody?)

(Shame on you, you're a taper at a Grateful Dead show!)

"And that's not whistling Winn-Dixie."

(Wow, big bro, a joke, of sorts, and one without a Grateful Dead reference.)

"Once in a while you get shown the light in the strangest of places if you look at it right."

(Well now you've ruined it. Anyhow, if this is my thirteenth show shouldn't I be concerned? Isn't that an unlucky number?)

(Are you kidding?)

(Thirteen?)

(BAKER'S DOZEN!!)

(Of course…)

"Hey everyone, we're finally moving!"

(I'll drink to that! I'll drink to anything at this point.)

"It's about time they opened doors. Don't these people realize how long it takes for me to erect my mic stand these days."

(You know—)

"That was a pre-emptive strike."

(Duly noted and well played. You won't hear me go on about how a few years ago you could get it up much quicker—wait, Ted, why'd you stop moving?)

"Have you seen Rez?"

(No, she wandered off.)

"I just remembered I have to take care of something. I have an extra that I've got to unload. The ticket originally designated for your betrothed."

(Big bro, let me do it. The last time I went to a show with you this took forever. You went through this noblest of Deadheads test. Just drop it in some stinky guy's hand. I'll reimburse you.)

"Stay here, I'll be right back. It shouldn't be hard to find a deserving face."

(That's right, it shouldn't. Don't forget. Why don't you make that an angelic face, remember your little brother is always happy to meet a new friend now that his old friend has slipped town with his expresso machine.)

"Even if that were the case, I doubt she'll actually sit with us in the tapers' section. But yes, statistically, I imagine it'll go to a woman. The ladies say I'm an old softie."

(I wouldn't broadcast that.)

How about that girl right there?

ROBIN

"I NEED ONE! PLEASE SELL ME YOUR TICKET! PLEASE SELL ME YOUR TICKET!"

(Okay.)

"Okay?"

(You want it?)

"Yes, yes, yes. Please."

(Hey, are you selling tickets?)

(No, I'm selling this woman a ticket.)

(You got any more?)

(No more extras. Sorry.)

(I'll give you twice what she's paying.)

(No, I'm sorry.)

(Someone has an extra?)

(Yeah man, you got an extra?)

(No, I don't.)

(Hey girl, better make sure that guy's not ripping you off. He could be selling you a fake.)

"It's okay, thank you. I know."

(It's a mail order.)

(I've seen fake mail orders.)

(It's a taper ticket, is that okay?)

(People can make fake taper tickets.)

(I'm not speaking with you, I'm speaking with her. What's your name?)

"Robin."

(I'm speaking with Robin. It's a taper ticket. Is that okay with you? If you were to sit down there with us, you'd need to keep a lot of your energy inside your head. But I imagine you just want in the door, right?)

"Yeah, that's fine. I'll be twirling in the halls."

(That's why I picked you. Twenty bucks.)

"No, twenty isn't fair to you. The price on the ticket is twenty-one-fifty plus there's handling charges. I've mail ordered before…"

(Fine, twenty-five. Please let's do this. The taper line's moving and I have to get in and set up my equipment.)

"Okay, here you go. Twenty-one…two…three…four…five…and a hug for good luck. Have a good show."

(Thanks. Same to you.)

I HAVE A TICKET!

I HAVE A TICKET!

(You better make sure that thing's real.)

(Well there's nothing she can do about it now.)

(No, no, it's real. It's a mail order taper ticket and that guy is definitely a taper. Watch him, he's heading over to the taper entrance.)

(Well just because *his* ticket is legit doesn't mean that *hers* is.)

"I appreciate your concern but I really don't need this trip right now. Have a good show, everyone."

I know that I will because I HAVE A TICKET!

At least I think I have a ticket.

No, no, I HAVE A TICKET! I HAVE A TICKET!

STEVEN

Shit, I hope those guys don't show up. They're gonna act all studly, do their college boy thing… Ooohh look, tie-dyed socks, very cool. I hope I brought at least fifty bucks… Burns and his friends are just gonna ruin it. Whenever those old Willington guys show up at our parties, the girls are all over them… Cool, a Jetsons tour T-shirt. I definitely want a Jetsons tour T-shirt. I don't care if I have to carry it around, it's *that* sweet. The Jetsons dressed as Deadheads. Even Astro is wearing a tie-dye.

"Excuse me?"

(What's up, bro? What can I do you for?)

"Hey, sorry, I didn't mean to interrupt you. I didn't realize you were talking to someone."

(That dude, nah, that's just Mr. Charlie. Cosmic to his friends. We weren't talking so much as occupying the same space. I'm here for you, bro. Give up your paw.)

"My paw?"

(Your phalanges, my friend.)

Right, right.

(There you go, that's what it's about. Strangers stopping strangers just to shake their hand!)

"Right on!"

Right on!

(Right on, right on! So what up bro?)

"I'm just digging that Jetsons shirt."

(That Jetsons shirt is there to be dug.)

"How much?"

(As much as you want to dig it, bro!)

"No, how much does it cost?"

(Right on, right on! Sorry bro, I was caught up in another time's forgotten place.)

"'Franklin's Tower.'"

(There hangs a bell. It can ring, turn night to day, ring like fire when you lose your way…)

I love this guy! I love this song! I love the lot!

"Roll away…"

(THE DEW!)

(Hey, Steven!)

Crap.

"So how much for the shirt?"

(Ten.)

"I'll take one. It's primo."

(Thanks, bro. A friend of mine at UVM designed it. Then he couldn't come on tour so I'm out here doing him a solid. Just breathing it all in. You dig?)

"I dig. Do you have it in medium?"

(Steven!)

(Ummm, no. Sorry, I don't have any more mediums on me. I have a bunch back in my vehicle, though. Do you want to follow me there?)

(Hey, Steven!)

"Well…"

(Saint Steven, get over here!)

(Are those your buds yelling for you? 'Saint Stephen,' sweet, sweet song, bro.)

(Yeah but my name's spelled differently, with a V.)

(Well Steven with a V, how about if I run to the car and meet you back here, pronto?)

"Yeah, that would be sweet."

(Little Steven, come over here!)

"Okay, okay, I'm here."

(What were you doing?)

"Buying a T-shirt."

(I thought we told you—)

"Well I don't mind carrying it around. It's got the Jetsons dressed up like Deadheads."

(Alright, fine. Whatever. Just come on over alongside this bus. Nate's making a deal.)

"Okay, okay, here I am…"

(So you're sure these are good?)

(Yeah, I've taken 'em myself. Guaranteed.)

(Okay, okay. How much a hit?)

(How many do you want?)

(Ten.)

(Five bucks a dose.)

(That sounds fair.)

(Hells yeah, it's fair. Come over here beside the truck, just one of you. The one with the cash.)

"Do you have enough dough, Nate?"

(Yeah, don't sweat it. We'll square it later.)

Well that's it, we've done it, we've found acid. We're buying acid. We're going to take acid.

Alright Steve-o, get your shit together, it'll be cool. It's not like you've never taken it before—okay, okay you didn't get off that time and it was only half of a half-hit after you tore it up. But that doesn't matter. What matters is that you took it. And if you took it once, you can take it again.

(Nate, man, we're styling now. What do they look like? Dancing skellies?)

(No, some old bald dude with a birth mark.)

(Timothy Leary?)

(Is he a bald dude with a birthmark?)

(You tell me.)

"Let me see… That's Gorbachev."

(So these are communist doses. Is that a good thing?)

"It's not a bad thing. Unless the doses are sabotaged like the exploding cigars we keep giving to Castro."

(Ha! Word to the wise!)

(So let's take 'em.)

(Okay, okay. Hold on. Let me pull out my Swiss Army knife. Man, my parents had no idea what was up when they bought me this. Mini scissors to cut the doses and a pair of tweezers to hold them while I'm doing the snipping. Okay, here we go. Zack, one for you. Jason, one for you. And last but certainly least, at his FIRST DEAD SHOW, the Virgin Steven Reynolds.)

No shit it's really happening. Here I am in the Grateful Dead lot, I'm standing in Shakedown Street, about to drop a tab of acid. I'm getting a rush just thinking about it. This is cool, this is definitely cool. There's nothing scary about it at all. The paper even has the Soviet leader on it which makes it pretty goofy. So here I go… On the tongue… Alright, that's it. Can't even taste it. That's the thing about acid, I guess. It's this little piece of paper and you don't imagine it can do anything to you and then look out!

(Do you usually swallow your paper or spit it out?)

(I used to swallow but now I spit—)

(I think that's another conversation for the two of you boys best left to the privacy of your bedroom.)

(—because I swear at the Hartford shows last spring I swallowed the paper and it caught in the back of my throat and fucked with my voice box or something. I had laryngitis for like a week.)

(Yeah, I remember that. But are you sure it was the acid? You told me that you walked around for an hour in the rain after the show looking for your car.)

"Apparently that's something of a theme in your life."

(Like I say, I gotta be me. But if was you, I still wouldn't swallow.)

"I just did."

(Steven, old man, it really doesn't matter. I believe we are done there. It's time to head in.)

"Wait. I thought you said we could grab something to eat. And some guy went to his car to get me a T-shirt."

(Look it's getting late. You already have something to eat. You have Alex's meat thing and I don't mean that metaphorically.)

(Yeah, maybe it'll bring you good luck with Shannon and I don't mean that metaphorically. Or maybe I do, I'm not sure. You're the wordsmith.)

(Listen, we gotta motor. The line outside is real slow. If you're still hungry after the meat thing you can grab something inside. And like I said before, you can get a shirt after the show. Is that cool with everyone? Jason?)

(Dig.)

(Zack?)

(Right on.)

(Alright, let's do it.)

"Yeah but this guy—"

(Steven man, come on. You can get a shirt after the show, I promise. Okay?)

"But I told him—"

(Well, I told Jerry you'd be in there for your first show before the show actually started.)

(Yeah, Steven, trust us on this, it's a fustercluck trying to get in.)

(Listen, you'll be hurting our feelings but if want to meet us inside that's fine, you're a big boy…)

"Well that Jetsons shirt is sweet…"

(So is that Shannon Phelps? Don't sweat it. Hopefully you'll be able to find us if we don't actually sit in our seats. We'll tell her that you blew her off for Astrid.)

(Astro.)

Crap.

(That Jane is a hottie.)

(Don't you mean June.)

(I think he means Judy.)

(No, I mean Jane. I've got a thing for redheads.)

(Gentlemen, lock up your mothers.)

(Well I've got a thing for Deadheads. Deadheads standing in line, so let's walk over and make my fantasy a reality. What's your fantasy, Little Steven? Are coming with us?)

"I am…"

(Of course you are.)

RANDY

(Shit Rand, where have you been?)

"Eddie, I got fucked."

(Seriously? I've been told these Deadhead chicks put out but you got laid?)

"No man fucked—screwed—my fucking car broke down. No, not my car, freaking Rennick's car."

(Well Mack's looking for you. His disposition is less than cheery.)

"Yeah, yeah I saw him. He fired me."

(Coach'll kill you.)

"Not if I kill him first."

(Yeah, right.)

"Nah, I figure if I do a good job tonight and then show up tomorrow, maybe Mack will let it slide."

(Good luck with that. You got the stuff for later?)

"It's in my backpack. I need to find Davis first."

(That's my crew. Davis went to take a crap. He'll be right back. Who'd you work for last night?)

"I don't know, some guy with a name."

(Really that's quite the eidetic memory you have there.)

"You know that's a myth right?"

(Marilu Henner, the fetching Elaine Nardo from *Taxi* has eidetic memory so I know it's *not* a myth, because as you as well aware, Nardo…)

"Has knobs. Yes, I've seen them. I'm not sure why that's germane but I'll concur. But even if I can't quite name any of the chimps who purportedly served as my supervisors last night, I can still memorize a playbook fourteen times faster than you.

You see, I had no single boss last night. I kept getting bounced around like Griffin Dunne in *After Hours*."

(Be careful you don't get bounced around like Griffin Dunne in *Johnny Dangerously*.)

"I never saw that one."

(Amy Heckerling. It was her follow-up to *Fast Times at Ridgemont High*. You never saw that one? Guess who's in it? Marilu Henner and her knobs.)

"No sale. I'm just not a Joe Piscopo guy."

(Talent squandered.)

"You're halfway right."

ZEB

(I'm sorry, I wish we could help you.)

"It's alright, brother, I understand. You're right on helping me as it is. Thank you for your patronage."

(Hey, thanks for selling us the beers. Say, if you don't mind me asking…)

Awww, not the dope question. Not from the little locals.

(How many shows have you been to?)

Right on.

"No, I don't mind answering that one. If I get in tonight, it'll be my sixty-third soiree with the Boys."

(Whoa, that's cool. That's a lot of shows.)

"Who are the Grateful Dead and why do they keep following me."

(Yeah! Hey and sorry we couldn't help you out with tickets.)

(Yeah but if we see you tomorrow and you need one—)

"Wait, you have an extra for tomorrow?"

(Yeah, one of our buddies was grounded—)

"Do you have it with you?"

(I think it's over in the car. Right, Keith?)

(It's in there. Our friend Max got grounded so his mom made me go to his house and take his tickets. We sold his ticket for tonight to our other friend who's over there looking at T-shirts because he was too chicken to buy a beer from you. He's not coming tomorrow, he's *definitely* not coming tomorrow, so we're gonna sell it then.)

"Would you mind selling it now, bro?"

(You don't have a ticket for tomorrow?)

"No, I'm—well no, I don't but that's not it. I'll take a tomorrow if I have to but with a little legwork I can trade it for a tonight."

(Really? You think you can do that?)

"Pie, bro. Pie."

(Yeah, sure. Then we'll do it. Especially after you sold us the beer. I probably shouldn't tell you this but we're not twenty-one yet.)

"That's cool brother, neither am I. So would you get it?"

(Sure, come on Brad.)

(We'll be right back.)

Crazy, I might not jones tonight.

Now *that's* why you gotta be kind to the custies!

Still need to make a trade though. Could go either way. Might as well start working it.

"Tomorrow for tonight. Tomorrow for tonight. I'll trade you tomorrow night's ticket for tonight. Nice cold tasty imports. Ice cold domestics a buck, imports a deuce. Kind Bud-weiser, kind Beck's."

There they are!

(Alright, so how should we do this?)

"Twenty-five. Does that sound fair?"

(Wait.)

Uh-oh.

"What?"

(The ticket says it costs twenty-one-fifty. We don't want to rip you off.)

"No, there's a service charge of three dollars and seventy-five cents. A little steep but that's what is. You got to add that to the price of the ticket. See? So it really costs… It costs a little more than twenty-five. I'll give you twenty-six."

(Okay, cool.)

"So twenty-six then?"

(Sure.)

Okay now I just have to find—oh shit shit shit. Here are my singles but where's my cheddar?

What am I—oh, wrong pocket.

"Here you go. And might I interest each of you, my kind brothers, in a complimentary beverage? Kind Beck's? Kind Bud?"

(Yeah sure that's great.)

(Yeah, cool. Thanks.)

"Have a good show the two of you."

(Thanks, brother, same to you.)

Those kids were alright. Sort of like me a few years ago. Of course I was younger than they are when I was them.

STEVEN

(Baaaahhh!)

(Moooo!)

(Baaaahhh!)

(Moooo!)

(Come on, let us in! Speed things up!)

(We're missing the shooooow.)

(Baaaahhh!)

"That's pretty funny. Did you guys hear that?"

(The dudes making animals noises? Yeah, I heard it. I've heard it before. What time you got?)

"Hold on, it's in my pocket…seven-fifteen."

(We could miss the first song.)

"That would suck."

(No, you'll be in by then. Once you're up here in the middle of the cattle call it goes quickly. Unlike say The Civic last spring when everyone was cutting.)

(Yeah, I was there.)

Owwww!

"Hey, don't push."

(Cut it out! Quit pushing!)

Awww, this is bogus. It's stuff like this that wrecks it for everyone, ruins everybody's vibes. I mean we all want the same thing—owww, shit.

"Come on, cut it out!"

Why do I need to get elbowed in the ribs while I'm trying to make my way into the show? This sucks. I've been to sold out Hartford Whalers games and I walked right in. This is out of control, it's a total mob scene. I wonder if it's like this everywhere the Dead play. Or is it just that they don't like Deadheads in New Jersey? It's definitely possible that they're trying to ruin the scene by letting us in extra slowly so that we'll push and stuff. And I bet some people can't help pushing, like if they have to piss or something. Shit, I can barely move my arms and I'm afraid I'm going to poke somebody with the Burnster's kabob thing. I'd dump it but I'm starving. Shit I hope he doesn't go to Emily's tonight.

Okay, Steve-o, chill. Just mellow. You're here on acid at your first show. Everything will be fine. Take another bite of the kabob. Uhhhh, it is sort of greasy and gross but at least it's almost gone. So just finish it up and then you won't be so hungry and you can go in and find Shannon and those guys and it'll be a great show and you'll know most of the songs and the acid will do what it's supposed to do without doing too much and you'll get the cool Jetsons T-shirt afterwards and you'll go back to Emily's and you'll finally hook up with Shannon. And all that seems like a lot but it's not, not here. Not at a Dead show.

(Baaaahhh! Baaaahhh!)

(Hey, who's poking me?)

"Sorry, that was my kabob-thing."

(Well shit, man get rid of it.)

"Okay, okay. I'm finishing it up now. See, see…"

(Okay.)

(Baaahhhhhh!)

(Mooooo! Mooooo!)

(Baaaahhhh!)

(Let us in!)

(Come on, let us in! We can't breathe out here!)

(Mooooohhhh!)

(IF YOU MUST TREAT US LIKE ANIMALS, AT LEAST TREAT US WITH THE BASIC RESPECT THAT WE GIVE TO ANIMALS!)

(Yeah, right. Slice our flanks into tube steaks and grind our ears into dog food.)

STELLA BLUE

"Mommy, I'm getting smushed."

(I know honey. I'm sorry, Stell Belle. Please everyone, please give us a little room. There's a child here.)

(Well maybe there shouldn't be.)

(Who said that?)

(Calm down, Jenny.)

(No, who said that?)

(Let it rest.)

"Mommeeee!"

(Okay, Stella. Want to sit on Mommy's shoulders?)

"Uh-huh."

(This is unreal. We should have gone in earlier.)

(We're okay now. You're okay, right, Stella?)

"It's pretty up here. Lots of colors."

(Can you see how close we are to the door?)

"This close."

(That close, huh?)

(You know it wouldn't have made any difference if the three of you had gotten here earlier. They only opened the doors a few minutes ago.)

(No shit.)

"Aunt Jenny!"

(Sorry, Stella… That's crazy.)

(Yeah and it was like this last night too. For some reason they won't open up the doors until quarter of seven and then there's this crush to get in. I missed the 'Half-Step' and the 'Minglewood.')

(You hear that, Alison?)

(Yeah. How you doing up there, Stella?)

"Great. I can see everything."

(I don't know, Jen… It's times like this that I wonder if Stella needs to be in here smashed together with all these people.)

(Hey, for all we know this is the way that people will be living when she grows up. She's fine. You're fine up there, right, Stella?)

"I'm fine up here, Aunt Jenny."

(Besides, it's important for her to get out and see everyone. It's an important part of life.)

(I know. It's just that she's this little kid and sometimes I have this overwhelming desire to smother her up and keep her away from everything.)

(Well that would be a mistake. That's what our parents did to us. That's why we're so fucked up.)

"Aunt Jenny!"

(Sorry, Stella… But really Al, you got to let the kid see and touch and taste and smell—)

(She's right, let the kid smell.)

(Yeah, let the kid smell.)

(Yeah, let her smell.)

(Let her smell!)

(Let her smell!)

(Let her smell!)

TAPER TED

(Hey, Teddy, can you come back here for a minute?)

"Just a second. Actually, Mitch, you can help me from there, what do you think?"

(A hair to the left for the proper Phil quotient. He's going to be pumping out the Biscuits tonight, I can feel it.)

"Thanks. Hold on, I'll be there in a moment. Tommy, can you stay here and watch my stuff? And please don't touch anything."

(Yes, Mr. Wilson.)

"Excuse me…excuse me… Oops, sorry, Kev, just passing through. I have to talk to this guy. Okay, Mitch what's up?"

(I'm almost embarrassed to ask but do you have any analog blanks on you? A pair of nineties or ideally one hundreds?)

"Not with me. I've been fully digital without analog backup for nearly five years now. Come to think of it, about as long as you have. So what's up?"

(In a few minutes I'm gonna be running on fumes.)

"How so?"

(I was having some problems with my deck. At first I thought it was the preamp but now I'm not sure. So I brought it to Audio Jack for a tune-up but with everyone in town for the shows, the only thing he had lying around that he could spare was this analog D-6. I was feeling sentimental so I went with it. I haven't run one of these in a couple years. The only problem will be the flip, it's like going back to the stone age.)

"Barney Rubble never went digital. So what's the problem? "

(As you pointed out, it's been a while since I've been analog. So I came in here slightly strung out, carrying my pack full of sixty meter digital blanks but no good old fashioned analog cassettes. I'll trade you blank for blank, sixty meter DAT for a Maxell XLII-S or TDK SA-X.)

"Sorry, while I do have my fair share of plastic ribbon-filled rectangles I just don't think I have anything that suits you. Do you have any analog blanks at all?"

(This kid over here who's running a D-3 said I could tape over his masters from last night if I promise to replace them pronto. Apparently, he was no fan of the 'Uncle John's' > 'Playing.' Or at least not fan enough. Personally I think Brent was on point for both of those and really pulled it out for them. And as you know that's something I'll rarely say.)

"Give the new guy a break."

(Yeah, it's only been ten years.)

"Plus, you don't want a retread."

(That's what I told him, which is why I called you over. My other option is I can use the clean portion of his first set master from last night until something else comes up. At least that way I can float him a signal.)

"Why doesn't he just patch out of someone else?"

(He's a bit on the timid side, you know how it can be down here. He's happy that he's found someone who isn't giving him shit about coming in with a tapers' ticket but without his own mics. Plus this is his seat, he's reluctant to move and attempt to make a new cranky taper buddy due to his lack of microphones and there's not much free space anyhow. Besides, Neumanns are Neumanns.)

"And he doesn't have another blank?"

(Just one for the second set. Kids today, they just don't come prepared.)

"But he knows that he's going to lose his signal when your tape runs out."

(I'm not sure he's thought that through but I promise it won't happen. If worse comes to worse I'll do a mercy kill and hit pause just before then so that he doesn't lose his signal.)

"Why don't you just give him first position?"

(I don't know if he can handle the Neumanns with his D-3.)

"Well then why not run the D-6 with his blanks for him."

(Would you like me to cut his meat for him too? I'm the guy with the microphones. I'm still hoping to come up with something. Plus, I'll admit, I find the dilemma somewhat charming.)

"You know what, Rez just may be the cavalry here. I haven't seen her in here yet but my guess is that she's got an analog in her bag. I doubt it's a blank. You'd probably have to go the retread route.)

(Listen, I'll have you spin me the show eventually so I can have a crispy DAT. I'm really just looking for something I can listen to on my way home and on my drive back in tomorrow night.)

"Just don't forget to pop the tabs."

(It hasn't been that long.)

ZEB

"Tomorrow for tonight, tomorrow for tonight. I'll trade my tomorrow for your tonight. MY TOMORROW FOR YOUR TONIGHT!"

What's that I hear? The whoosh of a nitrous tank. Somebody just busted out the hippie crack.

No balloon for me though, I've given it up. Even when I'm dosing and it can be as crinkly as it gets.

Lesson learned in Charlotte last fall when I took a hit, passed out for three seconds, dropped the balloon and then crawled through broken glass trying to grab it again before all the nitrous spilled out.

I had an out-of-body experience in that moment and I did not like what I saw. Plus my hands were bleeding, which is never a kind visual on acid.

Nobody's fault but mine.

What's crazy about the nitrous guys these days is they're so out in the open. They're not clandy about it at all. The whoosh draws in the Heads, who pay five bucks a balloon, wander around a little and then get back in line. The cops stay out of it because the nitrous mafia pays them off.

When the cops are on the take, the nitrous dudes can get real obnoxious about it too. Some of them tour with their own sound system that's heavy on the bass. So they get a dance party working and start whooshing out balloons. Disco lights too if it's after dark. The whole scene becomes demented real quick. Then once the custies finish their balloons, they try to keep up with the frantic pace of it all. That works for a minute or two until the droning bass makes everything sound a little bit off and slightly uncomfortable. The solution? Why another balloon. So it's back in line for more hippie crack. Again and again and again. A sad state of affairs. Positively diabolical. One night I nearly dropped fifty bucks that way, for myself and a sweet Sugar Magnolia I met on tour who was selling fresh pressed juice and crystals.

Those dudes never even think about going into the shows, it's a pure cash play for them. They make out like bandits too unless some competitor feels threatened and really hounds the cops. The way that story eventually ends is everyone loses because the cops force all the nitrous dudes to empty out their tanks. When that goes down the nitrous comes whooshing out for free and if you pick the right spot a safe distance away, it can be a religious experience. The thing to remember, though, is that the tank is pressurized, so if the cops and the nitrous guys don't pay close enough attention you'll end up with a chunk of tank in your head. I've heard stories.

Maybe I deserve a treat though. It's been six months and business *has* been good tonight…

Well…

No…

I can't go back and I can't stand still. If the thunder don't get me then the lightning will.

"Tomorrow For Tonight! Trading tomorrow for tonight. Tomorrow For Tonight!"

(Hey, I'll do that.)

"Really? Righteous!"

Righteous!

"To celebrate, can I interest you in a complimentary Beck's?"

(Yeah, man, great.)

Wait, where did I put my—here it is.

"Take a gander at this cutie. It's no countie… It's the real deal, on my honor… What's the problem? It's not a fake, I promise."

I think.

(So this is a ticket for tomorrow night.)

"That what it says. I mean, I didn't look at it too closely when I bought it from these kids but… No, that's what it is, a ticket for the Saturday night show."

(Bummer!)

"What?"

(I thought you were trading me tonight's ticket for tomorrow night's ticket. I already have a ticket for tomorrow night which I'm trying to trade for a ticket for tonight.)

"Ahhh, man."

(Bummer. Let me give you a buck for the beer.)

"Nah, keep it, brother."

A Beck's costs two anyhow.

(Well good luck, man.)

"Same to you, brother. Just a little less luck than me…"

(Ha!)

"Hey now, nitrous zombies! Tomorrow for tonight! I have in my hand a ticket for tomorrow night's show to trade for a ticket to tonight's show. You hand me your tonight and I'll hand you my tomorrow. My tomorrow for your tonight. MY TOMORROW FOR YOUR TONIGHT!"

ROBIN

Uhhh, I can barely breathe in here, I think I'm going to lose it.

All these elbows and shoulders and backs. Please let me get up there. And please let Mara get in. And please let me find her. And please let me find kind dancing space.

Inching forward…

And please let this not be a counterfeit.

Closer…

Closer…

Feeling the twinkles too. A little aloha from my Dark Star unicorn dose.

Closer…

Just one more push and…

Finally, I can see the ushers…

Here, we go…

(I just need to give your bag a quick check…)

A little pat down from the nice lady…

(Ticket?)

"Here it is!"

He's eyeing it, he's eyeing it.

Something's not right.

I can't believe it's a counterfeit. The taper guy seemed so kind. I can't believe I bought a counterfeit. It looked so real too. It can't be a counterfeit, can it?

(This is a taper ticket, do you realize that?)

"Umm, yes, but I'm not taping."

(You do realize that there's a separate taper entrance, don't you?)

"Yes I do but I'm at the front of *this* line and I don't have any taping gear and the show's gonna start like any minute now. So can you could please let me in here?"

(Let me talk to my boss. Can you hold on a moment?)

"Indubitably."

I learned that from Schoolhouse Rock.

(Hey, don't walk away, what about the rest of us! We wanna get in there before the show starts.)

"Sorry."

(What was their problem?)

"It's a taper ticket but I'm not going in through the taper entrance."

(Really? That's it? But it's a ticket right? This is so frustrating. It's not even opening night. You figure they'd get their shit together and get on the same page by now. It's like they can't quite handle what's going on out here and don't entirely understand what we're doing. This happens every time the circus comes to town.)

"Again, I'm sorry."

(It's not your fault, it's theirs. It's always theirs. Here they come...)

(Whose ticket is this?)

(It's hers.)

"It's mine."

(This is a tapers' ticket, do you realize that?)

"I do."

(There's a separate entrance for tapers around the other side of the building.)

(Awww, come on, let her in, you're holding up the line!)

"No, it's fine. Yes, I understand that but I don't have any taping equipment with me and the show is going to start any minute now, so can you please just let me in this door?"

(But if you have a taper ticket why do you want to come in this door?)

(SHE WANTS TO GO IN THAT DOOR BECAUSE THE SHOW'S ABOUT TO START!)

"I'm sorry. I just ended up in this line. I'm sure the tapers' line is much shorter but this is where I am now, so can you please let me in?"

(Well...I have to admit, I've never seen a situation like this before. Okay, I'll make an exception but tomorrow night use the tapers' entrance.)

"Absolutely."

(And you over there, the guy yelling, Old Yeller, get to the back out of the line!)

(ARE YOU SHITTING ME?)

(Yes I am. But please, no need to raise your voice. We're all on the same side here.)

(No, we're not.)

(We're not?)

(No, you're on the other side of the turnstile, which is where I want to be…)

(Alright, well hang on, this girl's first…)

He's tearing it in the middle just to be sure…and it's got those beautiful purple threads inside so it's not a counterfeit! He's ripping it! He's ripping the ticket! I AM IN!

"YAHOOOIEE!"

Time to find some dancing room and find some Mara.

BAGEL BOB

"Bagel Bob will barter or buy! Please enter into a transaction with Bagel Bob! Sell you extra ticket to Bagel Bob! Bagel Bob wishes to enter the coliseum. Bagel Bob wishes to enjoy the show."

(No go, eh, Bob?)

"Not as yet. Perhaps the time has come to contemplate a game of cribbage."

(Don't give up yet. Something might come through.)

"Bob doesn't think so. Something is askew. Bob feels wary."

(Yeah, I saw what happened before. That's the problem with this place. The yellow jackets trip on power. And their trips are ruining ours.)

"Bob does not disagree."

(Last night a gang of them tried to close me down. They tried to tell me that it's illegal to sell my spinach lasagna outside the show. Since when have they reclassified pasta as a controlled substance?)

(Man, me too. They gave me that same shit last night.)

(No ticket for you either?)

(No tickee, no showee. Man, last night they confiscated a whole pot of my three bean salad. I begged them to give it back. I told 'em, 'Please, pick out the kidneys and make it a two bean salad if that floats your boat but let me keep my livelihood.')

(And?)

(They walked away and came back a half hour later with an empty pot.)

(That's a bummer.)

(And their breath smelled suspiciously of waxed beans.)

(What do waxed beans smell like?)

"Jackie Straw!"

(Greetings, Robert.)

"No ticket?"

(No, Robert, I possess a ticket.)

"Well then you should proceed to the coliseum, the show is about to commence."

(En route. I'm just collecting my space.)

"Bob understands."

(And once I can fit it into the palm of my mind then a showing, I will go...)

(Just try not to spill any of it.)

(Come on, don't mess with me. I'm trying to hold it together so I can walk the gauntlet.)

"Jackie Straw, ignore Three Bean Monty. As you well fathom, one man gathers what another man spills."

STEVEN

(Finally! Have a great show, everybody!)

Sweet! She gave me a hug. Now this is what a Dead show is about, not about being stuck in a mob scene out front. Everyone is happy and skipping and hugging. And why shouldn't they, WE ARE IN THE SHOW!

INSIDE THE SHOW!

MY FIRST SHOW!

(Alright, let's move. It's like 7:25. They're gonna come on soon.)

"You guys have been here before. Take command, lead on."

(Zack, you run point.)

(Let's roll, brothers.)

This is very, very cool. Everyone is smiling and running to their seats. It's almost like they know that they have to get there so that everything that's supposed to happen can happen. We're all just moving past each other so that it can start, so that THE MAGIC CAN BEGIN.

Look at that. They're selling thirty-buck T-shirts inside here. I kind of want to yell at those people not to do it, to buy their shirts outside. It's too bad that some people just don't know what they're doing but—

Wharf Rats. Look at that sign: *Wharf Rats Meeting Here at Intermission.* What sort of thing is that? Is it some sort of Deadhead group for people who are into sailing? I should look into that for next summer, if they have an outpost in Connecticut. I've got to ask Nate and Zack about that. Without making it look like I don't know of course.

This is just so cool. I'm catching a buzz just from running around, hustling to our seats. When I go past the signs for each section, it feels different because they're not just telling me where each section is, they're telling me where each section is AT THE SHOW. And those guys selling hot dogs at the concession stand are almost cool or something because they're selling hot dogs AT THE SHOW.

Everything is like mystical, I can't explain it. And that smell, it's that perfume stuff that Deadhead women wear. We're changing the whole place in here, even the air. We're making it ours. Man, my adrenaline is pumping. I just want to get in there and start grooving.

(Nate! Zack!)

(Steven!)

(Hey, what about me?)

(Jason! Jas!)

Shit, this is like perfect. Shannon, Emily, and Meg.

"Hey, how are you guys doing?"

(How long have you been here?)

(Great.)

(We just got here. We were afraid that you already went down to your seats.)

"Nah, you had to know we'd wait for you."

I will always wait for you Shannon Phelps.

(Alright then, let's go in.)

(Wait, have you guys checked? Are they looking at tickets before they let people down into the sections?)

(It's not gonna be a problem where we are. If we were sitting one section lower they'd check our ticket stubs but not up here. They'll just let us go in. I was behind the stage one night last year and moved to these great seats on the side. No prob.)

(Okay then, let's go. You guys know the row, so lead us in.)

(Will do and if we can't all fit in that one we can look for another one or split up or something.)

Cool, cool. Maybe something for Shannon and me by ourselves. Now if I just keep her directly in front of me, I'll be all set. I can't believe I'm here with her. She's just so cute. I mean she's not just cute, she's someone who actually earns the word adorable, especially with those dimples in her cheeks. I remember when I couldn't even speak to her, the Dimples of Muteness did me in.

Whoa, look at it in here. Check it out, it's so colorful. People are all wearing tie-dyes or Guatemalan threads and everyone's bopping around balloons. And look at the stage with those monster speakers alongside it. There's no question that the sound at a Dead show rules. I bet the lights are wild too. And down on the floor there's the taper section with all those microphones up on stands, ready and waiting for the action to start. The Dead are just so awesome letting people tape their shows. They really understand what it's all about. This is definitely the coolest.

And I'm finally here.

I've imagined it hundreds of times but here I am INSIDE THE SHOW.

Hey, and this is a pretty good section too, in the middle on the side, not up in the nose bleeds and not down so far where you can't get a good view of everyone else.

(Check it out. This is our row and there's enough room for all seven of us.)

It's like destiny. We fit in here perfectly. And this is a Dead show so even if someone shows up with tickets for the other seats, they'll just find somewhere else to sit. Everyone makes room for everyone because we're all part of the community. We're all in the scene together.

This rules.

My first Dead show. Perfect seats. Great view. Nate on my right. Shannon on my left. This is it. Tonight it's gonna happen. Everything. The Dead. Shannon. Everything.

(Alright, game on! Does anybody have last night's setlist? It's in the Dupree's.)

(I heard someone in the lot saying they played 'Uncle John's Band.' I'd love to hear that tonight.)

(You're joking, right?)

(No, it's sweet. What's your problem, Jason, is that song not Deadheady enough for you? It's not like I said 'Far From Me,' which I still think is a good song even if they look cheesy on the album cover.)

(Emily's right. We play the song all the time. Even Jennica the perfect prefect likes it. Besides, I don't think that album cover is cheesy, it's a joke and they're in on the joke. It's semiotics. Like in Williams' class. Right, Steven?)

Crap. Put on the spot.

"Well, I think that's a reasonable interpretation—"

(But wait, what's a Dupree's?)

Thank you, Meg.

(Just keep your eyes open for a pink piece of paper. Dupree's Diamond News. It has setlists and cool ads on it. And they're not going to play 'Uncle John's' tonight because they played it last night. You know they don't do that.)

(Well, I can't see a pink piece of paper but I bet they played their drum and space jam last night and they're going to do that again tonight.)

(Yeah, but that's different every time.)

(Jason, be a Deadhead not a dickhead. Do you even listen to any of those live tapes you're hoarding back in your lair? 'Uncle John's Band' sounds different every time.)

(Psych!)

(Face!)

(Burn!)

(Sizzle!)

(And I also like it because Jerry sings 'Are You Kind,' which you Mr. Jason Baumgarten are most certainly not!)

(I hear you, Meg, I'm Bauming you out.)

(Get a room you two!)

(We'll see…)

"So, Shannon, how long were you out in the parking lot?"

(A couple hours. We got here really early to beat the rush. And to find shrooms.)

"Did you find any?"

(Yeah, we bought two eighths.)

"How much did you take?"

(Two eighths. A while ago. I'm already starting to rush.)

"Sweet."

Man, I wish I had taken mushrooms. They're better for you than acid because they're organic and—no Steve-o, you can't think like that. You'll bum yourself into a bad trip.

Okay, I took acid and I'm here at the show. We all have seats and any minute now the Dead are going to step on stage and it's gonna happen.

I just wish it would hurry up and start.

Then again, if they don't come on for a little while, I can hang with Shan and ease into my buzz.

RANDY

"So what exactly are we supposed to do here, Eddie?"

(Essentially, we walk through the parking lot and if anyone's doing anything really stupid, we stop them.)

"Sounds manageable."

(Yeah it sounds that way but none of these people want to be managed. And plenty of them are out of their minds. They yell at you, they give you shit and then they blame it all on you. I imagine you experienced that last night doing whatever the hell you were doing with your multiple monkey bosses."

"So how are we supposed to handle it?"

(However we handle it.)

"Second verse same as the first."

(Here comes Davis. Check him out, I think he did a few tours of duty in Vietnam and I'm not convinced he ever left. I'd call him Patton but that would be an insult to George C. Scott.)

"Or George S. Patton."

(Although maybe he can help us with our thing.)

"Except we can't tell him. Why does he get a golf cart?"

(I assume he wants to go play a quick nine before the show starts. No, that's what I'm telling you, that's his thing.)

(Robbins. Where's Schultz?)

(Went off to take a crap. I thought he was with you.)

(I take my craps by myself, Robbins. It's been that way for quite some time now.)

"Although from the looks of it, you're only a few weeks away from needing assistance again."

(Excuse me?)

"Excuse not accepted."

(Randy, what are—)

(Who the fuck are you?)

"Don't try to win me over with Who lyrics. Forget about me. YOU on the other hand are the worst referee in the history of New Jersey high school football. You cost my team the N.J.S.I.A.A. Group A North Non-Public Championship and I took a solemn vow to tell you as much the next time I saw you. I mean, Christ, blocking below the waist is only a penalty if it is outside the free blocking zone."

(That is a judgment call. What is your name?)

"Ellis."

(Ellis, that is a judgment call and given the limited self-control you are currently exhibiting, I have every reason to believe that if I threw a flag against you then a flag was in order.)

"Isn't it pretty to think so."

(Well, you win points for the Hemingway retort, I'll give you that. Are you assigned to this unit? Or perhaps I should phrase that in the past tense, as in *were* you assigned to this unit before your insubordination jeopardized that assignment?)

"Mack instructed me to report here."

(Well it appears that you're able to follow instructions. I will expect as much from you, along with an unwavering submission to my authority.)

No fucking way!

(Ellis?)

(Randy!)

"Absolutely, sir."

Absolutely no fucking way!

(Ellis, you're starting out on thin ice. Do you think you can keep yourself out of the drink?)

"Here's hoping that my two hundred and sixty-five pounds won't leave a crack."

STELLA BLUE

(Okay, Stella, I'm bringing you down.)

"We're here, Mommy, we're here."

(I know, honey, that's why I'm bringing you down.)

(Aww, you're bringing us all down. We'll miss you, Stella!)

(Yeah, Stella, we'll miss you!)

(Have a good show, Stella!)

(Thank you, Greek chorus.)

(Hey, this isn't the Greek. We're 3,000 miles away from Cali. No fair teasing!)

(Could you raise your arms, ma'am?)

(Hold on, Stella.)

"What are they doing, Mommy?"

(They're checking to see if I have anything illegal.)

"Do you?"

(Nothing they found. Just kidding, people.)

"How come they didn't check me?"

(Because you're an angel. And angels don't have illegal things. Okay, keep moving, we're almost there.)

(Tickets?)

(Here's your ticket, Stella. Hand it to the woman.)

"It's yellow."

(Yeah, it's pretty. Now hand it to the woman.)

"Here."

(Thank you. And here's your ticket stub. I hope you enjoy yourself young lady.)

(And here's mine. Hold on, Stella.)

"Look Mommy, everybody's dancing and making funny noises."

(That's because they're happy. They've been waiting outside for a long time and now they're inside where they can see the show. And they're happy because they know the Grateful Dead are going to make them happy.)

"I'm happy too, Mommy."

(Well I am especially happy that you're happy.)

"So can I scream too?"

(I should have seen that one coming. Absolutely!)

(And you can use your outdoor voice, even though we're indoors!)

"You're silly, Aunt Jenny!"

(Silly excited for the Grateful Dead!)

"Awooooo!"

(Me too?)

"You too!"

(Awoooooo!!!)

"Awoooooo!!!"

TAPER TED

(Are you all set here, big bro?)

"Just waiting on the band."

(Okay, I'm going to run up and grab myself a pretzel. I want to do some carb loading before the main event.)

"If you see Rez out there can you send her my way?"

(Will do.)

Hopefully she gets down here in time to help Mitch.

Let's see, what to do, what to do… Actually, nothing. It looks like I am altogether ramped up and ready…

(Excuse me, are you Ted Auslander?)

"I suppose I am."

(Can you come over here for a moment, I have a quick question for you.)

"Let 'er rip."

(I want to show you something, can you come over to me? It's easier than if I fight my way in to you.)

"That's fine. But we're getting close. Once Healy and Candace move in to position I have to step back… Excuse me… Excuse me… Okay, what's your name?"

(You can call me Chuck.)

"Then I shall. What's up, Chuck? "

(I want to talk to you about Whole Earth Access.)

Uh-oh.

"It's a store in Berkeley, right? I'm an East Coast Head but when I make the Bay Area pilgrimage for Shoreline or the New Year's shows, I'll stop in. Even if I don't buy something, it's worth it for the conversations I have on the floor. Where are you from?"

(Norfolk.)

"Scope Arena."

(April 3, 1982. I was there.)

"You were? You look a little young to have been there—"

(Okay, enough pleasantries.)

"Really? One can never have enough pleasantries."

(On a time available basis. We're up against it and we both know that I'm not talking about the Whole Earth Access store. I'm talking about the Whole Earth Access tree. I'm not on it and I want in.)

Uh-oh.

"I don't mean to me rude but I just don't know what you're talking about."

(Really? Because I have a printout right here and I see your name on this branch. Don't play games with me. Look over your shoulder, Candace just stepped behind the light board. The soundboard's still empty but I imagine that Healy's on his way.)

"How did you get that?"

(Someone printed it out and left it behind last night in the tapers' section. I was packing up and I found it. At first I couldn't figure out what it was, although I recognized a few of the names. But I spent some time on it today. I've been here for a few years, doing my thing, mostly keeping quiet. Over the past twelve months or so, I've heard pieces of a story about how a few tapers acquired a set of original soundboards that had been mixed live by Betty Cantor herself in the 1970s and '80s. Supposedly they were circulated weekly at the Whole Earth Access Store in San Rafael, not the original in Berkeley, by the way. So I stared at this for a while and then it all came together.)

"And what is it that you want?"

(I want in on the tree. I want you to supply me with all of the shows.)

"If you've seen the printout then you should also be aware that I'm not the one with the tapes. I'm not the trunk, why are you asking me?"

(The person on the trunk has a shielded email address. Besides, that individual could always run scared and shut down the operation. That's not my goal, I want more access to the Whole Earth Access, not less. You on the other hand are one branch away. Plus, I've seen you do your thing. You're not one of these obnoxious, elitist over-the-top tapers.)

"Don't sell me short, I think I'm pretty obnoxious."

(Well, from my vantage point, you're a good man.)

"Well if that's the case then what's a good man supposed to do here? What exactly you want from me?"

(I'd like you to pretend that I'm one of the leaves. I'll give you all the blanks and postage you need. I'm not asking you to dip into your pocket and pay for them. How many shows are there?)

"Ummm… Well…five or six."

(No, there's more than that. I have the printout folded up in my pocket. I can pull it out and everyone can have a look.)

"Okay, okay, my best guess is it requires about fifty tapes."

(I think you're right. In fact, you've jogged my own memory. I believe that each branch or leaf is expected to supply fifty-two unopened 60m DAT blanks. Would you like me to deliver those to you tomorrow night at the show or would you prefer to give me your home address and I can send them to you. I really want to be a mensch about all this.)

"I'm not sure you understand the meaning of the word mensch… And what if I won't do what you say?"

(Then I'll expose you all. You're sitting on *the* treasure trove of Grateful Dead tapes. Soundboards recorded throughout the 1970s, by the band's former audio engineer, Betty Cantor, who happens to have the best ears in the business.)

"Shhhh."

(I've had all day to think this through. If you don't play along I will send messages every hour on the hour to rec.music.gdead and ten different places on the WELL, providing the names and email addresses of everyone on this elitist tape trading tree. Aside from the fact that you will be inundated with emails and bad vibes from thousands of outraged Deadheads, it's also possible that the Dead's attorney, Hal Kant, will become involved. Some would say that you're taking a very cavalier attitude towards the band's property. Those soundboards you're exchanging were not acquired legally.)

"Now there you are wrong. As I understand it they were purchased at a collectibles auction. My wife is an attorney, we already looked into this. So long as we don't attempt to sell them, then we are within our legal rights."

(Well then I'm within my legal rights to respectfully request copies. Again, I'm not asking you to pay a cent. I will provide you with blanks and postage. There goes Healy. We can sort out the details after the show.)

"This is crazy. What you're talking about is blackmail."

(Don't be overly dramatic. It's not blackmail, it's blankmail.)

ZEB

Hey, there's one of the dudes I saw getting turned away at the door last night with a bogus ticket. I didn't recognize him but I could tell he knew what was up to. Maybe I should follow him and try to find the countie crew.

I'm not sure if he's one of them or just someone who's friendly with them but it certainly seemed like he was in on the scam. Nah, scam isn't the right word. If you're making counterfeits for yourself then you're not the victim or the crime. That's how the countie crew does it. Then they use the Jedi mind trick when they get to the front of the line.

It's all a game to them, trying to keep a half step ahead so they can make it to the promised land.

Photocopied tickets, taping two stubs together, erasing the printing on the ticket to some other show and then using a special pen and a real careful hand to turn that into a Grateful Dead ticket. It all can be done.

In the future, I bet ushers will have computers or something to stop all that but right now all you need are cojones.

The foolproof way is the voucher system. Some kid was explaining this to me at Spectrum set break last year. If you order your tickets over the phone from Ticketbastard then you can call them back a few days before the show, tell them your tickets still haven't arrived and they'll give you a voucher for the same seats. That means you have a free pass into the show for however many tickets you originally bought. *If* you have a credit card. *And* you have credit available to you on the credit card. *And* you don't pull that too many times.

At this point maybe all I have left is the countie crew but I'd probably need someone to vouch for me with them. I'm not sure who could do that. Maybe Peggy-O? I haven't seen her in a few nights, though…

Time to face facts. I could be jonesing tonight. It's almost time to start thinking about some outside show craziness. At least I'm in tomorrow night.

"Hey now, tomorrow for tonight, tomorrow for tonight. I'll trade my tomorrow for your tonight."

No show tonight, show tomorrow.

I'd rather be in there with the Boys but there's mischief to be made.

"Tomorrow for tonight, I'm looking to trade tomorrow's ticket for tonight."

(Wait, which way is that?)

"I have a ticket for tomorrow and I'm looking for a ticket for tonight."

(So you have a ticket for tomorrow…)

"And I'm looking to trade it for a ticket to tonight."

(Well you have found your match. I've got an extra for tonight that I will gladly trade you for one more Saturday night.)

"Deal."

(Comes a time.)

"Please ease me in."

(Nahhh. No disrespect but I'm going to have to disqualify you on that one. I can give you some license with the song titles but 'Don't Ease Me In' is the exact opposite of what you meant. You gotta chip it a bit closer to the flag. I would have gone with 'Simple Twist of Fate.')

"Right on."

(I was getting worried. I ended up stuck in that traffic. Everyone is willing to buy my ticket but I wanted a trade, you dig?)

"I dig."

(Here you go… Thanks. Hey, I'm Craig.)

"Thank *you,* brother, I'm Zeb."

(The seat's pretty good if you actually want to sit there. Mail order section too, so people know how to behave themselves. I have to ditch something in my car but hopefully I'll see you inside.)

"Right on, me too. Dank you very much!"

(That's why I'm headed to my car…)

BAGEL BOB

(GRILLED CHEESE FOR A BUCK, WHAT THE FUCK? GRILLED CHEESE FOR A BUCK, WHAT THE FUCK?)

(Nice salesmanship, Sal.)

(Well the show's started and I don't have a ticket, so it kind of sums up where my head is at.)

(No, hey, pithy, perverse, I love it. Bob?)

"Bob is charmed. Time to move along."

(Those yellow jackets have you spooked, don't they?)

"Bob is moderately unsettled."

(I can see that. You can't let them rattle you.)

"Rather than discuss Bob's mental state, Bob would prefer to undertake some heated cribbage competition in your recreational vehicle."

(Some crib in my crib? So I take it you are not going to participate?)

"In what activity?"

(The Thoreau thing. The book protest.)

"No, Bob will not be a participant. All day long Bob has counseled against this event."

(Come on Bob, we're talking about our constitutional rights. These people are taking away our fundamental liberties.)

"They are not. The Constitution only applies to action by the state. The Bill of Rights does not shield individuals from the atrocities of private entities. Your protest may be right-minded but it is certainly misguided. Or perhaps it is left-minded. Bob will leave that distinction to others. What Bob will opine with some measure of confidence is that this initiative is likely to yield harm."

(Man, I think you've got it all wrong on that Constitution crap… Hold on, I forgot. You used to be a lawyer, didn't you?)

"Barrister Bob was many lifetimes ago."

(When were you in law school?)

"Bagel Bob was graduated from Columbia Law School in nineteen hundred and seventy-one."

(Man, I was in grad school down at NYU around then. It would have been a trip to have met you back then rather than what was it? A decade later?)

"Bob feels fortunate to have made your acquaintance in any epoch."

(Why thank you, Bob.)

"Bob is grateful for the good fellowship."

(I wish that tonight we both could have been grateful for the Dead…from the relatively cozy confines of the arena. In lieu of that, though, why don't you join me for another performance. I hear that the Jevushuans have built a bonfire for their full-moon ritual.)

"An apprehensive Bagel Bob will accompany you if cribbage is to follow in short order."

STELLA BLUE

"Mommy, it's dark."

(Yes it is, honey.)

"They turned off the lights."

(I know honey, I can see.)

"No Mommy, you can't see because it's dark."

(That's very funny, Stella.)

"I know it is."

(Well it's not funny to me, Stella, I'm scared. I'm scared of the dark.)

"Aunt Jenneeeee!"

(Okay, okay I'm not scared, I'm excited. The Dead are about to come on stage. Are you excited, Stella?)

"Uh-huh."

(Well I'm so excited I think I'm gonna pee in my pants.)

"Aunt Jenny!"

(Jen!)

"Mommy, why is everybody clapping?"

(They're clapping for the Grateful Dead.)

"But where are the Grateful Dead? I can't see them."

(They're clapping so that the Dead will come on stage so that everyone can see them.)

"Should I clap, Mommy?"

(You should if you want the Grateful Dead to come on stage.)

"I'm gonna clap, Mommy."

(Good idea honey.)

TAPER TED

I don't even know how to process that last conversation but I don't have time to think about it. They're about to hit.

(Did you miss me, big bro?)

"How can I miss you when you won't go away?"

(The lights went out as I was walking up the aisle to get my pretzel. Everyone came rushing in and suddenly I was a salmon fighting upstream. All the traffic on the stairs become one-way against me. Not worth the battle. The trick is to surrender to the flow.)

"Are those song lyrics?"

(I figured you could tell me. I saw them on a shirt outside.)

"No clue."

(A rare admission, which I duly acknowledge and appreciate. Which reminds me, I know how this game is played, what's the first song gonna be?)

"It should be a Bobby. Jerry opened last night with a 'Half-Step.'"

(What's that one called again?)

"Mississippi Half-Step Uptown Tooteloo."

(Of course it is. So we know what they *won't* play. What *will* they play?"

"I'll go with 'Stranger.' 'Feel Like A Stranger.' Could be 'Bucket' though. Here they are, if you give me a moment and promise to whisper, I can tell you from the tuning…"

(So what's it going be? I'm on tenterhooks. To be frank, I think a few people in here are on tenterhooks if by tenterhooks I mean tenderhooks and if by tenderhooks I mean articulated wiggle shanks and if by articulated wiggle shanks I mean, *the drugs.*)

"Shhh—let me listen and I'll-'Bucket.' Definitely 'Bucket.'"

(We both know you're equal parts delusional and obsessive but can you really tell that from a few guitar farts?)

"Shhhhh."

(Shhhhh.)

(Shhhhh.)

(Ooops, here they go, the tension—)

(Shhhhhhhhh.)

('Hell in a Bucket.' You called it. Hail to the king. Hail to Taper Ted.)

"Shhhhhhhh."

STEVEN

There go the lights.

It is HAPPENING.

I'm buzzing all over this. Here I am in the dark with the Dead. Whoa, *In the Dark*, that's the name of the first Dead album I bought. It's like everything is synched. And with this energy, it's almost out of control.

Come on, get out here. Come out on stage.

No shit, no shit, there they are. The Dead. The Grateful Dead. All of them up there.

Jerry Garcia. I am in the same room with Jerry Garcia. He gives off these vibes that I can pick up just by standing in the same room with him.

(They look almost lifelike.)

(Ha!)

They do look kind of small. I wish we were closer. No, no I don't wish it, this is fine, it really is. Although it might be cool if we were closer. No, no this is fine. It really is.

There they are, the Grateful Dead, tuning their instruments.

This is going to be it. I've got to prepare myself. Okay, okay, calm, calm. Bake down, that's what I need to do.

"Hey, you guys want to bake down?"

(Yeah, sure. Whose herb?)

"I've got some. Hey, Shannon, did you bring your bowl? "

(Huh?)

"Did you bring your bowl?"

(Umm, uhhh, no. I left it in the car.)

(I've got mine. Let me pack.)

Hurry, hurry, I want a hit. I want to be toking when the music starts. That would be primo. The first note at my first show and I'm baking down with my buds. Buds with my buds.

"Buds with my buds, right, Shannon?"

(Huh? Uh-huh.)

(Here you go, Steven, first show. You can have the honors. Spark up!)

Sweet.

Here go the Dead, and the opener is…

("Hell in a Bucket!")

Choice! I know this one. A classic. From *In The Dark*. It's like this was supposed to be. That was my first album and this is my first tune.

But wait—shit, shit. I can't take a hit and dance too.

So should I stop grooving while I toke? How do people handle this at a show?

Okay, okay I'll slow down. No wait, that must look stupid because everyone else is dancing faster. No, okay I'll stop. No, then I'll look like I'm not enjoying the ride. Shit, I wonder if Shannon thinks I look hane.

Alright, I'll pass the bowl over to Nate.

Now I can do a little grooving… Whoa, he can toke and groove at the same time. Well shit, it probably comes from practice, he's been to way more shows than me.

When it comes back I'll try to take a hit while I'm dancing. But for now I'll just feel the music and let myself go. Look at all those people down there. They're all grooving and smiling and having a good time-oops here comes the bowl again. Okay, here I go, I'm gonna toke while I dance.

Shit, I spilled.

Mayday, mayday.

I dropped the buds all over the floor.

I can't believe it's my first show and I'm already acting like a dork.

ROBIN

They're out there, I can hear them.

Need some space though, need some space.

Where does this go—oops too many ushers on this level, I better run up.

Okay, okay, where, where?

"Ooops, sorry."

Here we go, okay second floor let's see where am I? No, too many people, no dancing space. Okay, okay…

Oops, there they go, "Hell In a Bucket." I have to get moving. Sounds good, sounds good. Maybe I'll sneak in a twirl. Here we go, here we go… Oops, Robin, look out for people with hotdogs. Okay, okay spin, skip, move.

Let's go—okay, okay here, how about here?

Nope. Still too crowded. I've got to move. Sounds good though, sounds good. I hope Mara is in here—we forgot to set a spot—wait, wait, where were we yesterday?

"Oops, excuse me. Sorry."

Okay, a little soda in the hair, at least it's not beer—

"Sorry, excuse me. I said I was sorry. Yes, it's clean…"

That's right, that's right, up one more flight. Come on girl, where are the stairs?

Skip, twirl, get that skirt flying. There we go, I can hear my bells.

"Oops, I'm sorry. Sorry…"

RANDY

(Welcome aboard, Ellis. Try to keep that rage in check or least properly direct it. Let me tell you how I envision this unit. They call us sweepers. I like to think of us as mine sweepers. There are plenty of bogeys out there ready to blow and we have to neutralize them. Do you understand?)

"I suppose I do."

(Alright then, let's head out on a run. We can leave Schultz on the crapper. Do you see those civilians over there? They are in triple violation of regulations. No unauthorized sales, no open fires and no frying of cooking oil. I want the two of you to neutralize the situation. I will observe you from this position. Go to it men!)

(Will do.)

"So this is what we do, walk around and tell people to stop cooking weenies?"

(You make it sound a lot easier than it is. Plus they are not cooking weenies.)

"So aside from being the most miserable third-rate referee in New Jersey high school history, do you think he was using the word bogey properly? I'm not so sure it means what he thinks it means. Isn't it like unidentified aircraft or something?"

(My intensive *Top Gun* training leads me to agree with you.)

"Roger that. Do they say Roger that in *Top Gun*? I've never seen it.)

(Seriously?)

"Not my thing."

(Have you seen any Tony Scott films?)

"I saw *Legend*. Tom Cruise is in that one too. Also the girl from *Ferris Bueller*."

(Mia Sara. No, that's his brother, Ridley Scott, who directed *Blade Runner*. Tony Scott directed *The Hunger*, a vampire film with David Bowie? Tony Scott also directed *Days of Thunder* which is coming out this summer. More Tom Cruise, this time as a racecar driver.)

"Which reminds me, I saw *The Wraith*, that ridiculous undead drag racing movie a few weeks ago on my free stolen cable, based on your recommendation. That film sucked. You owe me ninety minutes."

(There is no way I would recommended that you see that dreck, when there are so many better films that I know you haven't seen.)

"Absolutely you did. I can remember exactly what you said. You told me that *The Wraith* was underrated. That was enough to get me to waste an hour and a half of my life on it."

(No, no, you misunderstood me. When I said it was underrated, I meant it was PG-13 and it should have been R. I think that at the time when I said it, I was wondering how the producers were able to pull that off. I *can* promise you though, that *Days of Thunder* will be much more entertaining. I trust in the Scotts brand.)

"Too much Cruising in that family for my taste. Is Paul Newman in it?"

(No, Robert Duvall. I know what you're thinking though, Paul Newman does like auto racing. His only film with Tom Cruise though, is *The Color of Money*.)

"Now that was a waste of time. Why did we need a sequel to *The Hustler*?"

(You haven't seen *Top Gun* but you've seen *The Hustler*?)

"Jackie Gleason, man, that guy's a master."

(*Was* a master.)

"Well he lives on through his work."

(*Smokey Is The Bandit*?)

"Never saw that. The trailer was enough for me. That's the first place you go, the third *Smokey and The Bandit* movie? The first one was a classic and that's not something I say lightly but how about a little show called *The Honeymooners*?"

(I'm talking film not television.)

"Fucking snob."

(Okay, here we go. You be Maverick. I'll be your wing man.)

"Got it. Even without seeing the film. See, I'm not a cultural illiterate. Hey you guys… Hey you guys… I said, 'Hey!'"

(Hey now! What can we do you for you fine two yellow jackets this evening?)

"Well, I suppose what you can do is put out that open fire and stop selling whatever you're selling. You are in violation of arena policy."

(And what policy is that, a policy against eating?)

(Yeah man, or a policy against not forcing people to choke down overpriced, overcooked hamburgers inside the arena?)

"A bit of a double negative but I feel you."

(You feel us yellow jacket?)

"Listen, can you just put out the fire?"

(What fire?)

"This one right here beneath the pot of steaming oil which is also against arena policy."

(What can't you just let us be? Why is the arena so obsessed with its concession revenues?)

"Hey, I'm just doing my job."

(So was Himmler.)

"That's where you want to go? Don't be an asshole."

(Ignore Groovy George. Hey man, we're just doing *our* job.)

"He's Groovy George? This is a job?"

(I'm named after my dance moves not my winning personality. And yes, it's our job until the show starts.)

"So I imagine I'm about the millionth person to tell to you to get a real job."

(You don't have to be an asshole. We're selling three dollar falafel wraps to support our tour. Do you even know what a falafel is you bland, blonde, hulking robot?)

"Ground chickpeas?"

(Good guess.)

(Our falafels are perfection in a pocket.)

(Let us prove it you. We'll give you a taste and if our falafels are as good as advertised, then you let us go about our business.)

(Randy, I wouldn't. Remember, we're not supposed to eat anything in this lot. Everything could be laced.)

(You think we'd dose you? No, that's a mind crime I don't condone. You can grab one of those right there yourself that we've already prepared. Trust me, I'm not dosing the clientele. That would decrease our opportunity for repeat customers.)

(Although…)

(No chance, Groovy George. Bad for business.)

"Fine."

(Randy? You're going off script here.)

"Well I'm hungry. I had to deal with all that bullshit on the highway *and* at the gas station *and* with Mack and now with the crap referee. Okay, you're on…"

Mmmmmm.

"Mmmmm… Not bad, not bad. Not sure about perfection in a pocket. There's a little too much acidity in your tahini sauce."

(That's bullshit.)

"But if you give me one to go and shut down for five minutes until that old coot in the golf cart drives away, you're fine by me."

(Hey, that's bribery!)

(Can it, Groovy George. Yellow jacket, you've got a deal.)

STEVEN

Oh yes, oh yes this is sweet

"Bertha!"

Alright, time to

"Mooooove, really had to moooooove!"

Everybody loves "Bertha." The Heads are going crazy—dancing and singing, everybody in the arena is grooving, it's like waves and waves of colors. This is primo.

I caught a heavy buzz from the dope and away I go.

This is beyond description. Here I am a Head, dancing while Jerry Garcia sings "Bertha." THE Jerry Garcia. THE "Bertha."

Aww and check out Shannon, look at her, she's smiling and dancing. It's great, it's so great. She is just so happy. Happy and dancing like everyone here at the show.

I even know most of the words so I can sing some of the chorus along with Jerry and it's like I belong here. Me and all these people who have never met before and maybe never will be in the same place again—no no, we'll go to shows together. Okay maybe not all of us here tonight but most of us. We'll go to shows together but we probably won't talk to each other. But here we are, singing along with Jerry. We're unified. It's inspiring and that's what being a Head is all about.

Aww, and look at Shannon, kind of spinning with her arms moving up and down. She is happiness personified. Right there dancing next to me at the show is Happiness.

And I can dance along with her. It's breathtaking.

BAGEL BOB

(Hey, Bob, I'll take a Stella Blueberry, light on the cream cheese.)

"Alas, Bob is bagel-less."

(Bagel Bob without bagels? That's impossible. If you don't have any bagels, how can you be Bagel Bob?)

"The Lone Ranger is not always alone. At times he is in the company of other rangers. Yet he retains his title."

(Good point but where are your bagels?)

"Bob left them in his friend Michael's recreational vehicle. Bob intends to return there shortly to begin some recreational cribbage."

(Recreational cribbage?)

"Bob's days as a cribbage professional are long past. Although Bob would not rule out a Pro-Am event with a suitable partner. Despite an otherwise tranquil nature, Bob acknowledges a predilection for the Muggins variation."

(And you intend to play cribbage after *what* exacly? I mean what's *this*? A bunch of people dressed in rags dancing around a milk crate engulfed in flames? Tell me, Bob, what's their story?)

"Their story?"

(Why are they doing this?)

"Because they are Jevushuans."

(But what does that mean?)

"Bob does not know. He is not a Jevushuan."

(But you must have seen them before on tour.)

"Bob has."

(So then tell me, why do they dance around like that?)

"Lunar worship as Bob understands it."

(Okay, I dig that. But these guys follow around the Dead, correct?)

"Bob has observed the Jevushuans in the vicinity of other Grateful Dead performances, yes."

(Come to think of it, I think I've seen them a few times myself but only out here in the lot. Do they ever go into shows?)

"Bob has never observed them do so. Perhaps it is against their dogma to initiate eye contact with the Grateful Dead."

(Can that even be possible?)

"Possible? Why do you invoke such normative terminology within the lingua franca that is the music of the Grateful Dead? Cast your eyes in a three hundred and sixty-degree radius. Does any of this seem bound by the artificial constraints of vocabulary and grammar that you privilege by giving meaning to the word possible?"

(Other than the fact that I don't have a ticket?)

"Hail fellow well met."

(But seriously, if they have no interest in walking through the doors of the arena then why are they here?)

"Metaphysician heal thyself. Why are you here?"

(I asked first.)

"But Bob asked taller."

(What?)

"What's on second. "

(Who?)

"First base… Okay, why is Bob here? Was not Bob univocal with his lingua franca reference? Well then perhaps this is a question that Bob himself is unable to answer to his satisfaction. Perhaps Bob contemplates this interrogative with an increased urgency each day while outside forces assail his unflagging optimism and set ablaze his banderole—they seek to burn Bob's freak flag—an unconscionable act if admittedly a Constitutionally unviolative one. Bob fears for the health of his habitat."

(Awww, Bob come on, now you're bringing me down. I know why you're here. You're here because you belong here. You're here because people need you. Just like people need bagels. I've been to like fifteen shows over the past couple years and I've bought a bagel from you at every one. You've given me nourishment and stability and a smiling face. That's why you're here.)

"Does Bob know you?"

(We've never been formally introduced. My name's Kevin.)

"Welcome, Kevin, you speak of Bob kindly. But let Bob ask you, you talk of Jevushuans and you inquire as to the nature of their presence. Once again let Bob ask, why are *you* here?"

(Because there's nowhere else.)

"Indeed."

TAPER TED

Jerry lobs back a "Bertha." No, this is one of these late '80s, early '90s retro "Berthas." So it's not a lob, it's more of a slam. Almost back to the ping-pong days of the early '70s when Bobby would rip through one and then Jerry would fire back. Now they're slower, we all are. So it's more like they're on a tennis court hitting lobs back and forth. Except for an occasional high hard one like the "Bertha."

Rez really enjoys these latter-day "Berthas." Not me, I dig the late '70s versions, the slow, bubbling "Berthas." Like May 9, 1977 in Buffalo, which always gets overshadowed by the previous night's sick Barton Hall show on my home turf in Ithaca. What a year that was, even aside from the music, an admission that would likely blow my little brother's mind. Rez and I had just found each other and recognized the role that the Dead would play in our lives. We've been to most of our shows together—286 for me, while she flat-out refuses to count because she says her Dead experience is unquantifiable. Now there's some weird irony, coming from a tax attorney.

And the cream of '77 awaits me on those Betty Boards. The DATs should arrive next week, if they're not already sitting at the post office. The conversation about which show to put on first will be quite delicious in its own right. I can't wait until Rez and I sit down, paw through those tapes and make a decision.

Of course I have another decision to make before we get there, which was altogether unexpected and where I suppose my thoughts have been headed. Blankmail—which might be amusing if it weren't so peverse. What am I to do about that? On one hand I'm all for releasing the shows to the community but it's really not my call. I'm just stoked that I was selected to be part of the tape tree. Only two dozen of us made the cut. More shows to come too if Reggie has it right. Of course it could go all down the drain if this guy Chuck blows the whistle.

Maybe I should talk to Reg about it. He's in his classic spot though, landlocked in the middle of the section, I'll never make it there.

The person I really need to speak with is Rez.

Where is she, off talking to a client?

I remember that Hampton '88 run, right after they made her partner when she was out in the hall on the phone and missed two of the breakouts. That "Ballad of a Thin Man" hurt. Bobby's her guy.

STELLA BLUE

"Why do you like the Grateful Dead, Mommy?"

(I don't like the Grateful Dead, Stella.)

"I don't like the Grateful Dead either."

(You don't?)

"No, I *love* the Grateful Dead!"

(Ohhh, Stella, that's what I was going to say!)

"I know you were, Mommy."

(You wanna know why I like the Grateful Dead?)

"Okay, Aunt Jenny, but don't say you love the Grateful Dead."

(Party pooper.)

"Aunt Jennneee!"

(What?)

"No poop talk."

(Oh, sorry. But do you really wanna know why I like the Grateful Dead?)

"Okay."

(Their sweet dance moves. I think they inspired New Kids on The Block.)

"Who?"

(I like you more and more every day. Do you see Jerry though, how he rocks back and forth while he's playing?)

"No…"

(Well if you look a bit closer-you know, you may be right. But remember, during the first song Bobby was jumping around.)

"He looked like he was trying to get an invisible hat off his head."

(He did look like he was trying to get an invisible hat off his head.)

"Aunt Jenny you wanna know why I love the Grateful Dead?"

(Sure, Stella, why do you love the Grateful Dead?)

"Because I love cows."

(You do?)

"Just like Jerry."

(Jerry's a cow? I'm not sure if he'd appreciate—)

"Aunt Jennnneeee! No, Jerry sings to the cows because he loves them—'I really had to mooooooo!'"

RANDY

(Davis is not going to appreciate that.)

"Well I don't appreciate his douchebaggery. He flagged me three times for blocking below the waist. A, I was still in the free blocking zone and Two, even if I wasn't, it's still not blocking below the waist if the other guy is not on his feet because I already knocked him in the air and he was on his way to the ground. I was just carving room for the tailback. My level of respect for this guy falls somewhere just below no respect."

(Well coach is not going to appreciate that—the letting the falafel guys remain in business part, not the opening holes for your backfield part.)

"Fuck him if he can't take a joke. I'm already fired anyhow. Plus that falafel was nearly as good as he said it was, I might go back for thirds. I'm a growing boy. But first I have to call a couple guys from my high school and let them know I found that hack referee from our championship game and told him what we think of him."

(By him you mean your boss.)

"Eddie, that's very reductive of you. Is Bernie Lomax just a boss?"

(Lomax? Nice pull on the last name.)

"*Weekend at Bernie's* is on The Movie Channel this month. Did I mention that we have free stolen cable in our apartment? But seriously, what part of 'I'm fired' do you not understand. Calling out that bush league ref was the highlight of a piss poor day. That and the falafels. So do you know where I can find a pay phone?"

"What about our other thing?"

(How about I go make the call, you round up the guys and we'll do it.)

(Hey yellow jackets! Yellow jackets, come over here!)

"Why is everyone so obsessed with the color of our windbreakers?"

(There's someone over here who needs your help!)

(Over here!)

(Hey Rand, look at that guy. We gotta do something. He's bleeding all over the fucking place.)

"Hey, come over here."

(Come over here, we want to talk to you.)

(Fuck off, the two of you!)

"Shit, that fucking loon's running away. We gotta go after him."

(Hey! Come back! We just want to get you help!)

(You can do it!)

(Run, Joe, run!)

"We're trying to get him help!"

(After you did that to him!)

"No, we didn't!"

(No, we didn't! Come on, man, slow down!)

(Naarrrghhhh!)

"We just want to get you to a doctor, you're bleeding"

(Naaargghhhhh!)

"Come on…"

(Grab him!)

(Heyyyyy! Aruughhhhhh!)

"This guy's a fighter."

(Don't throw him back. He's a keeper.)

"He's slippery though. All that blood and sweat."

(Hey, yellow jackets, I saw what happened to that dude.)

"Yeah?"

(He was trying to scale that fence to get into the area over there with the tour buses and just when he got to the top, somebody on the other side, some yellow ja-some security guy started shaking it and he fell down, scraped the side of his face alongside the fence and then hit his head. I think he was messed up to begin with.)

"You don't say."

(Randy, hold him there and I'll go get a Dead Med.)

STEVEN

I think I just had my moment.

My GRATEFUL DEAD MOMENT.

It was like some sort of Zen experience or something.

I wasn't even thinking or anything, I was just shaking my bones alongside Happiness, sort of feeding off her groove and I looked across the arena and there was this girl, she was maybe a couple of years older than me, dancing in the lower section closer to the stage. I looked over there and this girl was just twirling and dipping her head backwards and I'm sort of dipping my head backwards too. And then I realize, I'm dancing with her. I'm dancing with this girl all the way across the arena. And I can't really see her face but I know that she's grooving back. The two of us are dancing with each other from hundreds of feet away.

That blows me away but I don't have time to think about it because I'm too busy grooving. But then as I dip my head a bit I can see that Shannon is doing it too. She's responding to me and the girl across the arena. The three of us are dancing together. That's way cool. I was part of something way bigger than me. It was totally better than when I was just singing with everyone. The three of us were in our own little Deadhead world dancing together during the "Bertha."

And now that the song's over I can't even really see that girl anymore. But I'm standing here while the Dead tune their instruments, and I'm raring and ready to start something like that again with some other people.

"Shannon?"

I guess I should tap her.

"Shannon?"

(Huh? What?)

"Wasn't that cool? The three of us were dancing together."

(Who?)

"You know, you, me and that girl over there."

(Wait, wait stop, you're confusing me. I can't understand you. Everything sounds weird. I can't even hear the Dead right. Everything was okay at first during 'Hell In a Bucket' but towards the end it just sounded like they weren't playing music at all. They were just making these loud, evil noises. And then during "Bertha," I mean that was "Bertha," right?)

"Yeah."

(And it—wait what's that? Are they playing a song?)

"Umm…yeah."

Although I don't know what it is. I-oh yeah wait I know this one, I know it, it's on that live album, what's that one called? Umm…*Dead Set* that's it and the first couple of words are the title…

"Yeah, yeah, it's 'Little Red Rooster.'"

(The music doesn't sound right.)

"Well I think they use a special guitar for this one."

(No, no you don't understand me.)

"Wait, Shannon, wait. No, I can understand you. Just give me a chance. Everything's fine. You were having a good time during 'Bertha,' right?"

(No, that's what I mean. You don't understand. I was in agony. I couldn't hear the music, I was writhing in pain.)

"No you weren't, I watched you smile. You were Happiness."

(No I wasn't. Just don't talk about it. Please, let me get my head together.)

"Yeah but—"

(No, please just don't, don't do anything. I was in this bad place and for a second you brought me out but now you're sending me back and I don't want to go back, so I can't talk. Please don't talk to me, please do not talk.)

She must be having a bad mushroom trip. I can't believe it, a bad mushroom trip. I've never heard of anyone having a bad mushroom trip before.

Okay, Steve-o, you've got to do something, you've got to help her through this. She can't communicate with anyone else, so you have to do it. You have to bring her through. And the Dead can help. Just you and the Dead, you and the Dead. Wait, huh, oh, she's tapping me.

"What do you want? I'll do anything."

(Could you move over a seat and then ask Emily to sit over here next to me?)

ZEB

Man, I can't breathe in here.

(Mooooooo!)

This is highly unkind. They must have started by now. Fourth time this tour that I've missed the opener.

Come on, come on.

The Boys are out there, Phil is rumbling and someone is sticking a lighter up my ass.

"Hey, watch it."

(Sorry, man, somebody pushed me.)

"Alright, brother, it's alright. But man are we ever gonna get in? This is the schwagiest schwag of all."

(Dig on that.)

"It's crazy. I was in line before the show started and I'd like to think I can make it in before the show ends."

(Dig on that.)

"Hey, are you feeling okay? You're not looking so right on, brother."

(Man, I can't take this. I'm claustrophobic or something.)

(It could be the tour crud. That shit's going around.)

(Yeah, I almost had to sit out the show last night. My fever was spiking.)

(Almost.)

(Then I full on raged it away. Fire on the mountain!)

(We can turn earth into heaven if we get high enough!)

(Wait, do you starve a cold and feed a fever or is it the other way?)

Help me.

(I've seen Bob Weir feed 'The Fever.' It made me uncomfortable.)

(Landover '87. I was there.)

(Doesn't cure the Tour Ick though.)

(It left me feeling kind of icky, though. It felt intrusive.)

(That's your problem, not our boy Bobby's.)

"Right on!"

(I'm still feeling dizzy.)

(Lucky you.)

"Don't sweat it, bro. Take it easy, think some kind thoughts. Pretty soon you'll be in there with Phil and Bobby and Jerry…"

If the first set isn't over by then.

Meanwhile Jerry is probably ripping into another killer "Shakedown" or a kind "Bertha."

(GIMME BACK MY TICKET! SOMEONE GRABBED MY TICKET! HEY! HEY! SOMEONE JUST TOOK MY TICKET! THAT WAS MINE! HEY GIVE THAT BACK! WHO TOOK

MY TICKET? GIVE IT BACK! SOMEONE FIND THAT PERSON AND STOP THEM!)

(Calm down man, calm down. What is it?)

(SOMEONE JUST GRABBED MY TICKET OUT OF MY HAND! I WAS STANDING HERE HOLDING OUT MY TICKET BECAUSE THEY TOLD US TO HAVE OUR TICKETS OUT AND SOMEONE JUST GRABBED IT!)

(Hey! Who took this guy's ticket?)

(WHO TOOK MY TICKET?)

That's nuts. It's like North Carolina last spring. This dude next to me took out his ticket just to look at it and then this other guy comes flying in, grabs it and runs into the crowd. We chased the guy but there was no way, he was gone. Bad craziness. Some guy couldn't find a miracle ticket so he made his own. A total breach of Deadiquette. And there was nothing to do. We couldn't catch him, there was no way he was he going to sit in the poor dude's seat. He just got into the show and the other dude didn't.

Shit like that happens on tour. Could even be the same guy here, hiding in the crowd and then reaching out to grab someone's ticket. It's too packed in here for anyone to tell what's going on.

Bad, bad craziness. Like gate crashing or leaping onto the field when you have a seat at a stadium show.

Okay, when I first started going to shows I thought that was right on. I jumped down at Foxboro and Giants Stadium. I figured I wasn't hurting anyone. Then I saw a bunch of Heads try to tear the doors off that arena in Pittsburgh. They showed it on the news and the mayor said we couldn't come back. It made me realize I don't need to do crap like that. That sort of stuff hurts the scene. And things are tough as it is.

But stealing someone's ticket that's-

KIND! I'M THERE!

No shit. I was spacing it, and now I'm there. Front of the pack, about to enter the show. I was drifting and now—

(Raise your arms please.)

Yellow jacket time.

"I will comply but I hope the smell doesn't offend."

I never tire of that.

Of course, I get that extra special loving treatment.

(Move along…)

Kind!

(Ticket please?)

"Here you go."

Kind!

I am IN!

KINDNESS!

The Rooster!

Bobby's sliding into the Rooster!

TAPER TED

(Psst, Bobby Weir is no Ry Cooder.)

"Shhhh…whisper. Here let's move to the end of the row… Your point?"

(He's no Duane Allman either.)

"Okay, we've established that he is a different human being altogether than the two other human beings you just named.

One of whom is no longer with us. I take it your point relates to his slide guitar work on 'Little Red Rooster'?"

(He's no Elmore James.)

"Really? Come on now, Tommy. Let me just say there are plenty of people who say he's the man, the real animating force behind the band. Aside from his really creative rhythm guitar work, on any given night he's the one who can pull them out of a ditch—"

(Now there's a metaphor.)

"You should talk to Rez."

(That's a schoolgirl crush.)

"If it were a 'Schoolgirl' crush, she'd be fixated on Pigpen. Alas, he's not with us either. Although come to think of it, Bobby did bust that one out a few years back, when Carlos Santana sat in with them. Angel's Camp. August twenty-second, nineteen eighty-seven."

(We've nearly reached the crossroads of I don't know and I don't care but let's review: Bob Weir is no Muddy Waters.)

"At least you're comparing him unfavorably to the all-time greats.

(Come one, he's just sort of preening up there, pretending to be a rock and roll star.)

"Well he kind of is one."

(Which reminds me. Kind. I've been meaning to ask you this for a while now. Some of these people use kind as an adjective when they overpraise what the band is doing, while other folks describe the same pablum as killer. Now both of these terms are favorable responses, right?)

"Yes…"

(Well how can that be? If something that's commendable is kind then how can it also be killer? Aren't those words contradictory?)

"I do not have time to think about that."

(Of course you do. What are you doing? You're sitting back in Tape Town watching some spools tum. And I hate to do this but I'll let you in on a secret, they don't need your help. In fact, if you really want my opinion, I think you make them nervous. So what else can we talk about?)

"We could just sit back and listen to the music play."

(Lyric reference?)

"'Franklin's Tower.' Which reminds me of this Red Rocks show back in '78. The second set ended with 'Franklin's Tower' > 'Sugar Magnolia.' Then they came back for a triple encore: 'Terrapin Station,' 'One More Saturday Night' and then 'Werewolves of London' with Bobby on slide..."

That one's in the first batch of Bettys. July 8, 1978. Damnit, I'm going to have to make a decision about that tree, what to do about Norfolk Chuck's threat. It's all just so bizarre.

(Ted? Ted? Is everything okay? As your doctor I hope you won't mind if I point out that you look particularly detached and somewhat piqued. This is supposed to be recreation, vacation... I'm serious, is everything okay? I can put my naysayer shtick aside for a little while.)

"No, don't worry, you've got to be you. As for me, I have a lot on my mind tonight. More than I had planned on for the evening. Let's just say it's gonna be a long, long, crazy, crazy night."

(More Dead lyrics? You said I gotta be me so even *you* have to admit those lines are a bit redundant.)

"As I've heard you mutter on more than one occasion, they can't all be gems."

BAGEL BOB

(Who was that kid speaking with you?)

"Kevin."

(Who's Kevin?)

"An admirer of Bob."

(An admirer of Bob?)

"Apparently Bob is something of a cult classic. Who knew?"

(Well said. And speaking of cult classics, what do you think of the moon dance?)

"Bob has seen it before."

(I know you have. With me. Summer of '88 at Alpine. That was the last time we caught it on tour. But I've never seen it like this. The last time we saw it they did it in some field up the road from the show. I've never seen them do it in a parking lot. I think they're in full-on recruiting mode.)

"Bob would advise an alternate method to secure novitiates. He does not believe that this new course of action is advisable. It will only antagonize the security forces."

(Well I was talking to Yoshni, one of Jevushuans. He promised it would be brief.)

"Bob hopes this is true. And Bob wonders as Kevin wonders, why is it that the Jevushuans accompany the Dead to their concert engagements?"

(Why are they here?)

"Yes."

(Why are *you* here?)

"It is an ill omen to invoke questions of ontology in a New Jersey parking lot."

(But, that can't—ahhh, you're jesting right? You almost had me there.)

"Bob almost had himself. But what Bob wishes to know is, do the Jevushuans incorporate the Grateful Dead into their religious tenets? And if so, then why do they not attend any of the band's performances?"

(Yoshni! Hey Yoshni! Can you come over here for a minute? We have a question for you. Yoshni, this is Bagel Bob. Bagel Bob meet Yoshni.)

(Greetings, Bagel Bob.)

"Salutations, Yoshni."

(How can I assist you?)

"Bob wishes to know, why is it that the Jevushuans accompany the Grateful Dead to their performance venues if they do not attend any of their performances? Is this an element of your religious dogma?"

(That is a provocative question, Bob, and one which I will answer. However, first I must tell you, we Jevushuans do not consider ourselves a religious group. To become a Jevushuan is to join a tribe and not a sect. We commune together in fellowship and family but we have no synagogues, no temples, no arks. To a Jevushuan the entire world is a place where we can offer our ritual thanks to the creator.)

"So you sermonize of God."

(Only to you. Jevushuans do not believe in a God per se, more of a spirit. It is something that Jevushuans come to understand through fasting, meditation and intellectual exchange. I say God because that conjures an image in your mind. What we believe in is inexpressible. It transcends words. Each Jevushuan has his or her own word for this entity, a privatized conception of this spirit.)

(I call mine Billy.)

(But to you who are not a Jevushuan I—Sorry, I must return to my people. Momentarily I will play a role in the ritual. Blessings to you both, Bagel Bob and Michael.)

"But wait, Yoshni Jevushuan, given all that just espoused, then you why are you here?"

(What?)

"Second base. Why are you here?"

(Why are *you* here?)

"Bob is now willing to modify his earlier assertion and definitively stipulate that it is a breach of decorum to answer a question with a question."

(He's gone, Bob, he can't hear you. But I'll answer. Why do they follow the Dead? You know the answer. In a word, recruitment. These guys are the bottom feeders of the tour. No, that's not true, the hardcore narcotics distributors are the bottom feeders but these guys get the residue, the mildew. When people are toured-out, dosed-out or just plain wacked-out they find the Jevushuans. Or the Jevushuans find them. And they do some good stuff. They feed people, give them shelter. Most folks just hang out for a few days, get some free food and then jump back onto tour full force. But there's certainly some weirdness and it's not always the good kind of weirdness. I've heard—Oh shit, don't tum around. Okay turn around but brace yourself, brace yourself.)

(PUT OUT THE FIRE!)

(They've gone to the megaphones already.)

(WE SAID PUT OUT THE FIRE!)

"At least eight of the jackets in yellow."

(Right on, check it out Bob, good for them. They're actually listening and extinguishing the fire.)

"That would be auspicious but cast your eyes in *that* direction."

(Oh, shit.)

(HEY! Why'd you make them do that?)

(What is it to you?)

(Please, please do not intervene on our behalf. The Jevushuans do not seek conflict.)

(My man, Yoshni. Sounds like you, Bob.)

"Although Bob's kindling is cream cheese."

(Well I don't care if these guys don't want to protest, I do! And I speak for the scene!)

(This is where the trouble begins.)

"This is where Bob departs. Once someone volunteers to speak for Bob, Bob wishes to select another spokesperson."

(That thinking will get you nowhere.)

"Most blessedly so."

(We refuse to accept your tyranny. These people were not disturbing anyone. You cannot use your bullshit bullying tactics on us!)

(The hell we can't! You are on private property, you must obey the laws of the arena.)

(NO ONE OWNS THE EARTH! IT BELONGS TO ALL OF US!)

(FUCK THE ARENA! THE ARENA DOESN'T EXIST, IT'S A FUCKING CORPORATION. FUCK CORPORATIONS!)

(AND FUCK THE LAW!)

(AND FUCK YOOOOUUU!)

"Bob counsels retreat."

(Fine. Listen, I'll meet you at my place in ten minutes, okay? Forget about the cribbage, though, I'm up for something a bit headier.)

"Bob has sworn off Scattergories due to irreconcilable differences."

(With me or with Scattergories? I am not budging from what I said down in Greensboro. Respiration is not a hobby. I'll accept Transcendental Meditation perhaps but not the sheer act of breathing. When you included both that was double-dipping.)

"Bob takes offense."

(But can Bob play defense?)

"Challenge accepted. Chess and Coltrane it is."

ROBIN

Here we go, here we go. Up the stairs.

Skip, skip.

Sounds good sounds good.

Okay okay okay.

Check it out, everybody's twirling in the hall out here.

This is kind, this is kind…and Bobby sounds good too.

Okay then right here. Clean floor, happy dancing people.

Wait, wait I should run in and see what it looks like?

Okay, okay.

Skip, skip.

Kind view, kind view. No ushers, a couple twirlers. Phil side too.

I love dancing Phil side.

Okay, move out, back to the hall.

Sweet sweet 'Rooster.'

"Oops, I'm sorry."

A little Mountain Dew in the hair, that's okay, a little caffeine treat couldn't hurt.

"Sorry. Yes, I wash it every day."

Geeesh.

This is nice. Lots of space and everyone's smiling and there's a great breeze and the sound carries out here too.

Okay, Robin, now think. When you were dancing you were trying to think of something...

No, no, you were trying to remind yourself of something—Mara, oh yeah, Mara. You were wondering where she is. I hope she got in. Seems like it's gonna be a hot show and there's some kind dancing room up here, I—

No, no, that wasn't it. Setlist, you wanted to remind yourself to write down the setlist. Okay, cool. Now, look for your stub.

Hurry, hurry, they're tuning, the next song's gonna start. Wait, wait I don't have any pockets so... Right, right, here it is.

Cool. Okay, Now I'll just-no wait, pen. I need a pen. Do I have a pen in here? Let me see... Okay, yes here we go, ummm okay, let's see...

Okay Robin think—right on! "Ramble on Rose!"

Come on Robin, do this first. Forget "Ramble on Rose" for now.

It's sweet, it's sweet though but come on, write down the list.

Write down the list and then you can dance-you can even run inside for a minute and watch Jerry sing.

Come on first song...

Okay it was a Bobby, I remember it was a Bobby—"Bucket!" Right, okay, second song was a sweet "Bertha" and then we had the "Rooster."

Oh, crud! Pen doesn't work though, not sure if stub is soggy or pen is loggy. Hey, I'm Rhyming Simon the pieman!

Now it's working!

Alright Rob, enough of that, put down your pen and dance.

ZEB

Okay, what to do?

I have this 100 level mail order ticket and he said it was a good seat but it'll be a ton of effort to make it down there right now. The wise Head's move is to wait until setbreak.

So what now? What now?

I guess it's the aisle hang. Phil side in the far left corner, there's a bit less congestion and the sound is great. Time to move in…

Just in time. They finished up the "Rooster." Time for some Jerry.

(We want Phil!)

(We want Phil!)

(We want Phil!)

Ahhh, maybe not…

Right on! There's some righteous crazy. They're chanting for my man. Chanting for THE man.

"We want Phil!"

"We want Phil!"

Awww, it's fading. Sometimes they listen, though. We want Phil and sometimes the boys give him to us. I could dig all over a "Box" right now. Or a "Tom Thumb's," that would be equally kind. I love it when they chant for Phil. A couple of times I tried to get people to yell "Let Billy sing!" or "Let Mickey Sing!" I think the boys would dig it and who knows what would come out of it but for some reason it's a non-starter.

Hmm, it's a little tighter in here than I thought. It seems like everyone in the 200 levels decided to clog the aisles in the 100 sections, making it uncomfortable for fellow cloggers like me. The ushers are bound to come in and bust us.

But what to do now? I could run up a level. The aisles are probably clear up there because everyone's down here.

Or I could spend some time in the hallways with the Heads in the skirts and bell anklets, that's usually a good trip. Nah, the first set is the wrong time for that scene. The jams aren't long enough. Second set's the time to catch a buzz off that action, when things get going and the jams start raging. Heads swaying, arms flying, the people become the music. On the right night whatever question anyone has about the Grateful Dead, those people are the answer.

So what should I do?

Ahhh…"Ramble on Rose."

Question asked and answered.

I'm staying.

STELLA BLUE

"Mommy, it's smoky in here."

(Yes it is.)

"My eyes are itchy."

(I'm sorry, honey. Do you want Mommy to put in your eye drops?)

"Nuh-uh."

(No? Okay.)

"Mommy, why doesn't anybody sit down?"

(Because everybody's standing up and dancing, honey.)

"But what if they get tired?"

(Well then they can sit down. Do you want to sit down Stella? Mommy will sit down with you.)

"Okay."

(Okay. Here, why don't you lie down and put your head on my lap… There you go. Now, why don't you close your eyes.)

"I don't want to, Mommy."

(Okay, okay.)

(Someone's getting cranky.)

(It's been a long day for her. If she falls asleep now and sleeps through the rest of the set, I can wake her during the set break and she can walk around and look at all the people. She'll like that. Then she can be up for the second set if she wants.)

"Hey, Mommy, Jack and Jill. They just sung about Jack and Jill."

(That's right, honey, and Jerry's going to sing about more people you know. Like Frankenstein. And Wolfman Jack, do you know who he is?)

"Mommy, I want to get up."

(Okay. Do you want me to pick you up and put you on your seat?)

"I can do it myself, Mommy."

(She can do it herself, Mommy… Hey, Stella, nice to see you back. And that's some fine dancing you're doing. You've got a nice little groove there.)

"I know I do, Aunt Jenny."

STEVEN

(What did you say to her?)

"I didn't say anything."

(Come on…)

"Emily, I didn't say anything."

(Well then what did you do?)

"I didn't do anything. We were just standing here dancing and then she freaked."

(You didn't touch her or anything, did you?)

"No I didn't touch her. Why would I touch her?"

(Steven. I know you've got the hots for her. We all know you've got the hots for her. Even *she* knows you've got the hots for her.)

Shit.

"I'm not hot for her. She's a friend of mine. I'm just a friend, I'm concerned. I'm a concerned citizen. A loyal patriot, a—"

(Alright, alright. Whatever. Ooooh, 'Ramble On Rose.' Hey Shannon, 'Ramble On Rose,' 'Ramble On Rose'… Whatever. She thinks you're a good guy. The rest I leave to you, just behave. I can't deal with this, I'm shrooming too and it's 'Ramble On Rose' so I'm moving back to my seat. I'm leaving her in your hands. Not literally.)

Leaving her to me. I can deal with that. I'll be mellow. I won't even turn my head and look over at her, not yet. She might freak or something. "Ramble On Rose" is a sweet song, I'll let her try to deal with it on her own for a little while. Then I'll check in and look over at her sideways. I definitely don't want to freak her out. Besides I've got my own business at hand. I'm here at the show and I have to get my groove on again.

"Ramble On Rose," I like this one. It's kind of hard to dance to it though. It's like a Broadway show tune or an old-timey song or something like that. It's cool though the way it names all those people. It's a song about America.

Hey that guy over there has it right, he's kind of dancing like a slinky, sort of letting his body collapse and then straightening himself out. No, no that guy there has it, more of a skip. He's just sort of standing there shaking his bones and kicking out his feet. That's the way to go.

Before my next show I'm going to work in some practice, maybe in front of a mirror. And I'm going to learn more lyrics, I definitely need to learn more lyrics.

"Just like Jack and Jill..."

Alright, I snuck in a couple. Okay, it's time to peak over at Shannon. Shit, she's sitting down. Everyone's dancing and she's just sitting down staring into space.

(Hey, what's with Shannon?)

"Nate man, I don't know. I think she's having a bad mushroom trip."

(Nah, can't happen. She just needs time to adjust. Watch her, she'll be up and dancing by Mary Shelley.)

"Who will she be dancing with?"

(No, no. In the song. By the time Jerry sings 'Just like Mary Shelley' she'll be dancing.)

"Oh yeah, right, I know what you mean. I was thinking of something else and I spaced."

Shit, I gotta learn some lyrics. At the end of the term that's what I'm going to do. I'm gonna sit down and write out the lyrics to songs on notecards so I can learn them before summer tour.

RANDY

(Where is he?)

"He's gone."

(What do you mean he's gone? He was barely conscious when I left.)

"Well while you were away he got a little more conscious and then he took off."

(Seriously?)

"He spit a big old nasty loogie on my face and then when I went to wipe it off he punched me in the gut and ran."

(Seriously?)

"Did I stutter? I'm covered in his blood."

(That's what you get in your house when you spill paint in the garage.)

(I'm not sure it's necessary for the two of you to make light of those with speech disfluencies.)

(Rand, this is Gil, the Dead Med. Gil, I don't think that's what we're doing, I'm pretty sure we were just sharing an homage to John Bender.)

(Yeah, *Breakfast Club*, I got that. It's not an obscure reference. But let me reiterate, why do you need to reinforce negative stereotypes?)

"You Deadheads are the most sensitive, delicate creatures to ever take a swing at me."

(Well—)

"Or threaten to take a swing at me."

(Well I've done neither.)

"Although you are unduly sensitive."

(Thank you.)

"I'm not sure that's a compliment."

(No, it is.)

"Can a compliment not delivered still be a compliment received?"

(Absolutely. Can an envelope not delivered still be an envelope received? Can a roundhouse punch not delivered still be a roundhouse punch received?)

"No and no. Didn't I already bring up the punching?"

(Okay maybe you're right. What about earthly salvation?)

"Are you serious?"

(Who wouldn't be serious about earthly salvation?)

"Jesus..."

(Really?)

"No, I didn't mean that literally, I was muttering to myself."

(Do the two of you really have to stand here and debate this? Isn't there something more productive we should be doing?)

(Okay, I wasn't serious about the earthly salvation either but I was serious about the stuttering. It's a medical condition. Just let things rest. There's no need to aggravate the situation.)

"I feel you, Doc."

(Just be gentle when you do.)

BAGEL BOB

(Spare change for bong hits?)

"Excuse Bob?"

(Spare change for bong hits?)

"Which do you seek?"

(Excuse me?)

"Which do you seek? Do you wish to inhale from Bob's hookah in exchange for coins or would you prefer that Bob offer you some change so that he may partake of your smoke?"

(I just want some change, dude.)

"Do you wish to receive this sum so that you may ingest marijuana smoke or is such smoke the legal consideration or illegal consideration as the case may be for the coins you covet? Of course Bob should inform you that illegal consideration is an oxymoron and the exchange would be invalidated in a court of law."

(Dude, I don't understand you, I just want some change.)

"People everywhere want change. But how to achieve it, how to achieve it…"

(What's that?)

"Perhaps Bob wishes to respond, to aid in your quest for change. However Bob also desires to learn the conditions you seek to allay and the reforms you hope to initiate."

(Dude, I don't know what to say to you.)

"Then perhaps you ought to say nothing. Bob entreats you to have a glorious evening."

STEVEN

No shit, Nate was right.

By the time they got to Mary Shelley, Shannon was grooving. I could see her in the corner of my eye.

"Hey, Nate, you were right."

(About?)

"Shannon. She was up by the end of 'Ramble On Rose.'"

(Cool. What do you think they'll play now?)

"An 'Althea' would be sweet."

(Steven, man, where's your head? Your dose must have kicked in. Two Jerry songs in a row?)

"Right, right. I thought you meant what would the next *Jerry* song be. Right, the next Bobby song, I—"

('Memphis Blues.' Never mind.)

"Right, cool."

"Memphis Blues." "Memphis Blues?" What's "Memphis Blues?" What album is that on? Of course Nate could be wrong, they're still tuning. You can't necessarily tell-although that guy in front of me said "Memphis Blues" too. Well here it comes, we'll see… Yeah, yeah I recognize this. I'm pretty sure I know what this is. It sounds familiar. Everyone else seems to know it. I'll sneak a peak… Yup, even Shannon's kind of swaying her arms back and forth…

(Killer…)

"Yeah."

Shit, what is it? Nate knows everything. I should have gone to one of the shows last year. I don't know any of the songs, I can't tell what they're playing by listening to them tune, I—wait I know this one. "Stuck Inside of Mobile with the Memphis Blues Again." Bob Dylan. They play it on that classic hits station.

Of course it looks like Nate knows all of the words. He's sort of mouthing them as he grooves. Man, after this semester's over I'm definitely going to sit home by the pool with my SAT book, a Dead lyric book, some notecards and take turns learning vocabulary words and Dead lyrics.

And then maybe when it gets too hot outside I can go up to Sarah's room, stand in front of her full-length mirror and practice my moves. It's like I'm too stiff or something. These other people move like they're liquid, it's the classic Dead dance. Their arms and legs and head kind of roll off their bodies. Even Shannon, she's just sort of staring out into space like she's a zombie or something, but she's making these little waves, almost involuntarily. And Nate, he's doing that plus some cool things with his hands when Jerry takes a solo.

I'm totally going to practice for summer tour.

ZEB

(Clear the aisles, you're going to have to clear the aisles.)

Bobby Weir! Feeling those "Memphis Blues" again!

(Clear the aisles. Everyone, you're going to have to clear the aisles.)

Smoked my eyelids!

(Sorry, you're going to have to clear the aisles.)

"The set is almost over. Just a few more minutes…"

(Fire codes.)

"Have you see the lines out there? By the time I got in I couldn't make it in to my seat. I was stuck outside and now they're playing 'Stuck Inside…'"

(Where is your seat, can I see your ticket?)

"Just a few more minutes? Then it will be set break and I'll find my seat."

(Can I see your ticket?)

"Sure. I… Here."

(Your seat is a few sections over. It's much closer to the stage than this. It's a better seat.)

"But this is where I am now. Please, brother, I just landed here. The Dead are doing Dylan. I'll move during set break. It's not that far away."

(You need to be out of the aisle.)

"Please. I was out there in line for so long, I'm finally in here and trying to connect. Please? How about if I scooch in here?"

(Fine, if it's okay by him.)

(It's okay by me.)

"Kindness."

Kindness!

RANDY

(So are the two of you Deadheads?)

"Is that a joke, Doc?"

(No but here's a joke: How many Deadheads does it take to screw in a light bulb?)

(I don't know, how many?)

(None. They don't change it. They let it burn out and then they follow it around for the next twenty years.)

(Okay…)

(Version two: How many Deadheads does it take to screw in a light bulb? Answer: Deadheads don't screw in light bulbs they screw in dirty sleeping bags.)

"I like that one."

(I thought you might. Last one: How can you tell if Deadheads have been in your house?)

(No idea.)

(They're still there.)

(Doc, you're a regular Hawkeye Pierce.)

"Eddie, a TV reference? I'm disappointed, you're slipping."

(Seriously, Rand? I don't I think ever watched that show. Come on, *M*A*S*H*? The great Robert Altman directed that one. I mean Alan Alda's okay, and I suppose he's a decent writer/ director in his own right. *The Four Seasons* didn't altogether do it for me although I liked *Sweet Liberty*.)

"My first Michelle Pfeiffer film."

(Really, what about *Ladyhawke*?)

"I saw it later on cable. Best Rutger Hauer film?"

(Guys, should that even be a category?)

(Don't be insulting, Doc, and Rand, can I remind you of a little something called *Blade Runner*? But, no, Hawkeye Pierce is Donald Sutherland.)

(Anyhow, do the two of you get my point?)

"Umm..."

(Deadheads look like all of us. We are everywhere. We're doctors, we're lawyers, we're carpenters, we're students. The whole point of Dead Meds is to offer non-judgmental medical assistance. We all volunteer our time and make every effort to treat and release our patients to their friends or family without involving the police in whatever may have transpired. So do you look like Deadheads? You look like Deadheads to me.)

"That's a beautiful speech, Doc. In fact, I suppose I look quite a bit like this other Deadhead because I have his blood all over my clothes and some of his loogie in my hair. And don't get me wrong, you Deadheads are fascinating creatures. I'm just not sure I'd let my sister marry one."

(Will the two of you please do me a favor? When you find that guy please bring him to me. We'll treat him the right way, I promise.)

"Your request is noted, Doc, although I might treat him my own right way first."

STELLA BLUE

"Hey, Mommy, I know this song."

(You do, honey, you do.)

"Aunt Jenny and I sing this song. Hey, Aunt Jenny… Aunt Jennneeeee…"

(What's that, Stella?)

"I know this song."

(That's right, Stella. This is one of the songs we sing.)

"This song's funny."

(You think so…wait here comes the chorus. You know the words, you can sing it.)

"Get your head back on Tennessee Jed!"

(Nice singing, Stell. Although you could do with a little brushup on your lyrics. You know what your mom and I used to say to the people who didn't quite know all the words to a song?)

"Nuh-uh."

('Better attend the meetings,' that's what we'd say. That means go to more Dead shows, so-wait here comes another part you know…)

"Tennessee…ain't no place I'd better beeee…black jack Tennessee…"

(Hey, Stella?… Attend the meetings.)

Giggle—

"You're funny, Aunt Jenny."

(I know I am Stella Blue. And you think this song's funny too. But you only think that because the dog gets kicked and you like cats. Well I don't think that kicking a dog is so funny at all.)

"Shhh, Aunt Jenny, I'm trying to listen to the Grateful Dead…"

ROBIN

Wheeaaahh! Twirlbuzz, twirlbuzz.

"Wheeaaahaaaa!"

Step-ba-ba-buh-turn-twirl-ba-ba-bu-bahoooo.

Whoaaah, look out, Rob, you almost turned into that woman.

Drink spill avoided.

Turn the other way

"Ooops. Sorry, ma'am…"

Well at least she didn't—

"Yes, my hair is perfectly clean!"

Ahhhhhrrrghhh!

Nevermind, nevermind.

Buh-buh-buh-step-buh buh buh-bu-twirl step buh buh twirl buh!

Step buh buh step twirl step-twirl-move it Rob step step bu-buh-buh-buh step step twirl!

"Aheeeeee!"

Jed Jed Jed Jed Jerr Jed Jerr-Jed Jerr-Jed Jerr-Jed Jed-Jer Jed Jer step step Jeddy-Jer Jeddy-Jer Jeddy-Jer Jeddy Jeddy Jerry Jerry Jerry je-je-je-je-Jeddy step twirl bu buh bu buh.

"Ain't no place I'd rather beeeeeeeeeeeeee!"

ZEB

Ten Jed!

The kindness potential is high.

High!

It's all up to Jerry.

Back when I started seeing shows this was one of my favorites. It has a high kindness quotient for the beginner. Jerry jams and the song makes you laugh. It's a total beginner song. It comes with the Dead starter kit.

It's always a treat but some nights with the "Ten Jed" Jerry sends out these mixed message vibes that seem to tell everyone that he's done this one too many times but he still does it because he knows the people love it, especially the newer Heads.

But other nights when he's up there, he tears off a lick and gives a look like "No shit, that was killer. And in the 'Ten Jed' too, I forgot I could pull off a killer lick in the 'Ten Jed.'"

Then he just smiles.

And there's nothing crazier than Jerry when he smiles.

STEVEN

Now this is more like it, this is what the Grateful Dead are all about. "Tennessee Jed."

I'm back into it. Man, going to a show is like a mushroom trip. You're up, you're down but it's always intense.

It all happens in waves, almost liked it was designed that way, to match the rhythms of a mushroom trip.

Maybe it was though. That would make perfect sense.

It's all in the *Electric Kool-Aid Acid Test*. That's how the Grateful Dead really became the Grateful Dead before they were the Grateful Dead. Whoa, that's a cool thought. But yeah, back when they were still called The Warlocks and they were playing for Ken Kesey and the Merry Pranksters at the Acid Tests, that's when they figured it out all out. So it would make perfect sense if their shows emulated the patterns of a psychedelic experience.

Whoa…

Of course "Tennessee Jed" is just good wholesome fun. It's such a Dead song. It's a total goof on everything. It's about how people are always getting kicked around but they bounce back. Just like me, just like I'm doing. Of course I don't have a talking dog, yet, but this is…well it's merry, like the Pranksters. I bet that's not a coincidence. Plus, I know the chorus…

"Tennessee, Tennessee, ain't no place I'd rather be…"

Oh man, so that's so true. I mean not Tennessee but here.

There is no place we'd rather be.

That's why we came together.

We're all back together again for the "Ted Jed."

Except for Shannon. She's sitting down, no, no… She's back up. She's back up for the "Tennessee Jed." And she's smiling. No shit, she's smiling. Jerry made her smile.

JERRY MADE HER SMILE.

TAPER TED

Mitch really must be running on fumes now. Unless he came up with something. From this angle it's hard to tell. Although he is hunched over the D-6 so he must still be running that kid's blank, likely with his own deck on pause so he won't cut the signal when the tape ends.

Where's Rez?

The whole situation reminds me of that night at the Greek in '84. They hadn't pulled a "Dark Star" in three years and I'd only seen two before that. That evening at the Greek there was supposed to be a lunar eclipse and people were talking about the "Star" but people were always talking about it. They're still always talking about it. Or about some other song about to make its miraculous return. I don't know how many times I've heard rumors about them bringing back "St. Stephen."

So the second set ended, it was a pretty hot "Sugar Mags" to close and I still had room on my tape because I figured we were due for a "Day Job" or a "Johnny B" but then they came out and started tuning and I KNEW. So I reached down and started fumbling for a blank but this was pre–Taper City and my blanks were hidden and it was too late. So I was standing there while they dropped the "Star" down on us and there was nothing I could do. So I just waited out that tasty, spacey "Star."

When my tape ended I fired in what was left of my first set blank which was the best I could pull off under the circumstances. I lost some continuity but what was I supposed to do?

Luckily Rez made the rounds and by the time we made it home a few days later, we had a crispy uncut version waiting for us at the post office.

Where is she?

There!

"Excuse me… Excuse me… Excuse me."

(Ted—)

"Where have you been? No, wait, do you have any analog blanks with you?"

(Sure, I think so. Wh—)

"Mitch is having problems. See him back there? Could you work your way over and hand him one?"

(Sure—)

"Give him anything you've got except the Phili 'Dark Star.' I might want to listen to that again on the way back to the hotel."

(Sure, sure.)

"No, forget it, just give him whatever tape you have that's already wound back to the beginning of a side. And thread it past the leader."

(I'll jump like a Willys…)

Okay… It's a good thing she's smaller than me so she can drift up there without freaking anyone out and… Bingo! Okay, he's got it. But let's see what he does. Will he stop, eject and insert a new tape, cutting the kid's signal in the middle of the

"Ten Jed," or will he hold off until after the song? Now that's a true measure of a man.

Let's see... Attaboy. That's the right call, he's going to wait out the "Ten Jed" and let the kid have a clean tape...

Boom! Song over, time to drop in the new tape. Ooohhh, Mitch still has it. Clean wrist action to make it seamless. He always had the knack.

It looks like the kid's gonna want that clean tape too. "Let it Grow." The band has been crushing these as of late.

ZEB

Bobby, you are speaking my language!

"Let It Grow!"

I know there was a reason I bought one of these shirts from Sharon. Other than that my other one was smelling ripe and not the good kind of ripe.

This is the Bobby song for me.

This and "Playing."

And "Cassidy."

Oh and "Jack Straw."

Right and "Sugar Mags."

And "The Other One." I cannot forget the Philtastic intensity of the "The Other One."

And "Estimated," that one's heavy.

Right and "I Need A Miracle," everyone's favorite chorus.

And "Playing" did I mention "Playing?"

"Stranger," right. "Stranger."

"Throwing Stones?" Yup, "Throwing Stones."

"Greatest Story Ever Told." So they say.

"Born Cross-Eyed" even if they'll never play it again.

"Black Throated Wind" because they just started playing it again.

I definitely said "Playing."

"Mexicali" not so much.

But "Let It Grow?" This can be a beast.

Bobby's passion, Jerry heating it up, Phil bombing away, the Devils pounding on and Brent lending a hand. Make that two.

There's gonna let this one grow deep and spacey.

BAGEL BOB

"So, you return. Back from the wars!"

(Robert, you are not one to talk. You've left casualties of your own in your wake. I just passed by some kid outside the camper shaking his head and muttering something about someone who sounded suspiciously like you.)

"Was this youth soliciting change?"

(He was, indeed.)

"It is possible that Bob engaged him in jest."

(The thing is Bob, that at times what you offer in jest others receive in confusion or even fear.)

"Fear of whom?"

(Of whom, indeed. That's what really gets me. Best I can tell, they end up fearful of themselves.)

"Perhaps people should unnerve themselves more often. It keeps them awake and aware."

(Perhaps, but with you it always seems to go further.)

"Bob is an advocate of going further."

(Generally I'm with you although I have found at times that you have a unique gift for creating self-directed panic attacks in the hearts and minds of complete strangers.)

"That is the beauty of being Bob."

(I know, I know. And in this instance you think you acted properly because you don't believe that kid should have been out there doing what he was doing.)

"The youth's presence is irrelevant although his actions are not. Bob does not care about geography, however behavior is significant."

(You don't think he should be in the lot begging for change.)

"Not until he is speaking metaphorically."

(Well I think you're being unreasonable there. People do that all over America. There is no reason why it should be any different here on Shakedown.)

"The distinction is that in the surrounding society most people have no choice about their condition, however this youth elected to enter the hothouse of our environment."

(I can't believe you're saying that. You wouldn't have said that fifteen years ago. That kid could have been you fifteen years ago.)

"Bob will not grant you that point. But no matter, the past is past. In the present we must work to preserve the sanctity and purity of our environment lest we lose it."

(And that's why you won't participate in the book protest.)

"Correct."

(Well I understand but I still think you're reading this wrong. *Reading this wrong*—hey now, there's a Bob-worthy turn of phrase.)

"Chapter and verse."

(Hey, no one-upmanship, the game is not yet afoot… Although that's what this all is about. Anticipation and response, because—and I know you know this to be true—sometimes you have to actively campaign to make things better. And that's what we're going to do.)

"Bob fathoms your motivations. Yet he believes that your efforts will only antagonize. What transpired at the fireside?"

(Nothing. The Jevushuans put out the flames and the yellow jackets walked away with a couple of angry Heads yelling into their backs.)

"And you deem this fruitful?"

(Hey, sometimes it helps to challenge Big Brother.)

"Only when they have the temerity to tour without Janis."

(Ahh, you surprise me there. I was expecting a more direct Holding Company pun.)

"Bob is happy that after all these years, he can still bemuse and bewilder. It was 50/50 on the pun."

(Seriously though, you should reconsider. Those are the same yellow jackets who tried to close you down.)

"True. But Bob does not seek confrontation. When it arrives he will not shrink from it but he does not actively pursue it. Except perhaps in his fervid quest of an opponent's king."

(Fine Bob, fine. We'll play chess. But listen, it's a quarter of nine. The protest is supposed to take place at ten. I have to leave ten minutes earlier. If we're in the middle of a game then we'll have to stop and continue when I get back.)

"That is satisfactory."

(I know you, Bob. If you think that this is a way to keep me occupied so that I don't go to the protest then you're going to be disappointed. There's a clock over your right shoulder.)

"Then perhaps a wager is in order. If Bob wins you will not attend the protest."

(And if I win?)

"Then Bob will permit you to go."

(Oh no. If I win then you will join me and participate.)

"Bob will accompany you but he will not participate."

(Fair enough. Deal?)

"Deal."

(Which they could be playing now.)

"Excuse Bob?"

('Deal.' They could be playing 'Deal' now.)

"They could be had they not played it last night."

(No shit, that's right. I forgot. I imagine you heard J.C.'s tape. So how was the 'Deal?')

"To employ a carcinogenic metaphor, it smoked."

STELLA BLUE

(Excuse me, but your daughter is pretty amazing.)

(Why thank you. What do you mean?)

(Your little girl right there, she's amazing.)

(Oh, right, sorry, I'm spacing. I get a mild case of flashbacks at the shows these days. No, no. She's not my daughter. It's just my turn to be the pillow. No, Stella popped out of that woman dancing to my right.)

(Stella? After the song?)

(Right.)

(It's just so amazing the way she's up and then she's down and then she's up. I even heard her singing some of the words to 'Tennessee Jed.')

(Yeah, Stella loves the 'Ten Jed.' I just hope they pull a 'Wheel' in the second set. That's her favorite.)

(Sorry to let Stella down but it's not gonna happen. We had one last night.)

(How was it?)

(Kind of tepid. A fierce wheel really gets me moving, doing involuntary arm motions for the big wheel and little wheel. That kind of wheel makes my hair curl up in appreciation, even the hairs on my beard.)

(What about the hair on the rest of your body?)

(Excuse me?)

(Does the hair on the rest of your body curl as well?)

(I suppose it does. Anyhow, I just wanted to tell you that I think it's amazing that Stella was up and down all through the set and now during this 'Let It Grow,' when the whole room's shaking, she's just lying there peacefully sleeping.)

"I'm not sleeping."

RANDY

"Come on, we need to sprint..."

(Rand, are you sure we shouldn't be out looking for that bloody guy?)

"The one who hocked a loogie on me and hit me in the gut?"

(You make that sound so unappealing.)

"Not, just anti-social. It discourages the tender reunion."

(Well we told the Dead Med guy we'd look for him.)

"I also believe we told him we'd ease up on the *Breakfast Club* references and I don't see that happening anytime soon."

(Screws fall out all the time, the world is an imperfect place.)

"Plus any commitment to the passive-aggressive overreaching Dead Med is less important than our previous commitments. Come on, let's move it, double-time…"

(I'm with you, Rand…)

"Where did you tell them to meet us?"

(Up ahead over there. I said all the way over in the corner of the fenced-in area. I figure no one will see us because we'll be blocked by the buses and the dumpster.)

"Colonel Kurtz will."

(Yeah, his camouflaged head will slowly pop out of the garbage.)

"And he'll throw an improper flag on the play—'I love the smell of Patchouli in the morning!'"

(Did you know that the Grateful Dead guys worked on that film?)

"I can safely say that tidbit adds nothing to my enjoyment of either *Apocalypse Now* or the Grateful Dead. In rapidly descending order. No matter what the Grateful Doc might say. To me, it's too much music, not enough words. Give me Anthrax any day. Or the Ramones."

(I'll give you anthrax—Holy crap, Ellis, what happened to you? Did somebody stick you with a shiv?)

"Schultz! Well, at least someone made it, although you sound like Eddie."

(No, I'd sound like Robbins if I said 'stick you with a shiv,' and then quoted dialogue from *Brubaker* or something.)

(*Brubaker*? Solid pick.)

(We saw it in criminology class. Christ, Robbins, why do you have to be a movie major?)

(Film major.)

(Why can't you be a criminology major like the rest of the team?)

"There are a few rogue chem majors as well."

(The less said, the better. But what happened to you, you're covered in blood.)

"Not mine."

(I gotta see what did you did to the other guy.)

"I didn't do anything. He hit me and ran. If I find him though…"

(I gotta see that.)

"But where is everybody else? We can't be here for too long. How are we going to do this, there were supposed to be six of us."

(They got called away. Some fire dance or something. Ellis, I know you want your devil's number but maybe the three of us can do it.)

"It's up to you. I already have a handle on it. I was just trying to be a good teammate."

(Then let's get started. If they show up, they can watch and then maybe they can jump in.)

"I suppose that can work if we all double up."

(Set us up, Rand. Let's get started.)

STEVEN

Strong set. That was a strong set. They've got the goods tonight, they've definitely got the goods.

Whew, we finally get to sit down.

I didn't realize how tiring it is, grooving for an hour or so with the Dead. I mean it's hard work. It's good we have this set break so we can regroup and get our faculties back.

Faculties, good word. Someone should teach a class in Grateful Dead 101.

Whoa, maybe I can do that when I get to college. I know a lot of places have those Experimental Sessions during the summer or over winter break where the students can apply to be the teachers. I think that by then after I've been to maybe a dozen or even two dozen more shows and I'm super on top of my lyrics and all that, it would be really cool to give it a go. That would probably look great on a grad school application as well, teaching a class as an undergrad.

For now though, it's time to rest, reflect and recharge. Look at everyone just crashing back into their chairs, they're exhausted. It's like the Dead knew how much we could take and then they had to stop. That last song was rocking. Everyone was going crazy, even Shannon was flying around. Shit—but now she's sitting there again with her hands over her face all hunched over. I've got to do something.

(Steven?)

"Huh? Yes, Emily?"

(Move over, I have to talk to Shannon. I don't understand it. I'm like totally flying. I'm having a totally great trip.)

"I can tell. You can't stop smiling."

(Really? Okay, I'll try to stop. There. Did I stop?)

"No."

(Well how could I, that 'Let It Grow' was so hot! Everyone was dancing and I could feel it. It was juicing me up, making me go faster and faster and making my brain go faster and faster until it absolutely stopped working. It just shorted out and I was out there in some nether world that the Grateful Dead created.)

"No shit!"

(Yeah, I know. And I think I can help Shannon get there, I just have to talk to her.)

"Go ahead."

Damn, she went off into some special Dead universe. That's so awesome, it's like she really had a Grateful Dead moment. Maybe my Grateful Dead moment wasn't a real Grateful Dead moment. Maybe I should have taken mushrooms. No, that's stupid, I couldn't take any, we didn't have any. No, wait but I took something, I dropped acid. Nate and Zack and Jason and I dropped acid. What happened with that?

"Hey Nate! Nate!"

(What?)

"Pretty hot set, huh?"

Look at him, look at his eyes, the way he's just staring out, kind of smiling. He's tripping. I can't believe it, he's tripping. Shit, I'm not tripping. I'm high but I'm definitely not tripping. Why aren't I tripping like he's tripping? I swallowed the paper and everything. Wait, maybe that was bad. Maybe I forgot to put it on my tongue and instead I just swallowed it so now I'm not going to trip. All my friends are going to have their Grateful Dead experiences and I'm just going to sit here like a dweeb.

(Did you say something?)

"When?"

(Just then.)

"Well yeah, just then."

(No, no, before that.)

"I don't think so. I was just sitting here thinking."

(No shit, I think I heard you. I'm pretty sure I heard you thinking. I mean I couldn't hear you clearly, it was like mumbling but I definitely was listening to you think. That's happened to me a couple times before when I've tripped. I am not making this up.)

"Man, you're definitely tripping. I'm not tripping that much."

(Yeah, man I'm tripping BALLS! BALLS!)

(Hey kid, keep your balls to yourself down there.)

(I'll see what I can do, sir… Sorry Stevie, maybe those first ones were duds.)

"What do you mean, first ones?"

(Zack and I each took a hit of this other acid.)

"Other acid? Where'd you get more acid?"

(Some dude at the end of the row. Zack saw he was taking some and asked for a couple hits. That's the way to go, get someone's acid they're not trying to sell, that they've brought in for their own personal use.)

"But what about me? Why didn't you get a hit for me?"

(Zack could only get two. Jason didn't get one either. Hey Zack, why'd you only get two?)

(I could only get two. I was grateful to get two. And now I'm grateful I had one. Real grateful. Yeeeehaaaa!)

(Balls, man! BALLS!)

No shit I can't believe they took more doses. Mine must be a dud or something. Freaking Gorbachev. Or maybe it was because I swallowed it.

"Huh?"

(I could hear you thinking again, I could definitely hear you thinking. I'm not sure what it was you were thinking but—)

"Do you have any more of those doses we bought outside?"

(Yeah.)

"Let me have one."

(Stevie, it's kind of late.)

"There's a whole set to go, come on."

(Right, right, okay, okay. Wait a second, I have to dig into my pocket… Ummm…okay, okay here you go.)

"Thanks."

(Hey Jason, you want one?)

(Huh? No thanks, I'm doing fine.)

(Yeah, he's doing fine with Meg.)

Sure he's doing fine. Everyone's doing fine but me. Okay now, here we go. Remember, on the tongue. Let it melt in your mouth. Not in your hands. Kind of like M & M's.

Alright, take it easy, okay, okay…I'm set. I'm ready to go. Once the set break is over I'll be dosed and primed for some Grateful Dead action, I just hope Shannon—

Hey, they're gone. Shannon and Emily are gone. Where are—Oh, there they are over in the aisle, Shannon's sort of clutching onto her. Well I hope a walk or something will make her feel better.

Although it kind of feels like everyone's left me. Jason and Meg are way over there huddling or cuddling or something. Nate and Zack are off tripping. They're next to me but they're not here. And Shannon is off trying not to trip. Or trying to trip differently.

And I'm left alone in this arena with 20,000 people.

All by myself.

ROBIN

(Good set, people! Good set!)

"Uh-gurgle-huh."

Robin… Whoa, Robin… WhooooooosH…okayyyyyy.

WhoooooosH! WhoooooosH! WhoooooosH!

"Heeeeaaaaahaaahhaaaa!"

Whoooooosh!

Setbreak okay Rob Setbreak.

Whoa let that pass…

Whoooooooshhhhhh.

"Ooooopsiesorry…"

Sorrryyyy.

Pretzel…

Mustarrrrrrd…

Messsssy…

"Yesssssittscleeeeeen."

Setbreak.

Setbreak.

Setbreak.

TAPER TED

"I'm with you on this. We are living in a 'Let It Grow' era. Mark my words, when we look back, 'Let It Grow' will define this epoch of the Grateful Dead. That version in Landover two weeks ago had power, grace and nuance. This one was damn close. Your boy Bobby is on top of his game… So where were you anyhow?"

(I was beeped.)

"During a show? Don't they realize the potential implications?"

(All too well. And just to be sure before we left I made my 'Ballad of a Thin Man' speech again.)

"So it was an emergency?"

(Of sorts.)

"Of sorts."

(An emergency social call.)

"An emergency social call?"

(Of sorts. Someone from our Manhattan office is here with her fourteen year old daughter and one of her daughter's friends. It's the girls' first show.)

"Old time Head?"

(She's attended the meetings. It's been a few years though, so somehow word came back to Portland. Paul beeped me and asked me to introduce myself.)

"How'd you find their seats?"

(It wasn't hard. I just went up to the suite and knocked on the door.)

"She's watching a Dead show from a luxury box?"

(Well watching might be a bit of an exaggeration. What she's mainly doing is trying to keep her eyes on the kids. The three of them are not the only ones in there as you might imagine. There are all sorts of people coming and going, puffing and pounding.)

"And what does she think about that?"

(She was a bit tense at first, trying to keep the kids from the booze. She did mellow a bit by mid-set though.)

"High from the second hand smoke?"

(No, high from the joint she pulled out when the kids went to the bathroom. I suspect to puff on a joint of their own.)

"Well she's got moxie."

(No, we have Moxie in the great state of Maine. She has whatever overpriced chichi fountain drink originated in Manhattan. She's a tough chick but also a single mom in a strange situation who was thrilled to learn there was help on the way. And more to come. Where's your brother, the girls need his stub.)

(Well it may not set any records but I'm not sure that I'd call it a stub.)

"He's right behind you on a mustard high."

(That's pretzel logic for you. See you're not the ones who can gracefully interject song titles. Did you say something about the girls?)

(Not quite for you. They're your typical fourteen year old neo-hippie chicks with hundred dollar haircuts and New York accents. I promised my new friend Stephanie that I'd escort them down here so that Ted can give them the grand tour during set break. So like I said, can they use your stubs? Tommy, not another word…)

BAGEL BOB

(Are you going to move?)

"No, Bob is quite comfortable where he is."

(A piece. Bob, do you intend to move a piece? I'm perfectly aware that you're trying to stall…)

"Patience, trusted friend of Bob. Patience—"

(Don't say it's a virtue. I don't want virtue. I am not a virtuous person. I haven't been since 1974.)

"That was a bad year for virtue."

(No shit, I—Damn it. I can't believe it, not another one. Come in…)

(Ummm, hi. My name is Cosmic Kel-Kel and I'm here on behalf of the Righteous Recyclers, we—)

(I know who you are. Garbage or money?)

(Excuse me?)

(Which do you want, garbage or money?)

(Garbage would be lovely.)

(Well my garbage certainly is. Right over there to the left of the fridge… There you go.)

(Thank you, have a nice night.)

(Bob, make your—come in!)

(Hey now, my name is Doug and I'm involved with the Garden of the Gratefully Deadicated.)

(Sorry, I gave at the office. Please, we're trying to play a little chess here.)

"Don't be so self-deprecating. While your end game needs work, Bob would not characterize the totality of your skill set as diminutive."

(Ha, ha, Bob. Good night, Doug… So Bob, do you have this problem with everyone knocking?)

"On Heaven's Door?"

(No on the door to your camper-Right, right, Heaven's Door, I forgot that's what you call it. Ode to Dylan. Why do we never play over at your place?)

"Eau de garlic, your sensitive snout."

(Eau means water, I might call you out on that one.)

"Bob produces his own garlic-infused cream cheese by a distillation process that also includes vidalia onions and leeks."

(Right, right. My bad. I never should have challenged you. I'll keep out of your idiom wind…)

"Michael is pleased with himself."

(Well, one Dylan turn deserves another.)

"Bob acknowledges this simple twist of fate."

(Okay, okay. Chess. Let's play chess. It's your move. You're gonna make me lonesome unless you go. Sorry, sorry no more *Blood on The Tracks* puns or references or distractions or whatever. We're here to play some chess."

"Let us not talk falsely now, the hour is getting late."

(Well, now you've jumped albums. Although I give you bonus points for quoting a lyric that just might come off the stage tonight. But please, as your host, I beseech you, let's resume our game.)

"Bob acknowledges you beseechment and appreciates your shelter from the storm."

(Fine, I have to give you that one, which miraculously gets us back to my original point. Do you have a problem with people knocking on the door of your camper when you're holed up in there?)

"Bob does not."

(And why is that?)

"Bob's door remains closed to anyone who cannot provide the proper salutation. Bob does not wish to present himself unawares to the representatives of certain authoritarian organizations."

(FBI? CIA? IMF?)

"ABC. One of their vice presidents went to school with Bob, spied him outside Madison Square Garden last fall and wishes to turn his life into a television docudrama."

(No shit, a docudrama, I can't believe it.)

"Well there would be some humorous elements as well."

(Arrgh. Again! WHO IS IT?)

(Coins or cash for a sister who was shut out?)

(COME ON NOW, I—)

(Just kidding. Hey now, Mike. Good evening, Bagel Bob.)

"Fair to middling evening Gershona."

(Tell me about it.)

"Perhaps Bob will."

(Perhaps you should but not now, I'm on a mission. That's why I'm here.)

(Another dog, Gershona?)

(We need you.)

(I'm sorry but I have to stop doing this. I can't keep on breaking into cars and liberating canines with you.)

(But they need us.)

(I know they do. And I would lock up all the assholes who leave them in there if I could but things got more than a little hairy last night. Those yellow jackets didn't share our outrage. Plus, I'm in the heat of the battle with Bob and I already signed on for the book protest. I assumed that you'd be in on that.)

(I will be. But we still have time for two covert missions.)

"Your literary demonstration will be far from covert. It will be as overt as it gets."

(Hear hear.)

(Let's hope.)

"Bob will keep his optimism in check while he aims to do the same to Michael."

(Finally, a move! Thank you, Gershona, at least you've liberated something.)

STEVEN

This is what I need, this is exactly what I need.

Shannon and Emily had the primo idea when they decided to come out here, it's like everything's right or something. I wonder where they are. I mean no big deal if I see them but if I do that would be sweet.

Set break is time to mellow out, walk around, get your head back together and prepare for the spacey second set. It's pretty crowded out here but it's not a bad sort of crowded. It's not like a real traffic jam because no one's trying to get anywhere, really. Except over there people are in line to get munchies and crap.

That's sort of weird, all those guys wearing tie-dyes in line buying hot dogs and candy bars. It's something you wouldn't expect. You'd expect them to boycott that sort of stuff because they don't eat meat or the package isn't recyclable or whatever. Like that guy with the long braids in his hair getting a cheeseburger and—

"Excuse me."

(That's okay. Buzzing past by the snack bar I see.)

"Sort of."

(Dig. I could rage all over an ice cream if I had the bread.)

"Yeah, me too."

(Well, have a good second set.)

"Nice bumping into you."

That was cool. Kind. No, kind doesn't cut it. Deadheads are peaceful, like there's this inner thing to them and that thing is mellow or whatever.

Not many people are going for the thirty buck T-Shirts. That makes sense. They're kind of cool but thirty is way too much. I could have bought a much cooler T for ten.

Wow, look at all the Heads over by the pay phones. I bet they're calling their friends and telling them what songs the Dead played. That way people don't have to call the 1-900 number where the guy reads the setlists.

There's a lot of grungy people too. People I wouldn't figure have enough money to afford a ticket. Of course maybe they got free tickets or something but some of them sort of look like the people you see muttering to themselves on the streets of New York. Like that guy over there behind the people in that circle who keeps saying "beautiful toys, beautiful toys" over and over again. That is kind of intriguing, though. I wonder what the toys are. Or who the toys are.

And over there on the floor, all those little groups of Heads are sort of huddling together and talking. And over there, they're sitting Indian style in a circle like they're going to play duck duck goose. They're totally sweaty, they must have been dancing like crazy.

It's wild out here. It's filled with all sorts of cool people, all sorts of Heads. It's like a giant Deadhead convention.

STELLA BLUE

"What did you say, Mommy?"

(I said, 'What, Stella?')

"I know you said that. What did you say before that?"

(I don't know, honey, I was talking to Aunt Jenny and her new friend.)

"I remember him. He thought I was asleep."

(Well I'll forgive him if you will.)

"Okay. What happened to the lights, Mommy? Why are they on?"

(Because the Grateful Dead stopped playing and now everyone wants to be able to see.)

"Oh."

(Any more questions?)

"Hmmm… Is there anything real that's nowhere?"

(Good question. Jenny, Stella wants to know if there's anything real that's nowhere.)

(This girl is Deadhead through and through. I don't care if she's three years old—)

"Threeandalmostfour."

(I don't care if she's threeandalmostfour, Stella Blue is asking *all* the right questions.)

(And are there any *other* questions you have for me, big girl?)

"Why are we here?"

(Why are we here… Wow, that is a really short question that calls for a really long answer. Where should we start? You know, this one is sort of connected to the last question, which also was an excellent one. Okay, Stell Belle, let's try to think back a long, long, long time ago—)

"Why are we here if the Grateful Dead are gone?"

(Ahh, ahhhhh…because they'll be back. They're taking a break. Jerry's taking a nap just like you do.)

"Mommy, Jerry's not taking a nap."

(I don't know, Stell, your mother may be right with that one.)

(Maybe he's not taking a nap but he is taking a break and then the Dead will come and play some more. Do you want to see them play some more?)

"Nuh-uh."

(No?)

(Fickle Head. Everybody's a critic. The kid gets a little upset with the first set so she stages a protest by sleeping through the 'Let It Grow,' then—)

(Jenny, extinguish it.)

(Right.)

(Stella, you don't want to stay to see Jerry and Bobby play some more songs?)

"I'm hungry."

(Hungry? Are you sure you're not sleepy? You don't want to go home and go to bed, do you?)

"No Mommmeee, I don't want to."

(Okay then, what do you say we get up and go for a walk and find you a snack? How does that sound?)

"Okay, Mommy, let's go."

(Hey I thought the two of you said Stella's been to eight shows. How come she can't remember the set break?)

(Take my hand, hon. Well, she was a Deadhead in utero and went to four or five shows prenatally. Then when she was an infant she went to a few, which was a treat because kids are free until they turn two. But we stopped coming for a while. This is the first show we've been to in a couple years.)

(Actually twenty-two months. I'll tell you because Alison wants to spare me. I did a little time for holding a few plants for a friend. A few dozen plants. So the local prosecutor decided it would be fun to hold me. A lot of holding went on but none of it was too tender. What *was* tender though was that during those twenty-two months, my touring buddy did some sort of vigil thing and stayed away from the Dead.)

(Heck, it was nothing.)

(Damn straight it was. She didn't have a baby sitter.)

"Aunt Jenneeee!"

(Sorry, Stell, but you were a baby back then.)

"No, you said a bad word."

(So I did. One should never say prosecutor in mixed company or there will be hell to pay.)

"Aunt Jenneee!"

(I know, Stell, I know.)

ZEB

G...F...E...D...Here we go...

Four rows off the floor, one section back from the stage, Phil side.

We are gonna be DEEP in the PHIL ZONE.

There's the dude who sold me the ticket—Craig, I think he said.

"Hey now, brother."

(Hey. Sweet seats, did I tell you?)

"You told me."

(You're gonna dig it here. I wasn't sure if I'd see you or not. So what'd you think of the set?)

"Missed about half of it. How about you?"

(I made it just before Bobby's first lunge during 'Bucket.')

"How'd you do that?"

(I have my ways. I zagged. I zigged. I zagged some more and then I Ziggy Marleyed my way to victory.)

"You cut the line?"

(I wouldn't call it cutting. Nobody out there got cut. I have my techniques and none of them involve laceration. Listen, it mattered more to me to be in here on time than most of those people, so I made it work. Plus I was serious when I said that I Ziggy Marleyed. I pulled out a bomber and made some new friends. That's a lesson for you kids today, perfect your craft. With all those pipes out in the lot, people have forgotten the simple art of rolling the perfect joint. Assuming you stick with me for the second set and go don't off seat surfing, you'll see what I can do. I have some dyno doojie.)

"Kind."

(The right kind. After 'Bucket,' it was 'Bertha,' 'Little Red Rooster,' 'Ramble On Rose'—)

"I was in for the 'Rooster.'"

(Then 'Memphis Blues' in Bobby's Dylan slot. I prefer 'Masterpiece' there or 'Desolation Row' but to each to his own.)

"I'm a 'Queen Jane' guy."

(Your secret's safe with me. Just, kidding. Tough to quibble with any song from *Highway 61 Revisited*. 'Queen Jane Approximately,' I'm a fan of any song with the word approximately in the title, although I can't think of any others right now. Back to our show, then we had 'Tennessee Jed' in your honor. That's your name right?)

"No, it's Zeb."

(Zeb? If you're going to make something up why not go right on point with Jed. Unless you were aiming for more of that Sci-fi, *Star Wars* kind of feel.)

"No, that's my name. Zebulon. I'm named after an explorer."

(I'm gonna my kids after explorers one day. I'll call 'em Jerry, Bobby, Phil, Mickey, Bill and sometimes Brent.)

"Come on now, Craig, don't be harshing on Brent."

(You're a Touchhead, aren't you?)

"Come on now, Craig, don't be harshing on Zeb."

ROBIN

Sit Robin sit find spot

So many people smiling skipping smiling sipping smiling sweating.

In the corner.

(OoooopsSorrrrry!)

Pizzaaaa.

"YesssHaaiiirzzzclean!"

Sitsitisit.

Against wall away.

(Hi.)

Theresss aperson.

No two personnssss lying together.

Nice.

"Nice."

Setlist.

In bag.

Okay.

After "Rooster" after "Rooster" after "Rooster." Jerry.

"After 'Rooster' Jerry?"

('Ramble on Rose.')

"Thankyooo."

"Ramble on Rose."

Next Bobby Bobby Bobbybobbybobby.

"Bobby?"

('Memphis Blues.')

"Thankyoooo."

(Show her your setlist, Annie?)

(Let her try, she can do it. She can do it. You can do it.)

"Memphis Blues." Next Jerry Jerry Jerry Jerry Jerry Jerry Jer-ry Jer-ry Jer Je-Je-Je-Jed-Ten Jed!

"'Ten Jed!'"

(You got it!)

"Ten Jed."

Then Bobby Bobby Bobby.

Bob-by Bob-Bobobobob-Bobby-bobby.

Bobbybobby.

"LetItGrowwwwww!"

(She did it!)

(She did it!)

(Our little girl's all grown up! She can figure out the setlist all by herself!)

"Haaaaa!"

RANDY

"Alright, gentlemen, so the name of the game is Diplomacy."

(Is that the actual name or are you giving us a strategy tip?)

"Schultzie, can you read what's directly in front of you on the game board? The actual name is Diplomacy. Although I suppose that is something of a strategy tip."

(Okay, now I see. It's in cursive.)

(Do you even attend class? We've been talking about this for two weeks.)

(What kind of a wack job political history class requires to you to play a game for 20 percent of your grade?)

(What kind? A wack job political history class filled with football players. Are you seriously complaining about this? That's part of the reason we're all taking this, it's a gut. It's no Geology 100, God bless Rocks for Jocks, but it's a pretty sweet deal.)

(But why does the game part take place on a Saturday? Who wants to play on a Saturday?)

(You did this past fall, when you were collecting splinters on the bench. Ouch!)

(Piss off!)

"Sorry, Schultzie, you might have played on Saturday, if I hadn't been ahead of you on the depth chart."

(Wow, you're so deep.)

"And you are the antithesis of that."

(I'm impressed with your big words.)

"I'm impressed with your big gut which is why you didn't play on Saturdays."

(Oh boo hoo.)

"Boo hoo, does that even make sense?"

(It makes as much sense as you starting over me when we both know I could take you in a fight. And I could take your woman if I wanted.)

"Take her where, to ladies night at the beauty parlor?"

(Well at least you're admitting that Angela and I are both beauties. Which is more than can be said about you. Which is also why we were made for each other.)

(Schultize, you and Randy were made for each other?)

(Robbins, you're quite the Charles Nelson Reilly. But you know, as a favor to Angela, I'd let him in on a three-way if he never made eye contact with me and she worked him from behind.)

"Alright, alright just simmer down. I knew that was what this was about. Stop talking about my girl. *My* girl. Simmer down and let me teach you how to play."

(Well you simmer down and one day I'll teach you how to be a player.)

"One day."

(Although some secrets I'll have to keep from you. Angela was telling me you're too dainty for her tastes.)

(Dainty?)

"Really, do I need this shit? I'd rather listen to the shitass high school ref try to defend his high school ref shitassery."

(Careful, Randy, you're going to knock over the board.)

"Listen, I already know how to play. Trust me, I'm going to crush you all tomorrow. But I offered to help. I said we could do it earlier in the week or even tonight after we finished up. You were the ones who said you wanted to do it here, not me. I was just trying to be a good teammate. But seriously, fuck it."

(Come on, Rand…)

"The board doesn't even really fit on this milk carton, we don't have everyone here, our demented supervisor is going to come looking for us any minute now, I'm starving, I'm covered in blood..."

(But other than that, Mrs. Lincoln, how was the play?)

TAPER TED

(Ted, this is Hillary and her friend Beth.)

(And I'm Tommy, just visiting the tapers' section from a warm and welcoming place I call reality.)

(Feel free to ignore him. In fact, he's leaving.)

(I am?)

(You am. I'm buying you a beer. Let's go. Ted, why don't you give Hillary and Beth the full tour. I'll be back in a little while to pick them up.)

"Right. Hillary and Beth. So how old are you? No, wait, I always hated it when people asked me that. How about, what grade are you in?"

(Ninth.)

"Both of you?"

(Yup.)

(Yup.)

"Okay then. Well, like Rez said, I'm here to give you the tour."

(Who?)

"Me."

(No, who's Rez?)

"Ohh, Rez, Kathy. She's my wife. Kathy. The one who brought you down here."

(Why do you call her Rez?)

"It's her nickname."

(What does it mean?)

'"It's short for...something."

(What?)

"What?"

(What?)

"Kathy. It's short for Kathy."

(Whatever.)

"Come on, let's start the tour though."

(Will we get to meet Bob Weir?)

(Come on, Hil, I told you. He's eating or something. He doesn't want to be bothered. Does he?)

"You're asking me?... Oh, you're asking *me*. Well actually I don't know."

(So we can meet him?)

"Uhhh, no..."

(Well then how about Jerry Garcia. Can we meet him?)

(Beth!)

(Well can we?)

"No, I'm afraid—"

(Well who can we meet? How about one of the drummers, they 're cool.)

"No, no. I don't think you understand. By the full tour I mean the full tour of the taping section and my taping gear."

(Ohhhh.)

(Ohhhh.)

(Wait, so you ARE a taper.)

"That's right."

(And you work for the band.)

"No, I work for a town in Maine."

(What does Maine have to do with the Grateful Dead?)

"Not much. They haven't been there since Oxford."

(What?)

(So you work for the Grateful Dead in Maine?)

"No, I…wait you think that I work for the band because I'm a taper?"

(That's what this friend of ours said.)

(Yeah, he said you get special passes and that sort of thing.)

"Well we do get tapers' tickets from the band through mail order that allow us to bring in our equipment. We have to pass through a special line just for tapers to get into the show. But that's all the special attention we get. I guess you'd say that we're freelancers, taping for our own personal reasons. I don't know if Rez-Kathy told you but the two of us have been doing this for a while. Back in the old days they didn't have this special area for tapers, everyone had to do the best they could. It was a lot harder too. The band didn't care so much but the venues would sometimes pitch a fit. So we had to come up with all sorts of creative ways to get our equipment into the shows and then to run tape. For instance, a couple times I pretended I had a broken leg and we put our gear in this hollowed-out cast. On a few other occasions Rez—I mean Kathy—pretended she was pregnant and… You see, I had a big analog deck back then, or at least big by comparison to what I have today. I assume that analog is the format that you have at home. Yes?"

(Well I have a CD player.)

(Me too. And a radio. And a tape deck.)

"Right, the tape deck. That's analog, correct? I mean it takes your average everyday standard cassettes? "

(I guess.)

(Me too.)

"The problem with analog is that the tapes last forty-five minutes per side—actually a little closer to forty-seven, which becomes an issue if you're taping because the Grateful Dead play for much longer than that, which means that you need to flip the tapes during the set which can become a real pain. You also have to do it towards the end of those forty-six minutes because the longer you let the tape record on one side, the longer you'll be able to record on the other side since there's no time to rewind. Plus the Grateful Dead don't always stop between songs, which can make it a challenge to determine the ideal moment to flip. Of course sometimes they take far too long because they can't figure out what to play. That all disappears with Digital Audio Tape. There's no flip with DATs because you can only record on one side but a 60-meter tape lasts 120 minutes. A 90m lasts 180 minutes but I wouldn't recommend those because the tape itself is thinner and DAT recorders can be fickle, generating error codes and shutting down for anything from dust molecules to dampness."

(So there's no chance you can introduce us to Bob Weir?)

"No, sorry."

(Can you introduce us to anyone in the Grateful Dead?)

"Again, sorry. Actually, I might be able to introduce you to the man who engineers their sound. Would you like to meet him?"

(Have you ever met Bob Weir?)

"No, I can't say that I have."

(How about Jerry Garcia?)

"No. Although now that you mention it I did spend some time with MG once. Mountain Girl. Although come to think of it, they should start calling her MW for Mountain Woman."

(She's not in the Grateful Dead.)

(Yes she is. She's that woman who used to sing with them.)

"No, that was Donna. Mountain Girl is a Prankster though. And I'm pretty sure she's still married to Jerry."

(But she's not in the Grateful Dead?)

"No."

(Why are you so interested in taping them if you've never met them?)

(Yeah, isn't that weird?)

"Well—"

(Especially since you're not an employee or anything. You're just this guy who follows them around with a microphone.)

(Yeah, isn't that weird?)

"You know Rez and I don't have any kids."

(No doy.)

(Yeah, no doy.)

STEVEN

(Do you go to Willington?)

"Yeah. Why?"

(I thought I recognized you. I'm Casey. Kevin Casey. Do you remember me? I knew your sister.)

"Yeah, you're a legend."

No shit. Casey Jones himself. In the flesh.

(I mean I still know your sister. I just saw her a couple weeks ago. I'm at Columbia and we have this crazy party house, with all of these bands playing our block parties who are embodying the spirit of the Grateful Dead. They are keeping the flame alive and it is ablaze! We are high minded! And there's a crazy, crazy new club that opened downtown, this hippie mecca, where you can burn one in the basement and then shake your bones in the sweat lodge upstairs to the latest psychedelic sounds. Better off Dead!)

"That sounds awesome. You know, we're totally keeping things blazing back at the big W."

(As long as the shrine survives. You dig?)

"Uh-yeah, yeah."

(It's a hand-me-down but the heart has its beaches.)

"Right."

(Although the shrine demands an offering, a sharing of the wine, dig?)

"Absolutely."

What?

(I don't mean to dominate the rap, Jack. But that's on you.)

"Um, sure—"

(Because the Shrine—wait, are you a senior?)

"Junior."

(Arrggh! I am a useless smile. Let the words be yours I'm done with mine…)

"Wait! Where? What?"

(Oh yeah and say hi to your sister for me…)

BAGEL BOB

(What the hell?)

"A quake! Quick, to the doorframe!"

(That's no quake. No, it is a quake but it's not an earthquake, it's a camperquake and it's not natural. It's man-made. Or woman-made. Hey! What are you doing?)

(We want to find the guy who sold us this bunk fucking shit.)

(Hold on, hold on I'm coming out. What do you want? Hey! And get him off there!)

(Joey, get off! We want to find the guy who sold us this bunk fucking shit.)

(So why are you shaking my van?)

(We think it might be you.)

(So you climbed on my house?)

(Well somebody sold us these counterfeit mushrooms.)

(Counterfeit?)

"Caveat emptor!"

(What's that?)

"Caveat emptor when judging a spore!"

(What are you saying?)

"Simple psilocybin jurisprudence. Since psilocybin has been prohibited by statutory means, the transgressor must appeal to the archaic realm of English Common law. Court of Exchequer… Or is it the Court of Common Pleas. Which is it, Bob forgets. Do either of you recall which is proper?"

(Is he tripping or something?)

(Just over his tongue.)

"Are Bob or Michael responsible for your consumer fraud?"

(I guess not.)

"Then perhaps it would be wise to locate the perpetrators and prevent them from further wrongdoing. But shake no more domiciles until you familiarize yourself with the proper precedents…and their occupants. Caveat Emptor! Bonam Fortunam!"

(Joey, man, let's just move on…)

(Wow, Robert. I mean, wow. One beautiful thing about you, is that sometimes I'm not entirely certain when you're full of shit.)

"A more beautiful thing is that neither is Bob."

ZEB

(I didn't mean to insult you by calling you a Touchhead, we all have to start somewhere.)

"It's all good, brother. Most of us here were touched in the head."

(Point well made. I mean everyone starts out as like a non-Head or let's say a shrunken Head. It's what happens next that matters. Some of us get on the bus...)

"Right on."

(It shouldn't matter when that happens. For me in was the early 80s, for you, let's just say you're In The Darker than me.)

"Dude..."

(And that's not meant to be racist. I mean we're both healthy, hearty Caucasians right? I mean the two of us, not the other 99% of the people in here who are healthy, hearty Caucasians.)

"Right..."

(That's what I figured. It's hard to tell, you've got that patina of dust on you from the lot. I don't want you to think I intended to insult you because of your ethnic origins."

"No..."

(When in reality I intended to insult you because of how long you've been seeing the Grateful Dead...)

"Come on, Craig."

(Just kidding. I kid because I care. By that I mean I care about what's happening out there. Too much excess. I'm all for excess *in here* but excess *out there*, just doesn't do it for me. That's why we can't do back to Providence or Worcester or Richmond where I saw my first show. When was your first show, if you don't mind my asking. Some people get all in a huff about that question, like I'm crossing some boundary and asking them when they lost their virginity. I just don't see it that way and frankly, not to be cruel about it, plenty of those dudes out there probably saw their first show before they lost their virginity. Am I rambling? Did I mention that I smoked some dyno doojie in order to cut the line?)

"I believe you did."

(So when was your first show, again?)

"I haven't told you yet but I'm happy to do so. March twenty-fourth, nineteen-eighty-eight, the Omni in Atlanta."

(Well you certainly are a Touchhead. I'm not trying to be insulting, think of me as your ace cub reporter here, just laying out the facts. Actually you're almost a post-Touchhead because when I think of Touchheads, I think of people who started touring in 1987 after 'Touch of Grey' became popular. Spring tour '88 had some fine moments though. 'So What' and 'Thin Man' in Hampton, the 'Louie Louie' bustout in Hartford. I have that whole tour on DAT. Crispy delights, first gens from the masters.)

"I was at Hampton and Hartford. I held my breath and jumped into the deep end. I did most of that tour. I had to break off after the Centrum shows, though. I was surprised I ever made it that far."

(It always seems easier than it is. That's why the whole Day of the Dead thing just crushed us. Too many people thinking they needed to be here. And again, not in here but out there. I can't believe the Dead even allowed MTV to do that. But that's when the train first jumped the tracks, back in '87. I imagine that's how you got the Dead bug, even if you didn't see your first show for an entire year later.)

"MTV? Craig, in my house we don't even have cable."

(Still, MTV has trained your entire generation. It's all about sharp cuts and immediate gratification.)

"So didn't grow up with MTV?"

(It didn't come to my town until I was a freshman in college. So it's not steeped in my soul, corrupting everything like it did with your peers. It's not your fault, I don't blame you, just like I don't blame you for being a Touchhead. You can't help how old you are.)

"And how old are you?"

(I'm a grand old man of twenty-six. And a half.)

ROBIN

Whattodo, whattodo...

So warm...

Water!

Have a drink, clean hair, have a drink...

Womensroom,...

"Womensroom?"

(That way?)

So many colors, people colors.

Smiling colors.

Smiling people.

"Womensroom?"

(Ooh, you look like you can use it. Over there. The line's really, really long, though…)

"Thankyou!"

Hmmmm

Where

"Womensroom? Womensroom?"

(Hi. It's around that corner. Can you see it over there?)

Ummmmmm

"Ummmmmmm…"

(No, that's okay. I've been where you are. So trust me on this, woman to woman, Deadhead to Deadhead. Go down those stairs, and then take a left. You'll pass the entry points to about four or five sections and then you can find the special bathroom. It's somewhat hidden in the corner of the hallway but it's well worth it. I never seen anything like it. You'll fly in and out. It can be a bit intense though.)

"Special? Intense?"

(What do you say, Katie, quick escort mission?)

(Fine, she seems a bit spun around and a bit—)

(Spun around. Agreed. What's your name?)

"Robin."

(Okay, Robin, take my hand and come with us. We're going to take you to this one woman's room, run by the stall sergeant. It's, what the right word, Katie?)

(Efficient.)

(That's exactly the word. We've never seen anything like it.)

(It's down the stairs on the next level…)

(We'll take you there. You're part of the stall sisterhood now…)

"Stall sisterhood! Hahhaa!"

(Okay, hold on, we're headed down the stairs. Take it easy… easy…one at a time…)

Oneatatime… Oneatatime…

(There you go…good…good… Good!)

(Now as a member of the stall sisterhood, you have to promise to share this info on another night with another dosed female Deadhead. And offer whatever assistance might be required. Agreed?)

"Yaaa… Hahahaha… Sissy-terhood!… Haaaaaa!"

(What's that?)

"Haaaahaaa… Sissy-terhood."

(What?)

(I think it's a variation on your joke, which was Tinkle-belles, remember?)

"Uhhaaaaahhhaa! TINKLE-BELLES!!"

(Shhhhhh, try not to call too much attention to yourself, no need to alert security that you have to urinate…)

(She's just kidding.)

(Come on, you gotta let me toy with the dosed girl a little. She doesn't mind. You don't mind do you?)

"Tinkle-belles! Haaaa…"

(I don't think she minds.)

(It's all fun and games until someone makes wee-wee while walking.)

(Urine, I'm out.)

"Tinkle—*hahahaa*—snort."

(Okay, okay, hold on, we're almost there…)

(Come up, keep on keeping on…)

(But keep it in.)

(Almost there, Sissy-ter.)

"Hahaaa…"

(Okay, here we are. We're not going in with you. Look over there, see the line, it's really short and it moves really quickly. No other women's room in this place is anything like this but you have to listen to the stall sergeant.)

"Thankyou…"

(You go, girl!)

(Seriously, you go, girl. And then hit that sink…)

"Thankyou…

(Our pleasure, Tinkle-belle!)

"Haaaaahaaaaa-snort"

Haaaaaa

(Four to the left! Three to the right! Six to the right! Let's go ladies!)

Huh?

(Three to the left! Five to the left!)

Hmm…line moving…moving…

(Five to the right?)

Huh?

Line moving…

Almost there…

(Maintain the flow. That's true of everyone on all sides of the stalls. We can't fall apart here, ladies. And don't forget to wash your hands!)

Almost there…

(Two to the left! Three to the right! Nice efficiency, former three to the right!)

Huh?

Ohhh, stall sergeant. What's my number? What's my number?

"Excuse me, whatsmynumber?"

(What?)

"Whatsmynumber?)

(No, you don't have numbers, the stalls have numbers on them can you see? That woman, the one in charge, the mad genius who works for this place has taped those numbers onto them, one through six on either side of the room as you're facing in, left and right.)

Eyesblurry…

(One to the right! Six to the left! Wash your hands ladies, don't forget!)

Gettingclose gettingclose

(Two to the right! Six to the right!)

(This place is amazing.)

(I'm gonna hire her for my sorority house.)

(I'm gonna hire her for my office.)

(I'm gonna hire her for my beach house.)

(Five to the left! Five to the right!)

Which?

Which?

(Come on, you in front! Five to the left! Five to the right!)

"Which?"

(Either, both, whatever you want! Come on we have to keep this moving. Five to the left! Five to the right!)

Tooconfused nonono.

(Let's go, ladies. Five to the left! Five to the right!)

(Either you're on the seat or you're off the seat…)

(Oh-ohh, we're losing her.)

(Let's go, ladies. The pressure is on but thankfully you can relieve that pressure… Five to the left! Five to the right!)

Ummmmmm.

Notsure notsure.

Nooooo.

(Another dosed dropout. She panicked and had the same problem as that girl over there…)

(You should talk to her. Over by the sink. Maybe the two of you can get your courage up together, while the rest of us pee…)

Mara?

(MA-RA!)

STEVEN

(Touch of Grape!)

(Good one!)

Shannon's back and smiling again!

Man and look how colorful it is in here with the lights on. It's like a liquid painting.

(What do you have for us, Em?)

(Hmmm…Beat It On Down The Lime?)

(Nice!)

(Steven! You're looking confused, I mean good, I mean confused.)

"If you get confused, listen to the music play!"

(It sounds like you're in the proper headspace for our game. Are you ready?)

(Nod your head.)

Uh-huh.

(Okay, fake Ben and Jerry's Grateful Dead ice cream flavors, go!)

"Umm…Stella—"

(Already said. And no Big Railroad Bluesberry or U.S. Bluesberry.)

"Ohhhh..."

(He's agonizing over it.)

(I can see those synapses misfiring.)

"Ripple?"

(Not bad.)

"Big Bowl of Ripple? Packed Bowl of Ripple?"

(Closer...)

"Fudge Ripple. Fudge Ripple!"

(There you go. That's our future yearbook editor.)

(Wait, he's still going...)

(Looks like he's gonna have a seizure...)

"Umm... Looks Like Rain... Looks Like Rain-bow Chip!"

(Saint Steven! Work it, girlie!)

"What's Become of the Gravy?"

(That one's a little obtuse for me.)

(I dig it!)

"Must Have Been The Doses?"

(Amen to that.)

(Is that even a flavor?)

(Not sure if that will pass muster with the FDA.)

"Pass The Mustard!"

(Okay, Stevie, sit down for a sec, take a deep breath.)

Whooo. Rushing. And all this ice cream talk is starting to give me the chills.

STELLA BLUE

"Mommy!"

(What, Stella?)

"Come here. Down here. Bend down."

(What, honey?)

"It's like the carnival in here."

(I know what you mean. That's why I like it. The people are all wearing clothes with pretty colors and smiling and dancing. I agree with you, Stell.)

"No, Mommy, it's like the carnival because it's like that time you and I went to the carnival and we were walking around and I couldn't see anything because everyone was too tall."

(Oh. Right. Would you like me to pick you up?)

"Mommy, I'm not a baby."

(Okay then, would you like to sit on my shoulders? Only big girls do that because babies don't have strong enough backbones so they would fall off their mommies onto the floor and splatter.)

"Mommy!"

(Sorry, Stell Belle, your mother is spending too much time with Aunt Jenny. So what do you say, up on my shoulders? Let me carry your load.)

"Okay."

(Alright. Up we go, one-two-three-uhhh. Whoa, you're getting heavy, Stell. I need to talk to Grammy about sneaking you those Keebler Magic Middles when you're at her place.)

"I like the elves."

(They are tasty, that's for sure. I don't know how many of them they grind up into each cookie to mix with that gooey chocolate center but I like my Keebler Magic Middles extra elfy.)

"Mommmmeeee!"

(Sorry, sorry. I won't blame Aunt Jenny for that one. Okay, let's go for a walk. Now remember if you want me to turn, ask nicely, don't pull on my hair like I'm a horsie and those are the reins.)

"I know, Mommy. Hey, look over there. Look at all the people. What's that?"

(Oh, they're all standing around the water fountain. They're hot and sweaty, so they want to drink some nice healthy water.)

"No, not the water fountain, over there."

(Oh yeah, that's the line for the bathroom… Do you have to go, Stella?)

"Okay."

(Yeah, I was afraid to ask. Not do you want to go but do you really have to? If you do, I'll stand in line with you and we can wait. But if you can hold it in we should probably go later when the line's not so long.)

"I can wait, Mommy."

(Good thinking, Stella, we'll go later.)

"No, Mommy, I can wait in line."

(Because you need to or because you want to?)

"I want to because I need to."

(Well I can't argue with that. Come on, let's go. Let me put you down.)

"No, Mommy, I want to stay up here."

(You want to stay on my shoulders?)

"Uh-huh."

(Okay fine, here we go.)

(Beautiful child.)

(Thank you… Did you hear that, Stella?)

"That man had big eyes."

(You're right, he did.)

(Remember jazz isn't dead, it just smells funny!)

"I think she smells funny."

(Stella!)

"Everyone here smells a little funny."

(And what do you think about that?)

"It's funny."

(What else do you think?)

"Are juice bags bad?"

(Juice bags? I'm not quite sure what you mean. Is that like a juice box?)

"No, a juice bag. A man over there yelled at his friend and told him not to be such a juice bag."

(Well-haaa-I'm not so sure, I… Hold that thought, honey. Oh my god. Megan! Megan! Stella, can I put you down for a minute? Mommy sees an old friend of hers.)

"No, Mommy, I want to go to the bathroom."

(Come on, Stella, take my hand. We'll come back to the bathroom in a minute, Mommy wants to see her friend. Megan! Megan! Come on, Stella, let's walk a little faster.)

"I can't, Mommy."

(Megan! Megan! MEGAN!)

(Alison? Alison!)

(Megan! My god, Megan! It's been, like, forever. How are you?)

"Mommy!"

(Megan, this is my daughter Stella. Stella, give Aunt Megan a hug.)

"I don't want to. She smells super-duper funny."

(Stella!)

(The kid reminds me of your old running buddy, Jenny. Do you still see her?)

(She's here. In fact she should be out here any minute now. Wow, it's good to see you. What have you been up to?)

I don't want to talk to Aunt Megan.

I want to go to the bathroom.
I'm going to run back and get in line.

RANDY

(Okay, Ellis, so where are the dice?)

(I always forget which is singular dice or die? They both sound right to me.)

"Die."

(Are you telling me something, Ellis?)

"No I'm answering Eddie. Schultz there are no dice in this game. There are dice in Risk, maybe you're thinking of that? Maybe?"

(Who can be sure?)

"You, perhaps. Risk has dice because that is a game of luck. It's unlikely you would receive credit in a college course for a game of luck."

(Although at Morristown you can never be sure.)

(Okay, no dice. Hey, did you hear what I did right there?)

"Can we just start?"

(If you take Psych 101, all the tests are multiple choice, which sort of makes it a game of luck.)

"Can we play?"

(Hey, Rand, do you know there's an *Escape from New York* board game? That sounds craptastic. I've never played it. No theory as to whether it would be better or worse than the movie based on *Clue*.)

"Guys, please. Let's just PLAY!"

(Play what?)

Shit.

Couldn't hear the damn golf cart over all these generators.

(He almost did just pop out of a dumpster like Kurst.)

(What's that, Robbins? Are you suggesting that Colonel Walter E. Kurtz is a garbage man?)

(I…don't think so.)

(What is it that you're doing here and why do you have barbecue sauce on your jacket? Have you been sampling prohibited foodstuffs?)

"It's not—"

(I heard you talking about playing a game. What exactly is going on here?)

(It's our break. We're taking our break.)

(And playing a little dice, wagering with the paycheck?)

(No dice, sir.)

(A few hands of poker?)

(No, sir.)

(We've been looking for you people. There was an incident with a fire. I've heard there might be something else planned and we can use all available assistance. But you're not there to assist and why is that? Because the three of you are hiding out back here playing Candyland. Now whose game is this?)

"It's mine, sir."

(What is it?)

"Can you not read or is it possible you have trouble seeing anything that's more than two feet away."

(You're fired.)

"Yes, I am."

(I just fired you.)

"No you did not."

(Yes, I did.)

(Rand, don't get worked up.)

"No, you did not."

(Yes, I did.)

"No, really, you didn't. You can talk to Mack."

(No, *you* can talk to Mack. He was the one who informed me you'd be cowering behind the waste disposal bins. Robbins, Schultz, follow me…)

"Hey, roll back here! Do you even know what a free blocking zone is? Do you understand that even if I'm out of the zone I'm still allowed to hit you while you're in mid-air if I've already knocked you off your feet? That's not considered blocking below the waist and so no flag should be thrown! And do you realize that this is not barbecue sauce, it's blood!"

(Don't forget to pick up your Candyland or else I'll cite you for littering.)

TAPER TED

(So what you think?)

Norfolk Chuck.

"What are you doing here?"

(What do you mean what I am doing here? I'm a taper just like you, I'm not an animal. Although at times it does feel like we're on display in here, no? Sort of like we're in the zoo? That's how they treat us sometimes too, just lofting their pre-stamped padded envelopes through the cage at us, expecting us to perform on command and spin shows for them. I am not an elephant! I am not an animal! I am taper! I am a human being!… Right?)

"I suppose."

(Come on, that's a quality riff. It's no Jerry during 'Eyes,' or Phil during 'Playin'" but I'm proud of my work.)

"Are you? Let's take a few more steps away from the crowd."

(Sure…)

"Okay, this is fine right here. Listen, I apologize but I am not feeling the mutual contempt for strangers who push us to spin tapes again our will."

(I suppose I understand that. But please recognize we're coming from the same place here.)

"You're a blankmailer."

(You make that sound so sinister. I'm a Deadhead. I'm searching for the sound just like you, it's just that you've found it. Or rather someone else found it and decided to gift it to you. I've decided to gift it to me.)

"Which is altogether at odds with the sense of community we try to nurture."

(Really? I'm not the one holding out on this community by hoarding tapes… Hey come on, don't get worked up. I'm just trying to point out that it's all a matter of perspective. And that's why I came over, not to go on about the Betty Boards and the Whole Earth Access tape tree but to hear your perspective on that set and the tour as a whole. I mean we all can get behind the Philly 'Dark Star,' but what else has moved you so far?)

"Well… It's tough to quibble with second night, second set Greensboro. The 'New Speedway' smoked and the 'Comes A Time' out of space? A treat…"

(And one that I would be happy to promise Jerry we would not take for granted if he served it up a bit more frequently. What else?)

"While that 'Dark Star' was without doubt the defining moment of the tour—"

(Thus far.)

"Thus far, as for the totality of a show, I think the second night Philly might have been the strongest. 'Attics' has never sounded better. Jerry was engaged throughout, Phil was animated, Bobby was on point and Brent was beefy, with his powerhouse leads and counterpoints. The band as a whole just connected."

(What about tonight?)

"I tell you what, that 'Let It Grow' was really stunning. It is not necessarily my favorite song but the places they're taking it are just above and beyond anything they've ever done with it before, and I'm talking all the way back to '74, which is when it really shined the first time around."

(I altogether agree with you there. This may be heresy to some but I really think a lot of that is Brent.)

"You're preaching to the choir on that one."

(I happy to hear that we're part of the some congregation. See we're all just Deadheads here, drawn to the music. Those are the insights I look forward to sharing about the Betty Boards. So do you want me to write you a check for DAT blanks and postage?… Should I leave you my address?… Would you prefer to give me yours?… Okay, we can finalize the details when we're breaking down our gear at the end of the night… Sounds good, Taper Ted, we'll talk later…)

ROBIN

"MA-RA!"

(Bobin! Bobin! Bob-in!)
"Con-fooosing."
(Numbers?)
"Leftright leftright."
(Leave?)
"Yessss, No Tinkle-belles…"
(Hahahaha No Tinkle-belles…")
Haaaaaa!
Ahhhhhh!
MA-RA!
"Dos!"
(Dose?)
"Dos!"
(Dose?)
"Two!"
(Hiiiiiiiiigghhh!)
"Dos Dose!"
(Dos Dose!!)
"Dos Dose!!"
"Missed yoooo!"
("Missed yoooo!")
"Good space up. Shall we go?"
(You and I?)
"While weeeee can…"
(Uh-huh.)
"Unhug me"
(Uh-huh.)

"Half-way is o-kay."

(Siamese-gurgle-dosers.)

"Uh-huh. Siamese dosers."

ZEB

(The whole Touchhead controversy has wider implications though. It's like that big debate over which shows are better, East Coast or West Coast. People on the East Coast assume that something better must be happening out there because there are fewer younger scene Heads and more old time music Heads. Meanwhile people on the West Coast seem to think that the East Coast shows are more intense. What do you think?)

"I don't think age should factor into this. A custie is a custie and a Head is a Head. Although sometimes it turns out that a custie *is* a Head."

(Lot talk, dig it. Plenty of sweet Sugar Magnolias out in those lots. But you know what they say about hippie chicks, right?)

"No brother, what do they say?"

(You gotta clean 'em to eat 'em… Yeah, just to remind you, I'm buzzin', cousin… But as far as the East Coast and West Coast shows, there are some major differences. First, the sound is usually different since out there more of the shows are outdoors, in amphitheaters. So of course the East Coast shows are more intense because spring and fall tours are inside where the sound doesn't float away. Plus the Dead just play more shows out there and so people are more blasé about it. Jerry Band plays at the

Warfield every month or so. But out here it's rarer, it's more of a treat. So people get really fired up about it and the band feeds off that.)

"It's that righteous energy circle."

(The guy who does all my envelope art for me, tells me his clients on the West Coast always get sweet seats, even for New Year's. But some of us back East don't always get the primo ducats because of the competition.)

"Your envelope art?"

(Yeah for mail order. I've got my own Picasso Moon. Really, that's what he calls himself. I know he probably should have picked an older song, maybe a better song but the art reference fits. He actually used to call himself Stanley Mouseketeer, which I for one, preferred, but hey, he's a kid like you. Actually maybe that's what we should call the next wave of Deadheads, people like yourself, who attended their first show after the *In The Dark* craze. Maybe we should call you Picasso Moonies. What do you think?)

"I'm not sure that'll catch on."

(I might try it. I like the way it references a Bobby song rather than a Jerry sorry. It's very diplomatic. And then maybe for the next wave we go Brent because he's the one contributing most of the new material these days anyhow.)

"Remember, Craig, no harshing on Brent."

(That wasn't harshing on Brent. If I had said he's the one contributing the non-Grateful Dead songs to the Grateful Dead, that might be harshing on Brent.)

"Just a bit."

(But I'm not even taking about Brent. Come to think of it, I'm not even talking about Bobby, I'm talking about a Bobby song. 'Picasso Moon.' Actually I'm not even talking about a

Bobby song, I'm talking about an artist who named himself after a Bobby song. Picasso Moon, that's why we're sitting here tonight, four rows off the floor. I pay him to do all the artwork for my mail order envelopes. He takes care of the whole thing, I give him a wad of cash, he pretties up the #10 envelopes, buys the postal money orders, fills out the 3x5 index cards and then waits in line to make sure he gets the proper postmark on the first day. I'm a crappy artist. You?)

"Not a source of pride."

(I'm with you there. So my guy, Picasso Moon, he does it for me and a few friends. He uses different styles for each of us. He lives in NYC, which is where I work, so he delivers the West Coast envelopes to my office, my secretary packages them up and sends them to my friends in Santa Barbara and Palo Alto. They have to buy their own money orders and send them from their local post offices so it doesn't look suspicious but it's a sweet deal for everyone. Those people in the Grateful Dead Ticket Office appreciate eye candy as much as the rest of us. Have you ever seen the photo of Steve Marcus and their envelope wall? One of mine's up there. I made the Hall of Fame.)

"You're a regular Pete Rose."

(Although Pete's not actually in the Hall. They won't let him in there because he didn't play by the rules.)

STELLA BLUE

"Mommy?"

"Mommy?"

“Mommmmmeee? Mommmeeeee! Mommmeeeeee!”

“Mommmmmmmmeeeeeeeeeeeeeee!”

BAGEL BOB

(Come on in!)

“Good evening, Morning Gloria.”

(I had forgotten you call me that. So Bob, are you going to join us?)

“In what endeavor?”

(No one’s told you about our book mobile? Speaking of which Mikey, it’s time for some mobilization.)

“Ah, some book mobilization. No, Bob is aware of this projected encounter with the jackets in yellow.”

(I prefer to call them the yellow in jackets. So are you two coming?)

“Not Bob.”

(Unless I beat you in chess.)

“It appears that we will not have time to complete our match before yours begins.”

(Well, I—come in!)

(Hey now, Gloria, Mike, Bob. What’s shaking?)

“Earlier this van. At present my viscera.”

(It turns out, Ryder, that Bob doesn’t approve of the book thing.)

(Why not? I mean we have to do something. The security is merciless here. Someone has to stand up to them.)

“Stand proud in front of them perhaps but not step on their toes for the sake of doing such.”

(You don't understand, we're not doing that. Passive resistance, that's what it's about. Maybe you don't understand the whole plan. Now the sign out front says something like *no possession of alcohol, no possession of drugs, no camping or vending* and get this—)

(*No solicitation or distribution of literature.*)

(Right, so we're going to gather at the side of the arena and have a big ol' swap meet. We've all brought our favorite books and we're going to go out there and distribute some literature.)

(And I might solicit some as well.)

(Right on, Mike!)

"And what result will this yield?"

(We're challenging the absurdity of the laws here and the brutality of those who enforce them.)

(Come on, Bob, admit it, you'd like to see their faces when I hand out my dog-eared Fitzgerald novels and try to solicit some of Faulkner's Yoknapatawpha Tales.)

"The nature of such an exchange appeals to Bob. As does its very pronunciation."

(Aha!)

"But the motivation behind it saddens him. And the results of this seem destined to sadden many."

(As many are saddened when these guys—and let me remind you, guys is all they are—)

"You would seem to be correct in that assessment, Morning Gloria."

(As many are saddened when these guys violate our civil rights by confiscating or even touching our personal private property. I saw one yellow jacket notice a tie clasp hanging down from someone's rear view mirror—)

"By tie clasp do you refer to an implement with which to sustain the burnt embers of a marijuana cigarette?"

(Well there no need to get all judgy about it. Sure, I suppose someone might call it a roach clip but there's no need to classify things. You don't need to make that jump and neither do the yellow jackets, which is why they had no right to search that woman's car.)

"Constitutional protections are not extended to those on private property."

(Maybe so. Maybe not.)

"No maybe. Not."

(But even that's not relevant. This is something we have to do. We have to band together to show strength and unity. And our strength in unity. Otherwise our scene will collapse. We have to take our stand and resist what we feel to be unfair infringements. And if you don't agree Bob, then don't join us but it's time to go.)

(I'm with you, G, I just came in here to get these guys.)

(Bob?)

(Bob?)

(Bob?)

"Bob?"

(BOB!)

"Oh, sorry. Bob thought that perhaps this was some sort of bonding ritual. The repetition of monosyllabic palindromes."

(Come on, Bob, what do you say, we can't finish our game, so our bet is moot. But we'd like you to be there. Even if you don't participate. Admit that you'll find it interesting.)

"Bob does not disagree. But this in and of itself does not ensure Bob's presence."

(Aha!)

"Back to the monosyllabic palindromes."

(Robert!)

"Bob can envision how the presence of observers such as himself might lend an air of civility to the proceedings, which could redound to the benefit of all."

(Or at the very least contribute some sublime weirdness.)

"Bob is happy either way."

TAPER TED

"So how'd it go, Mitch?"

(It turns out running analog is not quite as charming as I remember it. I was firing on fumes by the time we got to 'Tennessee Jed.' The tape almost made it to the end for a full-on stop and signal loss, which would have made the kid cry. Thankfully the cavalry arrived, via your lovely wife, so I can listen to that major 'Let It Grow' on my drive home. She also handed me a Maxell XLII-S 100, so I should be covered for the second set.)

"What did she give you?"

(Nothing much. Your beloved Augusta October 12, 1984 second set master.)

"Ehh, that's it?"

(She gave me your dupe of the first set, second night Landover that I guess you spun down from DAT for the car ride.)

"It was solid but certainly retread material especially as a dupe. Hey, Reggie, did you hear about Mitch's little choose your own adventure?"

(I had my eyeballs on the action. It was quite a spectacle.)

"If you wish to cut the patcher's signal while you insert a new tape during the 'Ten Jed' turn to page twenty. If you prefer to keep your own borrowed deck on pause so that your young friend continues to receive a signal until the end of the song, turn to page thirty-three. "

(It really wasn't much of a choice. What good would it have done me to drop the tape in there and cut the kid's signal? My tape already was shot, no need to be mean spirited about the whole thing. As they say, nothing left to do but smile smile smile.)

(Hey, Teddy, who were those kids I just saw you with?)

"Teen tour."

(How'd it go?)

"About as well as you'd expect, only worse."

(Kids today, they have no love for the Schoeps.)

(So who were they?)

"One of them is the daughter of someone at the Manhattan branch of Rez's law firm."

(Which of them was the daughter?)

"Don't ask questions I can't answer."

(So why the pow-wow? The set's going to start soon.)

"I'm in a quandary. Consider this to be something of an ethics colloquium."

(Is it about people tossing padded envelopes at you again? That's why you need to seek out a spot in the middle of the section. No matter what your assigned seat, you always set up too close to the end of the row. That way anyone can hand you blanks and postage. Your other problem is you make eye contact. NEVER make eye contact, that draws the beasties right in.)

"I'm near-sighted, what can I tell you? I don't always wear my glasses, so I stare and squint because I'm trying to recognize the faces of the people I actually know. Plus, I like the clear ingress and egress on the edge of the row. Most importantly, my recordings always sound fine from there."

(Which results in the problem where you're too close to the aisle so that anyone can thrust one of those mailers in your face. It's so passive aggressive, they stand there with their doe eyes, trying to connect so they can hand you a self-addressed stamped envelope. You know how that goes too, a pair of cassettes and they've already poached the Max Points, they don't even leave those for you."

(Is that passive aggressive or aggressive aggressive?)

"I've sought out Rez's counsel on this general topic after too many folks just started dropping them at my feet. Now I apply the process server's protocol. Unless I accept the envelope in my hand, I'm in the clear and I can abandon it free of dubbing responsibility."

(So you want to hear our opinions on this? It sounds like you've already got a tactical plan in place.)

"No, that's not quite it although you're not far off. Let me phrase it this way, what do you think would happen if people became aware of the Whole Earth?"

(Are you saying what I think you're saying?)

(What do you mean by people?)

(Hypothetically? Everyone on rec.music.gdead.)

(I think the Whole Earth would self-destruct. Okay, not the Whole Earth, just a special sapling that hasn't taken sufficient root quite yet.)

(I just received an update on that. I'm told that it should flower about two weeks after tour.)

"And are we committed to keeping all the fruit to ourselves?"

(That was our pledge.)

"What if we share a bite?"

(You're really one for extending the metaphor, aren't you?)

(Ted, are you familiar with the Hippocratic oath?)

"That's my brother."

(Attorney-client privilege?)

"That's my wife. I'm a librarian. Plus I'm not sure how either applies."

(What does apply is that you made a promise. If you can't honor it then I think you need to recuse yourself.)

(That may be more Rez's language than yours.)

(Or find someone else to reap your harvest, which may I remind you, starts off with six nights from the Capitol Theatre in February of 1971.)

(Whoa, Candace and Healy are up there, band is soon to follow.)

"Sometimes the needs of the many outweigh the needs of the few. Or the one."

(You're going full *Wrath of Khan* on us?)

"It's all I got."

(Let's hope not.)

STEVEN

(Are you okay? It looks like you're shivering.)

"Yeah, it's like I can feel cold water rushing down my spine. Hey, Nate, I had this baja hoodie thing in the car. Do you remember if I took it with me?"

(No idea. I don't see it under you seat, though.)

"Never mind. I'll be fine once they come back out and the limbs start rotating. Shannon looks like she's coming around, no?"

(Don't wig out, she had some help.)

"Why would I wig?"

(Hey, Saint Steven, could you move over one? I need to slide in there.)

Burns?

"You know it's spelled differently."

(I can't summon the energy to care.)

(Be nice!)

(Sorry, Shan.)

(Take a chill pill, Alex, that's his thing. He makes sure that letters are in their proper order. He's a total moto.)

Thanks?

(That's why we like him. But, Steven, can you do me a favor and let Alex in here. He's kind of helping me out. I had an epiphany in the woman's room. An epiphany. See, Steven, now there's a word for you!)

"He was in the woman's room?"

(No, we had one of those encounters in the hallway...You know...serendipity, that's it! Serendipity. How's that one? Doing you proud, no?)

No.

"Absolutely, Shannon."

There go the lights.

Deep breath. Deep breath.

(Alright, Stevie, second set! Now we're in for it!)

(The training wheels are coming off, big boy!)

Wheels? Wheels? Ahh, that reminds me...

"Hey, Nate, I saw Casey Jones out there in the hallway."

(*The* Casey Jones? Willington folk hero Casey Jones?)

"One and the same. He…he said something about a shrine. It was really confusing. He seemed to think I'd understand. Do you know what he meant?"

(Ummm. Hey, Jason, Stevie saw Casey Jones.)

(He's hallucinating, already? The music hasn't started yet.)

(No, Casey Jones from Willington. The one who practically did his whole gap year on tour.)

(That guy's the Headiest.)

(Yeah well Steven saw him out there and Casey asked him about the shrine.)

(We are *not* authorized to talk about that.)

(Sorry, Stevie.)

"What?"

What?

(Hey! Hey! Saint Steven, a quick heads up from Head to Head.)

"Yeah, Burns?"

(That kabob thing, I gave you outside. What'd you do with it?)

"I ate it."

(Shit, man, sorry about that. It might not have been the wisest move. I think there was something foul in there. I spent half of the first set in the bathroom. I was puking like a banshee.)

STELLA BLUE

"Mommeeeee! Mommeeeee! MOMMMMEEEEEE!"

Everybody's running and running and running.

Where's Mommy? Where's my mommmeee?

Is she in there? It's dark. It's dark in there and people are running.

"I want my mommeeeee! I want my-muh-muh-mwuh-mwah-wahhhhhh..."

RANDY

(Ellis, what are doing? I thought I fired you.)

"You did."

(But then Davis rolled in and told me that he fired you.)

"He did."

(Well your day isn't going to get much better because I just called your coach and he wants to see you bright and early in his office tomorrow morning.)

"I can't, I have class."

(Class on a Saturday?)

"I have to play a board game."

(What the hell kind of school is that? And what you need to do is stop playing games. I heard you're corrupting my men with some form of gambling behind the dumpsters.)

"That's not true."

(And what's that all over your jacket)

"Barbecue sauce?"

(Let's hope it is. GET OUT OF HERE! I don't want to see you on these premises ever again. EVER! You are officially banned. You are a man without a country. And give my regards to your football coach. Or maybe I should say, give my regards to your former football coach.)

FUUUUUUUCCCKKKKKK!!

ZEB

(You're not tripping or anything, are you?)

"Nope."

(I'm not a narc, it just helps to know if I'm having a conversation with you and all you're doing is watching my hands make trails.)

"Uh-huh."

(Cause if you were I'd make my hands do some really cool things. Nah, just kidding. No, yeah. Me neither. Of course tomorrow is another day. But there's always that problem when you trip, that problem of judgment. You lose objectivity. You can't always tell how the band's really playing. Like whenever one of my friends calls me after a show and tells me that the best part was 'Drums' and 'Space,' then I'm a little suspicious.)

"Right."

(Or 'Throwing Stones.' If someone calls me at 3:30 in the morning after a West Coast show and says 'Craig, man, you missed it, they just did the hottest "Throwing" ever,' then right away I know where his head's at.)

"Uh-huh."

(Or I'll make some other kind of mistake. After one of the Garden shows last year I walked out knowing that I wanted something, I had some basic urge that needed to be satisfied. So I bought a veggie burrito. And I'm walking up 34th St. about to take a bite of the burrito when it occurs to me, 'I'm not hungry at all, I'm thirsty.')

"An honest mistake, brother."

(But hey, I'm not knocking the kind veggie in general. There's been more than one night after seeing the Dead when

I've been back at my place or a hotel room somewhere and said 'The highlight of the evening was definitely was the kind veggie after the show.')

"Must have been some kind veggie, brother."

(Not that I'm knocking vendors or vending or anything. The ones I sometimes want to knock are the tapers. In general they're pretty cool and I respect what they do. Some of my best friends are tapers, as they say. But just once I'd like to mail order for a taper ticket and then come to the show with a beat up old cassette recorder that has a cheap built-in mic. Then in front of all the other tapers I'd open up a pack of C-120s, you know in the three packs you can buy at the grocery store. I'd stand there like an idiot with a bullshit tape recorder that can't record jack shit, turn to the guy closest to me while he's setting up his deck and ask him for spare D batteries. The guy would freak. They all would freak. Friends of theirs probably would have been shut out of the taper section and they'd look at me, like, 'Now there's an asshole.' You dig?)

"I dig."

(Ohh, we're getting close now. Candace Brightman just stepped forward. Can you see her over there? Do you know who I'm talking about? Down there in the middle.)

"I am familiar with her work."

(That pleases me. I'm happy to hear that you kids have an appreciation for what she does. Her light show enhances but never overwhelms. I tell you though, it always cracks me up that the woman running their lights is named Brightman. She's a pioneer. And her sister Carol's the real deal. She was a political activist in the '60s and now she's a literary scholar. I know someone at a publishing house, who's going to be working with her on a big biography of some writers from the 1950s.)

"Right on."

(And do you know who else is a literary scholar? Jerome Garcia. He—)

There go the lights.

(It's on! They're off! I mean the band's coming on! Man, we were so busy talking I didn't realize that Dan Healy was in place as well behind the soundboard. Alright, we're back in business. Should I spark up?)

"I'd be grateful."

(Well if they're gonna pilot the plane then the least I can do is provide the in-flight entertainment.)

"Right on."

(Or the entertainment insurance, if it's going to be a weak set. I'm optimistic though. I'm not one of those picky Deadheads, who are always so judgmental about the music. I can tell you though that even an average set delivers above-average enjoyment when you're sitting in these sweet seats.)

That I can dig.

This is going be Philtastic.

We are IN THE ZONE.

(Here you go. Take a deep hit but careful it's potent.)

The kind.

"The kind…"

(I told you. I have a guy for that as well. So what do you think? 'Eyes?')

"I'd be game. Or maybe a festive 'Aiko,' just to get things rolling…"

(They're talking about it, which is always a good sign. Can't hear any tuning yet… here take another hit…pregnant pause… Better butter your biscuits, you're gonna get your Phil!)

BOX OF RAIN!

"Kind! Kind! KIND!"

BAGEL BOB

"Ah, Morning Gloria, Bob is happy for you."

(And why is that?)

(Follow us! Everyone who is participating in the book demonstration, follow us!)

"Bob does not believe that you are violating the posted decree."

(Why not?)

(THIS WAY TO THE BOOK DEMONSTRATION!)

"Bob does not believe that Anne Tyler qualifies as literature."

(Bullshit!)

"Speak not to Bob. Bob admires Anne Tyler. She even quoted McGannahan Skjellyfetti in her fictional work *Breathing Lessons*. As you are no doubt aware McGannahan Skjellyfetti—"

(Was the pseudonym for the Grateful Dead in the songwriting credits on their first album. Yes, Bob, what sort of Deadhead do you think I am?)

"The sort of Deadhead who doesn't know that 'Golden Road' appears in Anne Tyler's *Breathing Lessons*."

(Ouch. Well I never read that one. I can't always afford new books.)

"Familiarize yourself with a lending library."

(But you're always on the road, where is your library?)

(FOLLOW US TO THE DEMONSTRATION!)

"The world is Bob's library."

(Meaning?)

(THIS WAY—meaning that he steals books from bookstores, reads them and then returns them. Eh, Bob?)

“This is a fact. But Bob also maintains a collection of nearly fourscore library cards which he employs when it proves fortuitous for him to do so.”

(FOLLOW US TO THE DEMONSTRATION!)

(Alright, that’s well and good. But what’s this crap about Anne Tyler?)

“Bob does not believe that the arena authorities will consider the products of her pen to be literature.”

(That’s crap. These people are lucky if they can read. And if they have heard of her and they don’t think she counts as literature, that’s because they’re a bunch of misogynist, impotent bastards who take out their inability to achieve erections upon the greater female reading populace.)

(PARTICIPATE IN A HEATED DISCUSSION ABOUT THE MERITS OF CONTEMPORARY WOMEN AUTHORS AND THE FLACCIDITY OF CONTEMPORARY YELLOW JACKETS’ SEX ORGANS AT THE BOOK DEMONSTRATION!)

“And simultaneously grant your detractors supplemental ammunition as well.”

(Bob, play nice.)

“I can tell your future, look what’s in your hand…”

(Always on point, Robert. The other Bob, Mr. Weir, would be proud.)

“Some folks look for answers, others look for fights…”

(Now, now. No piling on.)

STEVEN

(This is the second set chonger I've been saving for your first show. Rolled to perfection with two papers from the last of my birthday bud.)

"Thank you, man."

Owwww. Something's just not right…

(You're gonna dig this.)

"The herb?"

(And the song. 'Box of Rain' baby…)

How can he tell? I just hear blurps. This whole thing is a headgame. Or is that a Head game? And maybe's it's all not the innocent fun I once thought. Like with that shrine, whatever it is.

"Hey, Nate, about that shrine…"

(Shhh, just take a hit and pass it on to Burns…)

Mmmm, kind bud for sure. And kind 'Box.' Now I can hear it. Alright, 'Box of Rain.' An *American Beauty.* I even know most of the words. Alright, maybe I will pull through. This is the second set. The totally Grateful Deady one. I wish it weren't so damn cold in here but I got this. I'm in control.

(Yo, Saint Steven, don't bogart that joint.)

ROBIN

"Touching down. You?"

(Nuh-uh.)

"Clear the runways."

(Plane Jane.)
"Myyy middle name. Jane."
(Haaaa!)
"Plane Jane coming in for a landing. Yooou?"
(Nuh-uh.)
"Plane Jane back sooon."
(Nice up here.)
"Can see your smiillllleeeeee"
(Nothing left to do but—)
"Smile smile smile."
(Jerry knows.)
"Jerry knows. Whoaaah honey, lights."
(Jerry knows.)
"Wanna run in and see?"
(Uh-huh.)
"Take hand..."
(Ahhh—gurgle—coooooool.)
"Oooohhhhhh. Box..."
(Box Oooooooo.)
"Hallway? Back out?"
(Yesssssss)
"Okayyyy"
(Sweeeeettttt. Oooopps sorrrry.)
Sodaaaagainnnn
"Yesssss, it's cleeannnn!"

RANDY

(Ellis, man, we're going on the prowl!)

"Schultz?"

(Damn skippy. I've had enough of this shit. Literally.)

"What happened?"

(Pooch patrol.)

"Huh?"

(I believe he called it the canine corps. He deputized me and put me in command. I was supposed to regulate illicit canine fecal matter and issue fines. If I spied any of them in the prohibitive act of procreation, I was also supposed to uncouple them.)

"What's that?"

(He wanted me to clean up dog crap and stop dogs from fucking. So I said fuck that. Then I came looking for you. You know what we're going to do, we're going to find that kid who took a poke at you at we're going to teach him a lesson.)

"Man, I don't—"

(And we're gonna drink plenty of free beer along the way…)

"Well…I am plenty fucking thirsty…"

STELLA BLUE

"I want my mommy!"

"I wuh-wuh-waaaaaant my mommmeeeee!"

Mommeeeeeee

"I wuh-wuh-wuh-whaaaaaaaaaa!"

TAPER TED

Whoa, Samson!

A Friday night "Samson."

Now there's a semi-nugget.

I don't think they've played a non-Sunday "Samson" in quite a while, at least a year or so.

There were a few during last spring's Midwest run. I can remember a Tuesday or Wednesday at Rosemont but nothing after that.

Nothing East Coast for sure.

I wonder when. Let's see what Mitch has to say back there if he's not too distracted. He's turned his back to speak with someone so maybe—

Hold on, he's talking to Chuck, the blackmail—the blankmail—the arsehole.

Well Chuck is a taper after all and he is here tonight, so maybe it's a coincidence or maybe he's trying to extort something from him.

Oh, he's looking at me.

What is that?

Right, right September 23, 1988, MSG. Last non-Sunday "Samson" in these parts. That was the nine night Garden run. The next show was the biggie, the Rainforest Action Network Benefit with all the guests.

I want to flip through the DeadBase back at the hotel and chart the days of the week when they pulled out "Samson"s. When did it evolve into a Sunday School song, '85? They started playing it in '76, that much I know.

I'd also like to know a bit more about that Chuck guy.

Mitch has his head back down in his deck, so he's out of range.

Okay, Ted, just let it go, that's all for later.

Get yourself back in the game.

Keep pounding you Rhythm Devils. Make that "Samson" cook…

BAGEL BOB

(Kind Emerson, get your kind Emerson, right here!)

(I'm soliciting Henry James. I'm soliciting Henry James.)

(Who's got your Edith Wharton? Who's got your Edith Wharton?)

(I'm looking for one. I'm looking for Volume One of Marcel Proust's *Remembrance of Things Past*.)

(Proust, is that how you pronounce it? His name rhymes with boost? I always thought it was rhymed with Faust.)

(Forget the pronunciation, that whole thing is just brutal. It's like reading about brushing your teeth for 4,000 pages. Why don't you try something a bit more lively. How about Bukowski? I've got your kind Bukowski.)

(Bukowski? That man's a pig.)

(He's sure as shit unkind.)

(Yeah, that's not literature.)

(It is too, you Bay Area snob. We Los Angeles Heads claim him for our own.)

(Do we really?)

(Your opinion on all of this, Robert?)

"Bob thinks that Charles Bukowski belongs to us all, not just to Los Angeles, although Bob grants the misogyny and even the misanthropy—"

(The protest Bob, the protest.)

"So far Bob is in approval. Bob enjoys the comic far more than the confrontational."

(Well once the yellow jackets get here the action will pick up, I promise.)

(Who's got my Walt Whitman? Who can miracle me a Walt Whitman?)

(I've got his complete works for you. All 1,500 pages.)

(No, that's too much. Clearly my eyes were bigger than my stomach on that one. Can you just give me a side of "Leaves of Grass?")

"A Whitman's sampler, so to speak."

(Nice one, Bob!)

(You want me to tear those pages out of the book? Sorry, no ordering off menu. It's all or nothing.)

(How about Carlos Castaneda, I've got your Carlos Castaneda.)

(Hold on, that's nonfiction.)

(It is not. *A Separate Reality* is not intended to be read as a memoir. It's an allegory, a novel.)

(That's a polite way of admitting that he totally made it up.)

(Please do not splinter over this issue. We must stand firm. They'll be here any moment.)

(She's right.)

(This is all their doing. They're trying to increase our divisiveness by refusing to show themselves while we squabble about literary categories.)

(Yeah, and who was it that even offered the Castaneda? I've never seen him before. Maybe one of them has gone undercover, you know, as an agent provocateur.)

(No, that was Fred. Remember him? Are you high?)

(Well, now that you mention it…)

(Come on, quit screwing around. These are the people who are taking advantage of us, breaking into our cars, stealing our livelihoods. It's unreasonable and we have to stop it.)

(She's right, she's right. We have to. So who'll take my Wolfe, I'm soliciting Wolfe.)

(Tom or Thomas?)

(I've got both.)

(Mike, hand me the megaphone. ATTENTION PLEASE! NO, FUCK THE PLEASE. WE DEMAND YOUR ATTENTION! YELLOW JACKETS, WE DEMAND YOUR ATTENTION! WE REFUSE TO YIELD BEFORE YOUR ATROCITIES! THE ATROCITIES OF YOUR DECREES AND THE ATROCITIES OF YOUR ACTIONS!)

(You said it.)

(She said it.)

(She did. I heard it.)

(WHICH IS WHY WE STAND BEFORE YOU TONIGHT IN DIRECT VIOLATION OF YOUR PROCLAMATION THAT WE NOT DISTRIBUTE OR SOLICIT LITERATURE. WELL, WE'RE GONNA DO THAT! WE'RE HERE TONIGHT TO DO JUST THAT, AREN'T WE?)

(Hell yeah!)

(Damn straight!)

(You tell 'em!)

(Here they come, Bob. It's finally on. Now you'll see some flying shit.)

"Bob hopes he remembers to duck."

ROBIN

"Wahooooo!"

(SAMSON!)
"And Deeeliiii-laaahhh!"
(SAMSON-ITE! SAMSONITE!)
"Heeeeeahhahaahhaaa!"
Twirl twirl twirl.
Whooahhhhahhhaa!ll
Buh-buh-buh-buh-buh-BAH
"Samson-iyiyiyiyahhhahahaaa!"
(SAMSONITE!)
"Iyahhaaahaaahahahh!"
(SAMSONITE!)
"Iyyyitahhhaahayeahhhhahahaaa!"
Bobby! Bobby!
(LUGGAGE!)
"Buh-heeeahaaahhahaa!
(SING TO YOUR LUGGAGE, BOBBY!)
"Heeeeahahahaaaah!"

STELLA BLUE

(Why don't you look all prettied up with your beads and your dress. What's your name?)

"Stella."

(Why that's a lovely name. My name is Ernie, like the character on *Sesame Street.*)

"Uh-huh?"

(Do you know who Ernie is?)

"Nuh-uh."

(You don't know who Ernie is? Don't you watch Ernie on *Sesame Street*?)

"Nuh-uh."

(Do you watch television in your house?)

"Nuh-uh."

(Well that's too bad. Ernie is really funny.)

"I don't live in a house. I live in a 'partment."

(Ohhh. And do you watch television in your apartment?)

"Nuh-uh."

(Well you should. I let little girls watch television in my apartment. Would you like to watch television and see Ernie act funny?)

"Uh-huh, but Mommy says it's bad."

(She says watching Ernie act funny is bad?)

"She says television is bad."

(Oh, she does? Well where is your mommy?)

"I wuh-ant my mommmeeeeee!"

(Ohh, don't cry. Would you like to come with me? You could watch some funny Ernie on TV while big Ernie looks for your mommy.)

"Dunno."

(Would you like something to eat? I can get you something to eat.)

"Nuh-huh. I have to pee. I wuh-ant my Mommmeeeeee!""

(Let me take your hand. I'll bring you somewhere where you can pee. Okay?)

"O-kay."

ZEB

(Can you believe it? Jerry's wearing a black T-shirt tonight.)

Huh?

(Just kidding. Now there's something you should try. Buy yourself a box of Hanes black T-shirts and sell them alongside your beers and bumper stickers. Put up a little sign that says 'Buy Jerry's T.')

"Right on."

(Here's another one. Passover is coming up in another week or two although it usually lands in the middle of spring tour. Now I don't know if you're a Grateful Yid but I am. So what you could do is bring a few boxes of matzahs on tour and make your own logo for them or even just a sign that says Unleavened Dead. You can target Jewish Deadheads who forget about the holiday and aren't allowed to eat a burrito.)

"Right on."

(Food for thought, right? Next year. You have to keep thinking ahead. Although I'm not so sure if *they're* thinking ahead. 'Looks Like Rain' makes it two Bobby's in a row.)

"Fine by me."

(Just so long as Bobby stays out of the screamer. We need a balance of thunder, lightning, rain and shine. We'll see how it goes. So far it's been strong this tour. My guess is you're not tapped into the taping community like I am but you should run not walk to seek out the 'Looks Like Rain' from opening night of this tour. You really need to hear it.)

"I did, brother, from the twelfth row."

STEVEN

Looks like rain, feels like rain.

Those are my Dead vibes.

The sound is all wrong, speeding up and slowing down, speeding up and slowing down.

Burns is right, I should find a bathroom and blow chunks.

Look at him. I can't believe it. He's all over her, touching her, pretending that he's trying to make her feel better, like he's Mr. Sensitivity or something. He's such a phony. He's got her, I can't believe it, he's got her. He's not Mr. Sensitivity, I'm Mr. Sensitivity.

Uhhh. My stomach's feeling sensitive.

Eeechhhh, and I have this nasty taste in my mouth, like dried up chocolate onion donuts.

And what's with the shrine?

"Nate, what's with the shrine?"

(Huh?)

"What's with the shrine?"

(Let it go, enjoy the show. Hey, I rhymed. I'm a poet and I didn't know—)

"Come on…"

(Dude, you are not looking good.)

"Please?"

(Fine, if it'll make you feel better. It's a soundboard from the Shrine Auditorium in Los Angeles, August 24, 1968. The best tape I have ever heard in my life. Supposedly it was liberated from the Dead vault in the late '70s or early '80s by some Willington kid who copied it and then returned it before anyone noticed. Not sure how he did it. The tape is passed down to the biggest Head in each senior class but this year's senior class is so bunk that it was given to Jason and me. We have it for two years. There's a ritual that involves breaking into the chapel at 2:40 in the morning, baking down hard with the diggity dank and then at precisely 4:20 lying on the altar and starting the tape. We would have told you but since we're not even seniors and you're hadn't been to a show yet we decided to wait. But you'll get your chance.)

I'll never get my chance.

Uhhh, although I might get my chance to hurl.

TAPER TED

"Looks Like Rain."

Whenever I hear this one I think of Rez. I still remember that time in '81 when we had just moved in together. We had our problems and that song just said it for me. It reminds me of how lucky I am that it worked out and that she's stuck with me over the years.

When she came back here to pick up the girls she could tell that I didn't exactly wow them but luckily she knows that I'm occasionally a schmuck.

We've toured together for so long, we're linked. And sometimes it's easy to forget that. But damn, if this song doesn't remind me.

"Looks Like Rain."

I wonder who Bobby wrote this song for or who John Barlow wrote this song for and if Bobby thinks of that person when he sings it. It's weird. Pretty much this is the only song where my thoughts drift in that direction.

Then I return to other matters at hand like "When's the last time they opened a second set with three non-Jerry songs and what does that mean will come next?" That and the fact that my setlist prognostication is in the toilet. Our projected lists are back in the hotel room but I remember my second set opened with "China" > "Rider" > "Estimated." I'm zero for three.

For any number of reasons I'm tempted to say that it's just not my night but then again, I am here with Rez.

My glorious Resin Scraper.

BAGEL BOB

(You're making a big mistake here.)

(Oh, are we yellow jacket? No, this is our stand. This is our time.)

(No, you're making a mistake with Sinclair Lewis. All that simple, didactic realism from the 1920s goes down easy but I wouldn't call it literature. I'm keeping him out of my literary canon.)

(He just threatened us! This yellow jacket just threatened us! With a cannon no less! This is in unacceptable!)

(No, the literary canon. Hey, Tony, come over here. Do you buy into this? What do you think of Sinclair Lewis? Do you consider him literature?)

(Jesus, Jimmy, what do you have against Sinclair Lewis? For most people living in the era, he *was* the voice of the 1920s. Not Fitzgerald, not Hemingway and certainly not Gertrude Stein.)

(I'm just not feeling it. These people are playing a little too fast and loose for me.)

(Hell yeah, we are, yellow jacket!)

(Why are you calling us 'these people'? We're every bit your equals.)

(And we're probably your superiors. Where do you two yellow jackets have the right to tell us what is and isn't literature?)

(I thought that's why you called us over. Hey Tony, have you taken Professor Franklin's 1920s seminar?)

(No, he only teaches it in the fall and it conflicts with football practice.)

(That's why I went for wrestling. Better hours.)

(YELLOW JACKETS, WE ARE HERE TO PROTEST YOUR POLICIES AND ACTIONS!)

(Franklin really makes you grind it out. There was a month there where he had us read *Main Street*, *Babbitt*, *Elmer Gantry* and *Arrowsmith*. Now *Arrowsmith*, that was the worst of them.)

(The yellow jacket's right. Aerosmith sucks. I hope they break up again.)

(Are you kidding me, Frankie? *Arrowsmith* won the Pultizer freaking Prize.)

(Yeah, but Lewis declined it. I think that was his conscience talking.)

(I REPEAT, WE ARE PROTESTING YOUR POLICIES BY SOLICITING AND DISTRIBUTING LITERATURE IN DEFIANCE OF YOUR DECREE!)

(Do you get it? This is civil disobedience.)

(Oh man, I love Thoreau. I knew we could find some common ground. I figured that's why the big guy sent us over. Which one of you is the Thoreau expert?)

(The throw expert? Are you proposing some form of martial arts challenge? Are you threatening us again?)

(WE STAND BEFORE YOU TO CHALLENGE YOUR REGULATIONS. WE HAVE HAD ENOUGH OF YOUR PERSECUTION!)

(Do you assholes even understand what we're doing here?)

(Yeah, we're all talking about books, right? Listen, we might not agree but that's what great about this country—we have the ability to express our individual opinions. Do you do this every night? This is cool. So much better than that bullshit bonfire.)

(Yeah, this is like a parking lot oasis for us lit majors. Jimmy's into America but I'm not so self-absorbed. Is anybody here talking continental literature?)

"Bob recently completed *Crime and Punishment* yet again."

(Well this Bob is a man after my own heart. Digging some Dostoevsky. I really like *The Idiot*.)

(Hey, don't insult Bob!)

(Yeah, don't insult Bob!)

"Bob is not sure who is insulting whom. Bob's Fydor fave though is *The Brothers Karamazov*."

(The juggler dudes? They crack me up.)

(Didn't they once sit in with the Dead at the Oregon Country Fair?)

"Bob suspects you are referring to the Flying Karamazov Brothers."

(And there's a book about them? Is Jerry in it?)

"Bob is suitably dumbfounded."

(Don't give in to their insults.)

(Oh, shit. Sorry everyone but we're going to have to punt on the canon talk. Our boss Tony just walkied us.)

(Good stuff though. Will you all be back tomorrow?)

"Might as well."

ZEB

(So where are we headed?)

"Headed?"

(Not the two of us but all of us. Still could go 'Eyes.')

"I'd still be game."

(You know if you cup your hands around your ears like this, it really helps you cut through some of the distortion and chatter. Go ahead try, it.)

"Thanks."

(No, go ahead, try it.)

"I get that it works for you but I like to do things my way."

(Come on, Jed—I mean Zeb. Don't be so stubborn about it. Give it a try. Trust me I'm full of good ideas. It comes up at work during our department meetings. People are always telling me I'm full of it.)

"Right on."

(Nah, just kidding. That was a joke. I never cease to amuse me.)

"Right on."

(Yeah my co-workers they don't have any problem with me. I mean what problem could they have other than my coming up with too many good ideas. I'll never apologize for that, man. It's not my cross to bear. Oohh, have you seen the Allman Brothers band yet? I mean, I know they pretty much stopped playing when you were in your crib but now they're back. They have this killer guitar player Warren Haynes trading licks with Dickey Betts and a real forceful but melodic new bass player Allen Woody. I mean they're not the Grateful Dead, but there's nothing like the Grateful Dead. Still, they'll treat you right for a night. That's my non-Dead tip of the day.)

"Noted."

(My Dead-related tip of the day, is hold your hands like this around your ears. Come on you can do it. There you go…)

"It's my Dumbo impression."

(Consider that a bonus.)

Terrapin!

"Terrapin!"

(Indeed! You see most people haven't picked up on it yet. We're still just drifting in that direction. Thank you, magical ear cups! Any minute now, Jerry will hit those familiar notes and they'll be screaming.)

ROBIN

(Terrapin!)

"Terrapin! Terrapin!"

(I see turtles.)

"TerrapinTurtles?"

(Ninja turtles?)

"Terrapin ninja turtles!)

(We're turtles!)

"Turtles!"

(Turtles!)

"Ooops sorry…"

Popcorn… Mmmmm salty…

"My shell issss cleannn!"

(Feeeeed Turtles! Jerrry, feeeeed theee tuuuurtlees…)

"Moths!"

(Jerrry, feeed theee turtles Moth solos!)
"Tassteeeee mothssss"
(Jerrryyyyyy!)
"Tassteeeee mothssss"
(Haaaa haaaaa)
"Yessss?"
(Jeerrrrreeeeee)
"Yesssss?"
(Jeerrrrreeeeee Haaaassss Motthhhhh Baaalllllssssss)
"Haaaaaaaa!"

STEVEN

Way too here.

I'm waaayyy too here.

I wish it were tomorrow.

I know that tomorrow I'll look back on this and laugh, so why can't it be tomorrow.

I've been looking forward to this for so long. All I wanted was to be here. And now I am and I don't want to be. I—uhhhh my stomach—he poisoned me, Burns poisoned me.

No, that's crazy.

Uhhhh.

What is crazy? What does that even mean?

Maybe this is my defining Grateful Dead moment.

"Terrapin's" sweet but there's darkness and confusion.

Jerry can't figure out if it's an end or a beginning.

Uhhhhh—oowwww.

And neither can I.

What I can figure out is I should be going to the bathroom, I'm gonna be—

Uhhhh.

"Excuse me, Burns. Excuse me, Shannon."

Nobody even asked—uhhhhh.

That's fine because this is the end of my beginning.

STELLA BLUE

(Come on, Stella, take Uncle Ernie's hand. There you go. How's your popcorn?)

"I'm not hungry."

(That's okay, you can hold onto it for later.)

"I can't eat it if I'm holding your hand."

(Well, then why don't you let me close the box for you, so it doesn't spill all over the floor here and leave a little Stella trail. That would be silly. That's it, there we go. Okay now, would you like Uncle Ernie to pick you up and carry you?)

"Nuh-uh."

(Are you sure? Uncle Ernie doesn't mind.)

"Nuh-uh. I'm a big girl."

(You are, you are a big girl.)

"I know I am."

(And I like your big girl necklace. It's very pretty.)

"I know it is."

(What's it made of?)

"Beads and shells."

(Ohh, beads and shells. Can I touch it?)

"Uh-huh."

(It feels neat with all those different shapes and colors."

"You can't feel colors. That's silly."

(Maybe Ernie can. Maybe Ernie has magical powers.)

"Like the Grateful Dead?"

(Like the Grateful Dead?)

"They have the magical power to create smiles."

(That's what your mother says?)

"Uh-huh."

(Well some people say that Uncle Ernie has the magical power to create smiles.)

"Are you Jerry's 'ssisstant?"

(Jerry?)

"From the GRATEFUL DEAD!"

(I am not Jerry's assistant. You can say we're colleagues.)

"Collies? Will there be doggies too?"

(We'll see. We'll be there very soon, Stella. Very soon.)

RANDY

(Ready to quench that thirst?)

"I'm parched. That means I'm dry and thirsty. I get that way after I play a few quarters of football. I'm not sure what it's like to sit on the bench. Do you get parched?"

(Don't be a dick and follow my lead… Good evening boys, and how are you?)

(We could be better. Far, far better if we were in the show.)

(Drowning your sorrows?)

(What do you mean?)

(What's that in your hand?)

(Nothing.)

(That nothing looks suspiciously like a beer to me.)

(So?)

(Can I see some ID?)

(I don't know, can you?)

(Son, with all due respect and when I say with all due respect, I mean with absolutely no respect whatsoever, can you take a look at my colleague here. Do you see what's all over his jacket? Do you think he has patience for twerps like you?)

(So you want to see my ID?)

(I don't know, do I?)

(Fine. Hold on, my wallet's in the car.)

(No, actually I don't.)

(You don't want to see my ID.)

(I do not.)

(Then what is that you want?)

(Your beer.)

(Here you go.)

(Not the one in your hand. The rest of it. Open your hatch.)

(My hatch?)

"Your hatchback. I can see three cases in there. Now listen, we both know you're not even twenty years old. So if you promise not to consume any more alcohol on the premises tonight, we'll leave you a case. We're taking the other two but we'll leave you one.)

(Don't let him do this! They can't make you, that's yours. You're allowed to have it in your car if it's unopened.)

(Do you think so? Should we take all three?)

(No…)

(So then two is fine?)

(I suppose…)

(Or would you underage boozers prefer that we call in our supervisors?)

"And the local constables."

(Constables? What movie are you in?)

"*Raging Bull.* Wanna join?"

(No, no, I'm all set.)

(Then two it is. Open up. There you go. My oversized assistant will relieve you of your excess. You can thank us later.)

(We won't.)

(No, you probably won't.)

(Mean people suck.)

(They suck down your beer. Randall, let's head to the back of the lot where we can dispose of these properly.)

STEVEN

Uuhhhh, I can't even even puke.

I'm soooo sick.

I've been poisoned and I can't even puke it out of me.

Uhhhhh. It stinks in here. It smells like everyone's been yakking. That kind of makes me want to yak but I can't.

(HELP ME! HELP ME! AHHHH SHIT HELP ME SHIT THEY'RE-BU-BU-BLUHHHHHHH-OHHHHHH! AHHHHH!)

What?

(HELP ME! PU-PU-BLUAHHHH! HELLLLPP!)

Uhhh, I am not leaving this stall. I am not going out there.

(PLEASE HELP ME!)

(Hey now, brother, what's the matter?)

Good. Uhhhh. Someone came in. Thank you.

(Please, please help me I'm—bluuuhhhhhh.)

(Aww man, that's gross.)

(Someone clean him up.)

(Help me please. They're after me.)

(How can we help you? Tell us and we'll help you.)

(I need you to help me. They'll be here.)

(Hank, man, stay away from him. He's covered with chunks and he smells like shit.)

This is just so harsh…

(I'm telling you they'll be here! Help me!)

(Henry come on, let's get out of here, this guy's crazy, there's no telling who's looking for him.)

(Help me, it's not my fault, I didn't mean to bluhhhhhhhhh.)

(Awww, that's gnarly. Hank, that is gnarly.)

(We have to tell someone about this.)

(Fine with me but let's go.)

(After I piss.)

(Really?)

(Yeah that's why I came in here.)

(Help, hehelll-bluhhh-BLUUHHHHH.)

(You know, I'm good. Let's motor.)

(Thank you.)

(But we need to find someone and let them know.)

Shit they're gone.

(Ohhhman, help, help ahhhhuhhhhhhaakkkkkhh-awwwkkkkk)

He's making scraping noises—choking, he's choking. Gotta do something.

(Uuuuuakkkkkkkhhhhhh.)

Over by think sink he's-uuuhhhhhhhhh.

Owwwww.

On his back, I need to turn him over.

Shit, I don't know

(Ahhkkkk.)

Okay, okay, I can do it. Okay.

"Gonnahelpyou…here I come, I'm gonna help you. Here I—ahhh, uuuhhh, LEMMMEGO! LET ME GO!"

PLEEAASEEEEE

"LET ME UPPPPPP!"

(Uhhhhh.)

"Helpontheway…"

He's breathing

I'm outofhere.

TAPER TED

Not bad. Four song pre-Drums but Jerry let the "Terrapin" flow gently away. Sometimes he's too abrupt—like he has to run offstage and pee or something. I hate that. They're in the middle of this post–"Terrapin" jam, a really beautiful jam, and Jerry starts rushing it. And then while the rest of the band is speeding to catch up with him, he takes off his guitar. But tonight was up to snuff. A fine transition into the death of song.

"Drums" and "Space."

And of course my brother is going to come up to me and complain that it's boring and it's the same every time. But that's bullshit, I've never seen it the same. Sometimes there are similar elements and maybe it's rigid in the sense that now there's a specific point in the show for it but—

Whoaaahh. Feedback. Drum feedback. Where else but at a Dead show are you going to get drum feedback? Yeah, this is more than some tribal backbeat that-

(Mickey's looking frisky tonight.)

"Rez! How long have you been there for?"

(Long enough.)

"I take it you were watching me during 'Looks Like Rain?'"

(Once Bobby hit the first note I abandoned your brother up in the luxury box and hustled on down here. I love the way that song bonks you on the head and reminds you how fab I am.)

"Well fab you are."

(I appreciate Bobby for reminding you of that. How about that 'Box?' Phil's voice was in fine form and the harmonies were Dead on.)

"No argument there."

(I had that one you know. My scorecard's looking pretty good.)

"Do you have our lists with you or are they back at the hotel?"

(Back at the hotel. I can refresh your recollection though. We both had 'Bucket' and 'Bertha' with double points for the correct order. I also had 'Rooster' third with the bonus, 'Ten Jed' and 'Let It Grow.' You had the 'Memphis Blues.')

"Tell me about it."

(As Tommy would say, I just did. Second set you have nothing, you have bupkis.)

"You're kicking my bup. Another nod to my little bro."

(That I am. I have the 'Box' opener, double points. 'Looks Like Rain'—I predicted you'd be fabbing me up—and also 'Terrapin.' My lead is nearly insurmountable. You have nothing on your scorecard for this set—and don't say 'Drums' and 'Space.' It looks like I've got you tonight. One more victory will clinch the tour series too. You'll be washing dishes for a month. You seem a bit distracted though, is everything okay?)

"Everything's fine. That's the problem with 'Drums,' I space."

STELLA BLUE

(Come on, Stella we're almost there. Through this door.)

"It's tooooo faaaar."

(You can do it. Let Uncle Ernie open the door for you... There we go, we're there. Now come on, Stella, Uncle Ernie just needs you to—)

(Uncle Ernie? You sound like a pervert. Like that guy from *Tommy*?)

(I have no idea what you're going on about.)

(That's the problem with you old guys. You don't know shit. Ooops. sorry kid, don't make that face, I didn't mean to swear.)

(Stella, are you upset with Joey for swearing?)

"Uh-huh."

(Well it's okay, he's just a little stupid.)

"My Aunt Jenny swears."

(Aunt Jerry? Jesus, Ernie, this kid's a loon like the rest of them. Aunt Jerry? Who's your Aunt Jerry?)

"Jenny. My Aunt Jenny. I—she—bwahhhhhhh! I want my mommmeeeee!"

(Great, there you go, Joey start the kid bawling. Come on, Stella, it's okay. Joey is sorry. Aren't you, Joey?)

(Yeah, I'm sorry.)

(See, he's sorry.)

"Are you p'licemen?"

(No, Stella, we're not.)

(We're close.)

(See now that's your problem, Joey, that's the problem with you young people. No, Stella, we are not policemen and we're not close but we *are* going to help you find your mom because that's what we do. We work for this whole big arena to help lost little girls like you. That why I said we work with the Grateful Dead because we're all trying to do the same thing.)

(Funnel much needed dollars into the impoverished drug dealer community?)

(We'll all trying to make sure that people can enjoy themselves. They call us security because we want to make sure that little girls like you feel secure.)

"You're good guys?"

(We're good guys.)

"Aunt Jenny doesn't like s'curity."

(And is your Aunt Jenny here with you tonight?)

"Not here. She's lost."

(Well we're going to find her.)

(I'd like to speak with her.)

(Stella, we're good guys, I promise. We'll find Aunt Jenny and your mom. Everybody's smiling here. Christ, Joey, smile at Stella. Good. Now Stella, can you smile at Joey and Uncle Ernie? Remember, Uncle Ernie has the magical power to create smiles.)

(Is that a union job?)

"Nufting left to do but smile smile smile."

ROBIN

(Devils!)

"Rhythm Devils!"
(Jersey Devils!")
"New Jersey Rhythm Devils!"
(Billymick MaraRob!)
"Mickeybill RobinMar!"
(Billymick MaraRob!)
"Mickeybill RobinMar!"
(New Jersey Rhythm Devils!)
"Here we goooooo!"
Move Rob buh buh twirl left left right
Boom boom
Move Rob move
Buh-buh-buh-buh buh-buh
Buh-buh-buh
Spirals and circles
Circles and spirals
twirl right left
Boom boom
buh-buh
buh-buh
(Mickeybill RobinMar!)
"Billymick MaraRob! Billymick MaraRob!"
Whaaaahoooooo!

BAGEL BOB

(Come in! Bob! So where'd you disappear to, you missed the fireworks.)

"Bob did not see much in the way of fireworks. Although he suspects that is just what awaits him inside the pages of Hawthorme's *Blithedale Romance* which he acquired via bagel barter. It is a send-up of Brook Farm. Quality commune chortles from the mid-19th century."

(No, Bob. literally, you missed the fireworks. I think that's why the yellow jackets were called away before the real confrontation could begin.)

"Ahh, Morning Gloria. Bob did not notice you and your crayons."

(Fabric paints, Bob. I've got to earn my tour too.)

"Bob very much enjoyed the book club. Thank you for inviting him."

(There was a little less clubbing than I had anticipated but I suppose that's not such a bad thing. I'm always happy to make you happy, Bob.)

"Bob reciprocates."

(We all just need to come together and protect each other. It's not getting any easier out there.)

"Truer words were never said."

(On the other hand, none of us needs to protect the tourists. Sometimes I think that they're the real threats. They're the ones who set off the fireworks or the firecrackers or whatever it was. They don't understand the eco-system and they don't worry about stirring up a yellow jacket nest.)

"Agreed. Yet they also buy Bob's bagels, scramble for Michael's veggie scramble—"

(I understand. Listen that's why I'm in here adding some splashes of color to my "Bass Great, Lesh Philling" shirts. I only have twenty left. I came on tour with 150, although 15 were confiscated in Philadelphia. I already sold out of Air Garcia and Shakedown Calvin and Hobbes.)

(Classics, all. I should say though that on my way back here, I saw some kid selling shirts that were blatant rip-offs of Gloria's designs—)

"Infringing on her copyright infringements."

(But this kid had just been busted. They were shutting him down and he was working himself into a frenzy, blaming it on the Dead, going on and on about how they're the ones who hire the promoters who then hire the security. Maybe we should talk to somebody about it.)

(Great, we'll get Jerry on the bat-phone.)

(Well what do you think we can do?)

"An old question. There may be no new answer."

(There's always an answer.)

"There's always a reply but not always an answer."

(So speaks the zen bagel master.)

"An appellation that demands fruition. Bob is in motion. Good evening, Morning Gloria. Michael, Bob will return at a breakfoot pace after he dispenses his lifeblood, his lifebread, so that the chess can continue. Dick Deck promised to spin an extra set of tapes, so with any luck, tonight's show can supply the soundtrack."

STEVEN

Not working for me here.

Too much soundandcolor.

I smell.

Uhhhh.

Where did these people come from?

It's "Drums." That's why. Everyone's in the hallway. Some even have drums.

Never thought I'd be out here in a Dead drum circle.

Maybe if I dance I won't feel so cold.

Gonna shake my bones, shake my—

"Bluuuuahhhhh."

Uhhhh, all over the floor. I hope nobody slips on

"Bluuuaaaaahhhhhh."

(Are you alright?)

"Uhhh? Huhhhh? Ye-Ye-Ye-Bluuuuuuh."

(You need some help.)

Too loud.

Too loud my head is splitting. Splintering.

(Are you sure you don't want me to take you to a Dead Med or something?)

"Nuhhhhh-bluhhhhh. I'm uhhhh-right."

Toomuch.

Need fresh air.

"Uhhh-scuse muh-eeeeeee."

Huh?

Where?

Theresadoor.

(Son, are okay?)

“I’m uhhhh-right.”
(There’s no re-entry.)
Uhhh-Huhhhh.
Must head out.
Head
Out.
(Did you hear me, there’s no re-entry once you leave.)
“Uhhh-Huhhhh.”
Where to go?
Uhhhh.
Never wrote down parking spot.
Bad Deadhead.
“Haahhhha-bluuuuahhhhh.”
Drums outside too.
“Drums” inside.
Drums outside.
Cool.
Cool but need quiet.
Too much.
So many.
So lonely.
Must head away.
Head.
Away.

RANDY

(Shotgun?)

"Nah, I prefer to settle things with my fists. Sometimes even with my head."

(Well, you do have one hard fucking head.)

"It's knocked you on your ass quite a few times. But that's not what I meant."

(Whatever. You're soft.)

"Have you seen yourself in a mirror?"

(You're not good at taking criticism.)

"*You're* not good at taking criticism."

(That's exactly the attitude that leaves Angela cold.)

"Enough with my girlfriend."

(That's not what she said.)

"Already give me that shotgun."

(I meant a beer, you wanna shotgun this beer?)

"Why not, I'm off the fucking clock, right? Even if I am still wearing this bloodied up windbreaker."

(We're gonna get that guy, Ellis. That'll salvage the day for you. Ready? Coors Extra Gold in a can… Boom!"

Ahhhh!

"Hits the spot!"

(Seconds?)

"Why the hell not?"

(Alright, here you go! Pow!)

Yehhhhh!

(My turn. None of that Extra Gold for me. You heard what's really in there to give it that special goldiness, right?)

"That's Corona and that was bullshit. I'll prove it by ground pounding another one to ease the stress of a stressful fucking day."

Yahhhhhh!

"What are we going do with the rest of these? I mean I bet we could plow through the entire case."

(Hang on, let me Bud Light myself… Damn that tastes good… It's even sweeter because it was free! Damn, I am going to make the best cop one day.)

"Or the worst."

(Potato, potahto,)

"Well, you are already giving in to the starches…"

(Alright, let's go find that guy for you…)

"Why do you keep coming back to that?"

(Like I said, I love this cop shit. Mack even had me go in *Serpico* style. How's that for a film reference?)

"*Serpico*?"

(Maybe I got that wrong.)

"What about all this beer?"

(I say one for the road. Second thought, how about a double session?)

"I'm game."

Yeeeahhhhhhhh!

(Sweeeeeet! So we'll leave the two cases out here, right on the edge of civilization in this corner of the lot. Then after we go pop that guy, I'll come back for them. You had a problem with Rennick's Chevette? Maybe you can go grab Robbins' car and swing it back here. But for now our focus is this other guy. We are officially on the prowl! Ready?)

"Shut your hole, Wang Chung. I got all three of you guys for the rest of your natural born lives. You're mine. Next time I come in here I'm cracking skulls!"

(What?)

"*Breakfast Club*!"

(Any time of day is fine by me.)

ZEB

(You ever think about what you'd say if you met him?)

"Who?"

(Who? Who. Jerry. Isn't he just infiltrating your head right now? It's almost insidious.)

"Actually I'm having my Phil—"

(We were talking earlier about how he's a literary scholar. He owns the rights to a Kurt Vonnegut novel. Not *Slaughterhouse Five*, maybe *Breakfast of Champions*. So if I ever met him that would be the conversation starter. I'd ask him what he's gonna do with that.)

"Right on, if that's what interests you."

(Well actually, it doesn't. Not really. Maybe a bit. Perhaps even more than I realize but I'd have to be strategic about it. Okay, what I really want to know is when they're gonna bust out the nuggets. I've never seen 'St. Stephen' or 'Cryptical.' Sometimes, I feel like I'm chasing both of those. How about you?)

"I've never seen them."

(I realize that. They stopped playing both of them when you were in nursery school. This is the part of the show where I just start thinking about those possibilities, you dig?)

"I dig."

Craig is right on about that because this is where the big time craziness begins.

'Drums' into 'Space' into Whatever. That's the killer part, the righteous part, the into Whatever.

I think the Rhythm Devils are misunderstood. Some brothers and sisters just don't get it. They go off and get a hot dog or something but some of them, like the dancers in the halls, they groove all over it, especially if it's one of the more tribal 'Drums.' But I totally get into the edgier stuff, where the drum sounds are going back and forth through the speakers and it builds and builds and builds and then BOOM the loudest sound I ever heard. So loud it pisses me off because I forgot that a sound that loud even existed. It rattles me.

But then 'Space.' Now that's THE PLACE.

All kinds of Space and the Boys know all of them. Outer Space. Inner Space. Already in My Head Space. Space that's forced into my head. Space they extract from my head.

Last night it was all UFOs and orchestras.

My number one right on Space though is that burpy Phil bass Space. It takes me down into the ground and I'm a dinosaur fossil playing with all the other dinosaur fossils.

But sometimes they'll even go back further and I'm not a fossil, I'm an actual stegosaurus. Then I'm a stegosaurus who turns into a fossil who turns into oil. I'm way below ground but when they play little bits of songs that I recognize I bubble up closer and closer to the surface.

And then ZWAPPP! They do it! One second I'm a dinosaur and then I'm a fossil and then I'm oil and then they go into a song and I come gushing up through a hole in the earth and I'm dancing along with 20,000 other people. I don't have any arms or legs or anything because I'm still liquid but I'm already dancing.

(I can tell, you're thinking about your special Jerry question, aren't you?)

STELLA BLUE

(Ernie, for once you're actually right about something. It is indecent that this little girl—)

(Stella—)

(That Stella has never watched *Sesame Street*. But she's heard of Ernie and Bert, right? You've heard of Ernie and Bert right?)

"Nuh-huh. I wannnnt my mommmeeeee."

(Sorry, Stella. we'll find your mommy. Ahh, now here's someone who can help. What's the story, Roberts?)

(We put it out there through the walkies on the open channel. We also have a few people walking around this level of the concourse with the specific goal of reuniting a missing three-year-old girl—)

"Threeandalmostfour."

(with the specific goal of reuniting a missing three-and-almost-four-year-old girl with her mother. As long as said mother isn't tweaking out somewhere—not sure how I'd lay the odds there—we'll be fine.)

(Hey Joey, where's that old black and white TV set we used to have in here?)

(The basketball game against the Pistons was so painful a few weeks back that I traded it for early release so I could go home and watch *Cheers*. I've been getting back into it lately, despite the whole Boston thing.)

(Really?)

(Yeah, I used to like it better with Coach but I'm really warming to Woody. He cracks me up. Plus I think that Frasier has come into his own now that he's part of the ensemble.)

(Ensemble? That's a rather hoity-toity way to describe a bunch of barflies.)

(I'm taking an adult ed class. Did you realize that the families on both *Full House* and *ALF* are named Tanner? I think it may be more than just a coincidence. There's something a little unnerving about it all.)

(Yeah it's like the Lincoln and Kennedy assassinations.)

(Do tell.)

(They were both replaced by their Vice Presidents, who were Southerners named Johnson, born 100 years apart. Lincoln was shot in Ford's Theatre, while Kennedy was shot in a Lincoln, which was made by Ford. John Wilkes Booth and Lee Harvey Oswald both have fifteen letters in their name. Booth committed his crime in a theater and was caught in a warehouse, while Oswald committed his crime in a warehouse and was caught in a theater. Kennedy's secretary was named Lincoln, Lincoln's secretary was named Kennedy...)

(I've heard all that, I thought you had something more to contribute on the eerie similarities between *Full House* and *ALF*.)

(Which reminds me, you traded away my television, my personal TV set, so you could go home and watch TV?)

(When you put it that way it does sound ironic.)

(It sounds moronic.)

(Well at least I have the good sense to know that Lincoln did not have a secretary named Kennedy, that's an urban myth. Next thing you're going to say is that three weeks before Lincoln was assassinated, he was in Monroe, Maryland and that three weeks before Kennedy was assassinated he was in Marilyn Monroe. Which I find distasteful, by the way.)

(Well I find it distasteful the way you trade away someone else's television so you can slack off on your job. And that you make imbecilic allegations regarding the Tanner families.)

(I haven't even started there—)

(You know the two of you remind me of Ernie and Bert.)

(Roberts, that's insulting.)

(What's your problem, Joey?)

(What's my problem? There's something wrong with the two of them. They're grown men, well two grown puppets, who still don't have the alphabet down and haven't quite mastered counting past ten.)

(That's not what I had in mind and it's not their worst problem.)

(Which is?)

(They seem to have a special manly attraction to each other.)

(You think they're lovers? No, they're committed bachelors.)

(They share a bed. Ernie?)

(Joey's right. They do not share a bed.)

(That's not their problem. That's not even *a* problem, don't be insulting. Their problem is that I have long suspected they are the product of some weird puppet inbreeding).

(They're inbred? The brothers are inbred?)

(Not so loud.)

(Ernie and Bert are inbred? You think the brothers are inbred?)

(Now I'm taking Roberts' side. You think the brothers are inbred? You're sick.)

"I wuuuht my moooommeeeee."

(Well played, Charlie Brown.)

(I think you mean Schroeder.)

(I think he means Lucy. She's the one who holds the ball when Charlie Brown tries to kick it and he end up falling on his…on his tushie, right Stella? His name's Charlie Brown?)

"Who?"

(We have to find this mother.)

BAGEL BOB

(We've got your bobbleheads! Bob Weir! Bob Dylan! Bob Marley! Bob Denver! Step on up, we've got all your Bob needs!)

"All Bob's Bob needs! Bob Denver! Bob loves Bob Denver… Maynard G. Krebs, where is Maynard G. Krebs? Excuse me, Bob, but where is Maynard G. Krebs?"

(What are you talking about, honey?)

"Where is Maynard G. Krebs?"

(I don't think I know him. Is he vending out here in Shakedown? There are three or four entire rows of people with tables, so I'd look up and down and then over that way on either side. I'm sorry, I can't help, we're just getting set up for the post-show. If he's by himself and has a cooler or something maybe he's over that way, closer to the arena. They're gonna be done soon, so people are starting to stake out their turf.)

"No. Maynard G. Krebs."

(Who?)

"First base. Where is Maynard G. Krebs?"

(I'm sorry but I don't know where your friend is. I need to get back to work. We've got your bobbleheads! Bob Weir! Bob Dylan! Bob Marley! Bob Denver!)

"Yes, Maynard G. Krebs!"

(I'm sorry, I don't know…)

"Third base. Maynard G. Krebs aka Bob Denver!)

(Ohhh, you mean Gilligan! Hold on, I'm about to put them on the table. They're custom. Gilligan's holding a little bong made out of a coconut… Kind custom Bobbleheads, right here! Bob Denver, all bonged up! Perfect for your dorm room! We've got, trinkets, we've got knickknacks, we've got gewgaws and that's not insensitive because my last name's Goldberg, which is why we've got *tchotchkes.* Plus of course we've got your bagels! That's right we've got it all right here at the original famous Bagel Bob's!)

"What?"

(Second base. I'll handle this custie, Sugaree.)

(Okay then, Gilligan fan, I leave you in the capable hands of Bagel Bob. I'd be happy to have you chat me up after we close. To a lot sister like me, you old-timers, you're like sages. That means wise men.)

"No flies on your glossary."

(Thanks, it's the cream rinse.)

(Suge, can you shake it over there and get the Christmas lights out of the van, apparently some people are having trouble reading our banner and we want everyone to know that the ORIGINAL FAMOUS BAGEL BOB'S HAS WARM, TOASTED BAGELS, FOR WARM, TOASTED HEADS!)

"This is wrong."

(That's right the ORIGINAL FAMOUS BAGEL BOB'S! WARM, TOASTED BAGELS, FOR WARM, TOASTED HEADS!)

"Bobbleganger!"

(Come visit us at the ORIGINAL FAMOUS BAGEL BOB'S!)

"You are not the original Bagel Bob!"

(Are you sure, because I have a vinyl sign that says otherwise.)

"Bagel Bob is the original Bagel Bob."

(Do *you* have a vinyl sign?)

"Do you have a vinyl heart? Bagel Bob is Bagel Bob. All other Bagel Bobs are redundant, superfluous, gratiutous."

(There's enough Bob to go around.)

"Bagel Bob says no."

(Bagel Bob says yes. And Bagel Bob reminds everyone that THERE'S ONLY ONE WAY TO MAKE SURE THAT NO ONE STEALS YOUR BAGEL. PUT LOX ON IT! RIGHT HERE AT BABEL BOB'S.)

"Oy vey. Well now you've done it. This is a first for Bob…"

(Oh, and what's that?)

"YELLOW JACKET! BOB NEEDS A YELLOW JACKET!"

ZEB

Whoaaahhh.

Kindness.

Crazy crazy kindness.

Out of nowhere.

It delicately floated down.

"China Doll."

Jerry was making those harsh sawing noises and then he just stopped and let it drop, like a beautiful net on top of us.

Nothing kinder than a "China Doll" out of chaos space.

It's dainty and delicate and sort of wistful, I think that's the word.

And it's not a net, it's a lace doily. Homemade and beautiful and just barely touching our skin, just barely touching us.

ROBIN

"Oooooohhhhh."

(Ahhhhhhhhhh…)

"Yeeeehhh"

(Yahhhhh…)

"So…"

(Beaaauuutiiiifullll…)

Deeeeeep breaattthhhh

"So…"

(Saadddd…)

Deeeeeep breaattthhhh

"So…"

(Sorry…)

"Sorrrrry?"

(Misssed you firstset?)

"Hugs?"

(HUGS!)

"Ahhhhhhh"

(Oooooohhhhh.)

"Yahhhhh…"

(Yeeeehhh…)

"So…"

"Happpppyyyy"

"So..."

(Hugggggyy.)

(So...oooooaaappppp... So...ooaapppp...SOOOAPPPPP!)

"Huh?"

(What?)

(SOAAAPPPPPP!)

(You girls could use some soap. We heady sisters have to stick together. Am I right ladies?)

"Ummmm..."

(Nooo?)

(And not just soap. Some shampoo will do you right too, you have all sorts of crap in those stringy locks, it looks like someone used your head as a mop near the hot dog stand over there.)

"Huhhhhh?"

(Nahhh, nahh, just playing... I'm on my own trip heady soul sisters...)

(Byyyyeeeeee!)

"Byyeeeeee..."

(Sheeee!)

"Shhhhh... Oooooohhhhh."

(Ahhhhhhhhhh...)

"Yeeeehhh"

(Yahhhhh...)

RANDY

(Holy shit, there he is! There's the tie-dyed prick who that attacked you. Go teach him a lesson)

"I don't see him."

(Right there! He's ten feet away! He just walked around the corner to the next row of cars. Come on, let's go! No one's around, just pop him one clean!)

"Hold on, let me crack a beer. This jacket actually came in handy for once, deep pockets for bonus brews."

(Crack his head first.)

"Too late, hang on…"

Ahhhhhhh

"Alright let me check him out first."

(That's the guy. HEY! He's ignoring me. He's ignoring us. HEY YOU! No respect, man. That's the guy, that's the one! He's the one who fucked up your day. Just one swing to remind him who's in charge here."

Fuck.

(You let him get away once, don't let him do it again. He got you fired. Hit him!)

FUCK.

(HEY! He's still ignoring us, that asshole. He attacked you! You've got to let him know that there are repercussions! That asshole is just like all of these other Deadhead assholes out here! HIT HIM!)

FUUUUUCCKKKK.

(He's the one who got you fired! He's the reason Davis was looking for you and found out about the game! He's the reason Mack thinks you knocked someone off the top of that fence!

He's the reason your car broke down! He's the one who's going to get you KICKED OFF THE TEAM! He's the one who's going after your girlfriend! He's the one responsible for all the foul shit that's landed on you ALL DAY! You better fucking HIT HIM! If you don't HIT HIM I'm gonna HIT HIM! I'm gonna FUCKING HIT HIM! SO YOU BETTER FUCKING HIT HIM!)

ARRRRRRRGGGGGHHHHHHHHHH!

STEVEN

Uhhhm-here.

I-uuuhhhm here.

Toohere.

Toomuch.

Somany.

Solonely.

So—

"OOOOWWWwwwwwwwwwuhhhhhhhhh"

RANDY

(What the fuck, Randy? Why did you hit me?)

"Why the fuck did you hit him?"

(You weren't going to do it and he deserved it.)

"YOU deserved it. You ratted me out. *You* were the one who knocked the guy off the top of that fence. That's how you fucking knew about it and it sounds like you told Mack that I did it. You probably told Davis that I was back there playing the game that *you* set up. That's the *Serpico* shit you were squawking about. You did it because you want me off the football team, so that *you* can start. There's probably some bullshit play for my girlfriend in there as well. You must have done something to fuck up Rennick's car too or you knew about it. My head's a little fuzzy from the beer."

(You're crazy, man, you're babbling. Let's get out of here. Let's go pick up our beer, put in it Robbins' car and you can drive us home. Fuck this place.)

"What about that guy, you took him out. It looks like he hit his head on that car bumper on the way down."

(Let me take a quick… No he's fine. He'll sleep it off. Plus, he's the asshole who attacked you.)

"Is he? He's lying face down, I can't really tell."

(Just leave him there. We shouldn't turn him over and revive him. He'll go apeshit or something. He's out of his head on acid or angel dust or goofballs. He's an animal.)

"Man are you sure? He doesn't seem like much of an animal. Well okay, a smallish, youngish human animal…"

(No, no, let him sleep it off. After the lame-ass Grateful Dead finish their lame-ass concert people will come out to this edge of the lot and they can deal with him.)

"I don't like the way his neck looks."

(Of course not, you shouldn't. His neck looks like someone popped him good which is what happened here. Someone popped him good. But he'll be fine other than a raging headache, which he deserves, considering all he did to you. Whatever happened here, retaliation was a reasonable response. Let's just leave him behind and put this whole nasty day behind us.)

ZEB

Watchtower!

Double Dylan night!

Go to it, Bobby!

(I'm telling you, you should play Dead, think about it…)

"What's that?"

(It's the perfect vending opportunity. Baseball and the Grateful Dead. Like I said, I'm full of ideas. You're clearly a baseball fan.)

"Not—"

(When you mentioned Pete Rose earlier that got me thinking. I have a killer idea and it's all yours. Grateful Reds caps. You put a Stealie on top of the Cincinnati Reds logo. Do you know that logo? It's a guy with a baseball for a head in a Cincinnati Reds uniform. What surrealist genius came up with that? He's the one who should be decorating my mail order envelopes. So then you replace the baseball head with a Stealie and change the C on the shirt to a G. Cool beans, no? What do you say?)

"That *is* a good idea."

(Surprised you again, didn't I? Well you know what they say about me—I'm substance masquerading as style. I'd say the same about the Grateful Dead. Although I've been saying that less frequently as late, the more they play 'Watchtower.' I'm getting a little tired of it.)

"Wait and see bro, wait and see."

(I am waiting and seeing. I'm waiting for a 'Lost Sailor' because I've seen too many 'Watchtowers.')

"Double the Dylan tonight…"

(I appreciate The Bard as much as the next guy—if the next guy knows his shit as much as I do—but I still wouldn't mind something else.)

"It's the Grateful Dead, you get what you get."

(Depending on where and when you get it. '87 was a big year for 'Watchtowers.' But '85, now that really was the year of the crazy lists: 'Day Tripper,' 'Walking the Dog,' 'Big Boy Pete.' Richmond, November 1, 1985 had a killer 'Sailor' into 'Drums' and 'Space' and then on into 'Saint.' 'Comes a Time' before 'Sailor' too. I don't think really I appreciated it. I mean I did and I didn't. Some nights the band didn't quite connect but I'll admit it I have soft spot for '85."

"Right on. I have a soft spot for 'Watchtower'…"

(I got you. I can pick up these subtle clues. I'll leave you to your 'Watchtower.')

"Right on."

(I've enjoyed my fair share of 'Watchtowers' in my time…)

"Right on."

(Come to think of it, the Landover one from earlier in the tour, sounds great blasting out of the DAT player I have I my office…)

TAPER TED

There must be some way out of here...but if there is, I can't figure it out.

What am I going to do about this Whole Earth Access tree?

It's the Kobayashi Maru but unlike Kirk, I can't game the system...

I wish Rez hadn't lit out for the luxury box during the "China Doll." I should have said something to her before she left.

Blackmail. Blankmail. How could one of us, a taper no less, attempt this. It's extortion...a takedown, a shakedown and not the right kind of "Shakedown."

It's a Hobson's Choice...

Sophie's Choice...

Bear's Choice.

Okay, maybe I've been swirling in the secondhand smoke a bit too long.

But whatever it is, it is the very definition of unkind.

While I do think that charges of taper elitism can be well-founded, no one ever sees it from our side. People just want the tapes when they want them. They should invest the time and the money if they care so much.

If I let Chuck go wide on the boards, people will overreact and the tapes will disappear down the rabbit hole again. People will rage about it for months—they'll call it the Betty Battles or the Cream Puff War or something clever that eludes me right now.

I'd feel better about the whole thing if Chuck presented himself as some sort of freedom fighter or social activist trying to liberate the boards on behalf of the people rather than just a selfish Deadhead.

Maybe I should just take a stand, call his bluff.

The hour is getting late.

STELLA BLUE

(There she is! STELLA!)

"Mommeeeee!"

(Oh, Stella, Stella, Stella. Stell Belle. My little Stella baby.)

"I'm not—"

(Oh, I know you're not, honey, Mommy's just so glad to see you. What happened to you?)

(I don't know, Mommy. I went to the bathroom and then you were gone.)

(Excuse me, ma'am, you let her go to the bathroom by herself?)

(I certainly did not.)

(Then how did she get away?)

(She's not an animal, it's not like she escaped. I just saw an old friend of mine, went to hug her and then somehow she disappeared.)

(Was there a magician involved?)

(Why would there be a musician involved? Are you trying to blame the Grateful Dead for this?)

(No, not a musician, a magician.)

(Does that seem more plausible to you?)

(You're the one who started talking about mysterious disappearances. It's my job to ask.)

(Is it, though?)

(And are you married, Mrs., uh Miss—)

(Miss no I am not. How is that relevant?)

(And where exactly do you live?)

(Look, this is my daughter. We need to get going—)

(I'm afraid we have some more questions for you first. Do you think that this is an appropriate place to bring your daughter?)

(No, I do not. In the future I'll keep her away from arena security.)

(Come on, now that's unnecessary.)

(But it's necessary to start blaming magicians or musicians for all this? You lost me back there. Look, this is my daughter. We have to go.)

(I just want an answer to my question. Do you think this is a proper place for her?)

(Yes I do.)

(With all the drugs? And the crazies? Do you realize how many people we've seen today who are totally zonked out crazy on drugs?)

(And how many have you seen who aren't?)

(I don't think—)

(Apparently Stella's Aunt Jerry told her not to trust security.)

"Aunt Jenneeeee!"

(What are you smiling about? I don't think that's funny.)

(No, you're right. I'm sorry. Listen, we need to go.)

(And she doesn't know about *Sesame Street*. You don't let her watch *Sesame Street*? That's unhealthy.)

(I don't have a television set.)

(Well, that's no excuse.)

(And why is it unhealthy? Do you think she's missing out on good role models and that sort of crap?)

"Mommeeeee!"

(Sorry, Stell. Well tell me this, how many of those puppets are female?)

(What's that?)

(How many of those puppets are little girls? You know, Ernie, Bert, the Cookie Monster, Count Chocula…)

(Count Chocula is a breakfast cereal.)

(I believe the Count's proper name is Count Von Count.)

(Well done.)

(College Trivial Pursuit club. Traveling team, five years running.)

(Five?)

(I'm better with the trivia than the pursuits.)

(The problem with those puppets is that the only one of them who's a female is Miss Piggy. And that's why I don't let my daughter watch TV. We're leaving. I appreciate your taking care of her but it's time for us to go. Again, thank you.)

"Bye-bye."

(Goodbye, Stella, it was nice meeting you. I hope to see you again at the Ice Capades or the Circus. Ma'am, please think twice before taking her to another Grateful Dead concert.)

(And let her watch *Sesame Street*! Charlie Brown cartoons, too! Lucy is a doctor! Say, Ern, did you know that Oscar The Grouch was originally orange?)

ROBIN

Oooooohhh thhhhheeeee DeeeewwwWWW

Ooooohhhhhhh

Thhhheeeeeee Deeeewwwwwwww

Ooooooooooh

Muh-muh-morrrrneeeeeeng Deeeewwwwww

Muhhhhr-neeeeeeeeeg

Deeewwwwwww
Deeeeeewwwww Noooootttttt?
Deeeeeeeewwwwww

BAGEL BOB

"YELLOW JACKET! BOB REQUIRES YELLOW JACKET SATIFACTION!"

(That sounds a tad obscene, no? And is it really necessary?)

"YELLOW JACKET! BAGEL BOB REQUESTS YELLOW JACKET ASSISTANCE!"

(What do you think, they're like genies? That you can just call out for them and—)

"There!"

(Well your summoning powers are a bit off, Bob, IF THAT EVEN IS YOUR NAME, because those two are skulking off in the distance.)

"And the yellow jackets had such good taste in books…"

(GOOD TASTE? TASTES GOOD, THAT'S RIGHT, WE HAVE IT ALL, RIGHT HERE AT THE ORIGINAL FAMOUS BAGEL BOB'S: BOBBLEHEADS, BAUBLES AND IF YOU PUT US ON THE SPOT WE CAN EVEN FIND YOU A BOBBY PIN! OF COURSE WE'VE GOT YOUR BAGELS, TOO! TOASTED BAGELS FOR TOASTED HEADS! THAT'S RIGHT, THEY'RE MADE WITH WHOLE GRAINS. AND IF YOU REALLY WANNA FLY, THEN HOW ABOUT A PLAIN BAGEL?)

"You truly are the anti-Bob."

(OR FOR SMALLER APPETITIES, TRY OUR BAGEL BITES, OUR BOBBERS, ALL AT THE ORIGINAL FAMOUS BAGEL BOB'S!)

"This isn't a parallel universe, it's a subordinate one."

(I'm sorry to interrupt the two of you sages but I have a question. Bob?)

"Yes?"

(Yes?)

(Where do these lights go?)

(Just place them around the sign, so that anyone walking past can see us. The show's ending soon and we need a healthy line of custies. Shake it, Sugaree... So what did you say your name was, again?)

"Really?"

(Come over here where we can talk.)

"Is language proscribed near your coven?"

(Just step over here. Not you sir, HEAD OVER THERE FOR THE ORIGINAL FAMOUS BAGEL BOB'S!)

"Bob is wary..."

(Just come over... Look, Bob this isn't personal, it's business. People have heard of Bagel Bob. I needed some help with name recognition. It's a Dead eat Dead world out here in the lots.)

"It's highway Bobbery."

(Did you ever have Famous Ray's Pizza? How about the Original Famous Ray's Pizza? There are like fifteen variations on that name. The Real Original Famous Ray's, the Original Real Famous Ray's and on it goes. Which was the original? Even Ray doesn't know and does it even matter? No one cares.)

"Bob suspects that Ray might have a rooting interest."

(Which, Ray? I mean, maybe I am the real Bagel Bob.)

"You are the *surreal* Bagel Bob. Although that may be a badge of honor you do not deserve."

(Listen, it's all a front anyhow for my other enterprises. I'm a do-er. If you want tickets: real or counterfeit, I can get it done. If you want doses: real or paper, I can get it done. If you want to meet the band, backstage passes, I can get it done. If there's something you need, something you want I can get it done.)

"Bob wants his name back."

(The Doo Dah man. That's what I should have called myself.)

"Consider it done, Mr. Dah."

(I looked into that. It's all a little loosey-goosey but R. Crumb has rights there. Those dudes with the big feet, they're the Doo Dah Men. But again, you can't trademark yourself. Or at least *you* can't because I filed the paperwork a few weeks ago.)

"M'lady spurned, the law, thy wrath is acrid."

(You really are one of a kind.)

"Bob has his moments."

(Which is why there should be two of us. I can use you. Join the team. Be the face of this operation. One might say you already are.)

"Bagel Bob would make that assertion."

(You can continue to do your thing and keep all your profits. I'll even cut you in for a piece of the action from our little table. I just need your good will and your street cred. Oh, and the shirt off your back—I'd like you to wear one of the promotional T's that I'm in the process of creating to help promote the business. You can't lose. So why not be our front?"

"Bagel Bob is affronted."

(I'm sorry to hear that, Bob. It's the very best I can offer you. If you don't find that acceptable then I suppose this is where we must part ways. Let the record show that I've made a good faith effort.)

"Good faith?"

(Well let's just call it an effort.)

"So be it. Bob's energy wanes. In lieu of due process, Bob will let lot justice prevail."

(What did you say?)

(When all legislation fails, Bob must turn to the commonest of laws: vendor vigilance… Hmmm, perhaps Bob's story would make for a compelling television docudrama, after all.)

(ARE YOU THREATENING ME?)

"Brother Esau bears a curse."

(Seriously, are you threatening me?)

"Bob is elevating you. Shadowboxing the apocalypse."

(I don't like the sound of that.)

"The Grateful Dead concur. They shelved it in eighty-seven."

(Reference eluded. Okay, come over here where we can *really* talk.)

"Are adverbs not permitted here?"

(Just come over here. I need absolute privacy.)

"Such absolutism seems improbable amidst ten thousand automobiles."

(Jut follow me to the edge of the lot…please?)

"Is the cone of silence going to drop?"

(Come on, just a few yards ahead, I just need to make sure nobody's eavesdropping… Okay… Listen, Bob, I'm sorry. I did everything you think I did and probably more.)

"Bob did not devote much thought to the manner, although now he is ill at ease…"

(I just never figured you'd be here. To be honest, I assumed you'd retired. I've bought a bagel or two from you a few years ago and I just expected that you'd moved on.)

"Where to?"

(Wherever else you go.)

"There is nowhere else for Bob."

(But the Grateful Dead aren't always touring.)

"There are always songs to fill the air."

(Maybe for you because you're living the dream. Not for me because I'm living in Connecticut. This is my weekend fun pass. My wife has no clue. I stole the toaster, fired up the Rambler that's been sitting idle in my mother's garage and here I am. Do you have any idea how difficult it is to come in cold and fight my way into the pecking order for a few shows? Do-er? I'm a do nothing. I'm going to take a bath this weekend. Metaphorically speaking.)

"Literally as well, Bob advises."

(That I can promise you, with a few of these honeys I met at my local head shop but in order to pull that off, I need to make them believe I am so much more than I really am. Which is why I need to be Bagel Bob. You know originally, I was going to approach this differently, I saw it all as something of a retro, tribute thing. I was going to call it Na-Bob's. I even created a Bagel Bob bobblehead. I can sell you a gross at cost, great marketing.)

"Gross, indeed."

(Then I figured the better path was what if I became Bagel Bob myself. Not only would I have plausible deniability with the wife but I could also leverage all the goodwill you've developed over the years. The only problem was all the Bobbleheads I had created in your image. I tried to rebrand them as Bob Vila but so far, no takers.)

"Perhaps Bob Ross?"

(Good call, that! I know we'd get along, like smoked salmon and a schmear.)

"There shalt be no false Bobs."

(You see, that's my point, I don't want to be false. Why don't we start at the beginning?)

"Bob is a fan of tautology."

(My name is Jack Novick. No, no, I want to be one hundred percent on the level. I go by Jack but my given name is John. There you go.)

"Uncle John?"

(What's that?)

"Catfish John?"

(Oh, CRAP. That's it. Uncle John is a little on the nose but Catfish John. *That's* marketing. It's got that Jerry Garcia association but you have to be a bit more in the know. I can do a little fish fry. Maybe go southern and theme it out that way. The margins are probably higher than with the whole rounded bread thing, which feels a bit dated, if you don't mind my saying.)

"Bagel Bob is proud to be on stale."

TAPER TED

That one hit the spot.

Monster "Dew."

And it was due as Tommy would say if he knew enough to say it. Of course if he knew that, he probably wouldn't say it on principle.

First time this tour. I was starting to think they were going to retire that sucker. Like the "St. Stephen" that Mitch may never hear again. Or the "Cosmic Charlie" that Rez would welcome. Or the "Golden Road" that I bet a lot of people here may not realize the band retired in 1967.

This "Dew" was dynamic, with a proper build and powerful peak.

That's the way to go out in style! That's also why you can't just look at a setlist and count the number of songs, it's all in the delivery. And on that one, Jerry was my delivery man for sure. When he fanned it at the end I felt like Homer Simpson when he sees a processed pork product, all week at the knees.

Of course *I'm* going to be week at the knees after a month of dishes. Rez just dominated the setlist game. I had the "Watchtower" but not in the right spot. She had the "China Doll" and the "Dew." Who wouldn't want to see *that* post-"Drums?" Maybe tomorrow night she can predict "Stephen," "The Eleven" and "Cream Puff War" while she's at it. Apparently she has the power.

Man, that was the way to end a set!

After all that blankmail bullshit, it scratched my itch.

The "Dew" flat out raged.

Just when I was feeling outraged, the "Dew" out raged me.

ZEB

(The 'Dew' does not disappoint!)

"It good to hear you say that."

(Well, maybe it on rare occasion, it doesn't live up to its billing but this was not one of those nights.)

"If you're excited, I'm excited."

(Well you're wise because given all of my experience, if I'm excited about something I've heard, then it was something worth being excited about. For the record, I wouldn't describe myself as excited so much as content. Still, praise is praise.)

"Hey, Craig, I'm gonna watch most of the encore from up there near the hallway so I can get back out to the lot and do my thing. But thank you for the ticket and the smoke and the convo."

(I hope to see you out there down the road. Quick game before you go?)

"Well…"

(Look over there. The fourteen-year-old-kid in the dye with his parents, are they older Heads reliving their youths with their youth? Are they people who saw the band a few times in the '60s or early '70s and thought it would be a hoot to check them out again? Or are they bored drones slumming from the suburbs with their neo-hippie kid? And if they *have* been to shows before, when was their first and how many have they seen?)

"Ummm…"

(Cogitate on that when the band comes back out and we can pick it up next time. I always enjoy spending time with the next generation of Heads, it leaves me optimistic for the future. I have to say, the music does too. This tour has been sponsored by 'Let It Grow' and 'Terrapin' and that's a beautiful place to be.)

"Right on!"

(Here they come, you wanna guess?)

"I don't enjoy that game as much as you do. I prefer to keep my mind blank."

(Well you excel at it.)

"Thanks?"

(That might have come out harsher than it was intended. I was funning around.)

"I just prefer to have no expectations."

(I'll take my cue from that and go with The Stones. I'll guess 'The Last Time' again. 'The Last Time' again, get it…)

"I think—"

(And I'll be wrong. Whoa, I'll amend my guess to 'Sugar Magnolia' because that's what it is. Can you hear that in the tuning? 'Sugar Mags,' I don't think we've had a full-on 'Sugar Magnolia' encore since my magical '85. I like it when they keep us on our toes.)

"I'm with you there. Everything's an experience. That's why I'm out here. I try to take inspiration from the Boys. You know what they say, 'Never play it the same way…once.'"

STELLA BLUE

(Where have you two been? You missed the entire set. And, Alison, my dear, this was the set for you… 'Box of Rain,' sweet, sweet 'China Doll,' 'Morning Dew…')

('Morning Dew?')

(It was poetry at the end.)

"Mommy, the Dead aren't playing anymore."

(I see that, honey.)

"Then how come everyone is still clapping?"

(Because if we stand here and clap loud enough then the Dead will play one more song.)

(Sort of like in *Peter Pan* when everyone claps for Tinkerbell. If you believe in Jerries, then clap your hands.)

"Aunt Jenneeee!"

(What? What? There wasn't a swear in there, I swear.)

"Nope."

(Then why did you Aunt Jenny me?)

"You're silly."

(That I am. Although your mom doesn't seem to appreciate it. Alison, I'm sorry, I did mean to gloat about the 'Dew.')

(That's not it. I am just so burned up about these security a-holes—Stella, that one slides by on a technicality. I just—)

"Look, the Grateful Dead, Mommy!"

(There they are and—wow, 'Sugar Magnolia.' Now that's a sweet one. Stella, you know this song.)

"I do, Mommy."

(Do you want to stand on your chair?)

"Uh-huh!"

(Alright then. Enough talking about security, let's just sit back and listen to the music play.)

"But I thought you said I could stand, Mommy."

(The kid's got spunk but she's got to brush up on her lyrics. Stella, your mom's quoting 'Franklin's Tower' back at you. That's it. No more disappearing during the second sets for you. You really need to—"

"'—tend the meetings. I know, Aunt Jenny, I know."

ROBIN

"Sweet sweet set. Running in to see..."

(Me tooooo.)

"Everyone. Look at everyone."

(Lights, lighters…lighters, lights)
"Whahooooooo!"
(Yahheeeeeeeeeeeh!)
"Vavoooooooom!"
(Jeereeeeeeeeh!)
"Buhbuh-beeeeeeeee!"
(There. There they are.)
"They're ba-ack."
(Uh-huh.)
"Uh-huh. Nice Dew Jer, nice Dew."
(Uhhhh-huuuhhh nice Dew, Jer. Nice hair-doooooooo!)
"Hahhahahaaa… What?… Sugarmags! SUGAR MAGS!"
(Sugar Mags! YEahaaahaaahhhhh!)
"Back out! Move back out!"
(Back back back!)
"Sugar Mags. Sugar Mags. Su-gar Mags."
(Sweet sweet sweet.)
"Sugar is sweet. Sugar is sweet."
(The Sweetest.)

RANDY

Schultz is off with waiting with the beer.

There's Davis idling outside the admin office on his ridiculous golf cart.

Time to make my move.

"Excuse me, sir."

(You!)

"Listen, I want you to know that I certainly appreciate that you feel I was disrespectful to you. And I also want you to know that I sincerely apologize for anything I said to you that was untrue.)

(Thank you…)

"Ellis."

(Thank you, Ellis)

"I also have a particular respect for the military, because a football squad is something like an army platoon. And while I haven't served, I do know some men who have. I think of American heroes like John Winger and Russell Ziskey who earned their stripes and I salute them. Anyhow, while I recognize you've made your decision to let me go, I hope you will stop by Mack's office. I just dropped off a pint of small batch Kentucky bourbon and three boxes of Girl Scout cookies for the two of you to enjoy and possibly reconsider my situation."

(I don't cotton to disrespect.)

"I can understand that."

(Not here and not on the football field. Disrespect will receive no housewarming party in either venue.)

"Agreed."

(So I make no promises about reassessing your situation.)

"I understand."

(But you know, Ellis, it's been long day, and at the very least I promise to receive your offering in the spirit with which it was intended.)

"That's all I can ask."

(So why don't you stop by after the parking lots clear out and we can continue our parley.)

"Why thank you, sir"

Keep walking…keep walking…keep walking…a bit faster… keep walking…Boom!

Sucker!
Key's still in it!
Gotta motor!

TAPER TED

Rez. Tommy.

"The Gang's all here!"

(I wouldn't quite call us gang, we're more of a pep squad.)

"Little brother, I rarely find you peppy."

(Then how about this…Kind show, big bro. Kind burrito show. Or should I say killer? I'll never get the lingo down.)

"You actually do seem chipper. What happened ?"

(Tommy made a friend.)

"Let's hope it wasn't a fourteen-year-old. It wasn't a fourteen-year-old was it?"

(Please give me some credit. It was a fourteen-year-old's mom.)

"Noohhh."

(Yes.)

(Yes.)

(She was everything I like in a woman. That ideal mix of beauty, brains and unabashed contempt for most of what she sees.)

"I hope you didn't do anything stupid that might hurt Rez—"

(He was fine.)

(I was fine. Which reminds me, when I was on my way down here, I saw a few folks writing SSDD on their setlists. What was that?)

"Sunshine Daydream. It's the epilogue to 'Sugar Magnolia.'"

(Ahh, I assumed it was same shit different day, which sounds a bit defeatist but that can be my motto for tomorrow.)

"So you'll coming back tomorrow? I wasn't quite sure if you'd be on the bus or off the bus."

(I don't know about any bus but I'll be in the luxury suite. Free drinks and hors d'oeuvres. And you know me, I can be something of a hors for the d'oeuvres. Although they did have some chafing dishes with little Grateful Dead insignias on them.)

(Stealies.)

(Which felt a bit like warning labels. Good grub though in spite of it.)

(Speaking of dishes, my darling husband…)

"That's a weak segue but you've earned the right to gloat."

(You must be off your game, hon, I can't remember another tour where I've clinched so early.)

(And what game is that?)

"It's our setlist prognostication series—and don't say 'You can't be serious!'"

(Okay, Groucho.)

Oh crap.

There he is.

Just when things were back where they should be.

And I still haven't spoken with Rez about this.

(What's wrong big bro, you seem agitated. I was comparing you to a Marx Brother and not even Zeppo, who I think was the handsome one but his name always reminds me a big gassy balloon, so I'll toss that in as a sideways insult.)

"Listen, Rez, can you break down my gear, there's someone over there I have to speak with. Tommy, can you go with her? I just need a moment."

(Who? That guy over there?)

"Tommy, please don't point."

(Point at him?)

"Tommy, come on, I told you, this is something private."

(Okay then, big bro. Calm yourself down. Let me see a *blank* expression on your face.)

"I'll do what I can."

(Just be zen about it. Have your brain create a *blank* canvas.)

"Why do I have the feeling you're trying to tell me something?"

(Because your mind has gone *blank*?)

"Tommy!"

(Take it easy on me. If you really want me out of your prematurely receding hair you're going to have to write me a *blank* check."

"TOMMY!"

(Don't push me too far, don't make me resort to…wait for it…wait for it…)

"Blankmail."

(You didn't wait for it.)

(Ted…)

(Mitch.)

(Ted…)

(Reg…)

(Ted…)

(Rez…)

(Taper Ted, welcome to April Fools' Day, Deadhead style.)

"But it's March twenty-ninth."

(That's why it's Deadhead style. We're never on time. Usually we're late. But sometimes we're early because Deadheads are space cases and time is an illusion anyhow.)

"So what's the story with Chuck?"

(We'll explain it all outside. There's still some of this we need to keep close to the vest.)

(Which may be challenge for you big bro, because your vest doesn't quite fit the way it should. But as your doctor…)

ZEB

(Hey, wait, hold on, hold on!)

"Craig, I gotta haul ass out to the lot…"

(I know, I just wanna go on the record and apologize if I oversold '85. Sometimes that's how it goes. Richmond '85 was my first show, so sometimes, I go a little over the top with my praise. Especially after burning some of my heroic hoobah.)

"No, no. You know of what you speak. I've heard that show…"

(Yeah, like I said, I don't think I fully appreciated it until a few years later. I bet the same thing will happen to you, when you've been out here a bit longer.)

"Right on."

(I also want you to know I'm rethinking my first Jerry question too. Maybe I don't need to start off with something quite so calculated or maybe my calculations are off and I should get right to the meat and potatoes, or the 'Stephen' and the 'Cryptical,' as it were.)

"Right on."

(So you'll be out there tomorrow?)

"Out there is where I will be."

(Look for me. If we see each other, I might even be able to kick you a ticket. Not the lame seat you traded me but another sweet one by my side. The envelope art did it again. Saturday night I'm seventh row.)

"If you already have Saturday seats then why'd you want to trade with me in the first place?"

(I had an extra ticket for tonight and I wanted the company. It's happened a couple times before. What I've come to learn is that someone with a Saturday ticket who understands he can make a trade is usually a Head with his head in the right space, who makes for an enjoyable show buddy. Which you did and you were. Winner winner chicken dinner.)

"Dead ahead, Craig, Dead ahead..."

ROBIN

"Sugar Mags was suh-weeeet! You okkayy?"

(Uhh-huhh. You?)

"Uhhhh-huuuhhh."

(Head out?)

"Haaaa! HEAD...OUT!!!!"

(Should weeee sitttt?)

"Uhh-huh... Kind kind Dew."

(Dooooooo!!!)

"Sweet Sugar Mags."

(Terrrrapiinn TIME!)

"Setlist. Second set. Setlist second set... First song..."

(Okay-okay. Ununmmm—)

"Right. Uhhh-it was-ummmm—"

(First soooonggg. Secondset... Ummmmm—)

(‘Box of Rain.’)
(Ahhhh… THANKYOU!)
“Second song.”
(Second… Bobby…or…Jerry?)
“Second song…”
(Hmmmmm…)
(‘Bertha.’)
“No, second set.”
(Second set.)
(‘Samson.’)
“Thank You!”
(Third song third song third song)
“Third song… Third song…‘Looks Like Rain!’”
(Ro-bin!! ‘Looks Like Rain!’)
“Yeah, Robin looks like Rain!”
(Robin looks like Rain?)
“Wet mop Head!”
(Haaaa! Lemme try some… Mmmmm tasty… Encore hair!”
“Encore hair?”
(Sugary sweet!)
“Ha!”
(And Mountain Dew-y)
“Morning Dew-y”
(Robin double Dew’d it!)
“Robin and Mara double do’d it!”
(Grateful Heads!)
“Forever! Fourth song, fourth song…”

BAGEL BOB

And so Bob returns. Back to his spot. Soliciting concertgoers.

Bob wishes he had been a concertgoer. Bob wishes he had concertwent.

"Blueberry bagels. Stella Blue-berry bagels. Consumer Reports ranks Bob's bagels as the most nutritious and scrumdelicious on tour."

(Oh man, I've been thinking about this since the second set. I was hoping I'd find you. Your bagels *are* the most nutritious and scrumdelicious on tour.)

"Bagel Bob appreciates the accolades."

(Somehow I missed you the past few nights. Come to think of it, I don't think I've seen you since all the way down at the Miami shows last year. I was feeling a little bit frisky that night and I went for the Loxy Lady. It was quite a revelation Bob. Quite a revelation.)

"Indeed."

(So what it'll be for me tonight? I really have been thinking about this since midway through the second set. I started migrating at the end of 'Sugar Mags.' I watched 'Sunshine Daydream' from the stairs thinking I'd have a better chance to find you before the congestion. I just can't tell you how good it makes me feel to see you again. You are comfort food. Hmm, maybe I should go for the Simon and Garfunkel. Then again, while I dig the parsley, sage and the rosemary, I'll end up with too much thyme on my hands.)

(Well done!)

"Ahh, now there's the answer. Something toasted. I'd like the Elvis, please. A dab of peanut butter, a dollop of honey, light on the bacon, heavy on the bananas."

"A wise selection. How was your show?"

(It was a weird one for sure. And not in all the right places, at least not at first. Odd vibrations.)

"Bob has lived that sentiment."

(It seemed that everyone was a little out of sorts, then they made some adjustments and now everything is in its place. But we'll do it all again tomorrow. That's the thrill of the game. Forget about me, how was your show?)

"A dab of confrontation with security personnel, a dollop of board games, heavy on the burlesque, a little light on the show."

(You didn't make it in?)

"It was a tough ticket."

(Tomorrow?)

"Another tough ticket."

(Not for you.)

"Alas, yes."

(No, not anymore. Thank you for my Elvis. Enjoy tomorrow night's show. Here's your money and here's a ticket. It would be an honor if you actually sit in the seat. I'd love to rap with you. That's your call, of course, but I'm a fan of your work.)

"Bob is not looking for this."

(You don't need a ticket? I'm sorry, I misunderstood.)

"No, Bob is not looking for a free ticket."

(Well that is *my* decision. It'll be a real hoot to be able to say I miracled Bagel Bob.)

"What is your name?"

(I'm Evan.)

"Well Bagel Bob thanks you, Evan. Bagel Bob is moved by your gesture. Bagel Bob will see you inside tomorrow night."

(My pleasure Bagel Bob. Remember, we are everywhere.)

"We are indeed. And Bob is truly, deeply grateful."

(No worries, Bagel Bob. No worries.)

TAPER TED

"Okay, we're out of the building, out of earshot, just who are you?"

(I'm not Chuck from Norfolk. I'm Pete from Petaluma.)

"Pete Sinnegan?"

(C'est moi.)

(You're the branch ahead of me on the Whole Earth Access tree.)

(That I am. I was going to introduce myself last night but these fine fellow tapers had other ideas.)

(I'd like to give Mitch and myself credit but really, it was Rez…)

(I figured when all was said and done, you'd appreciate a good ol' April Fool's prank in the Grateful Dead tradition. We let Tommy in on it in case he saw you interacting with Pete and involved himself in some awkward way.)

"Tommy making things awkward. Gee, I wonder how likely—"

(I was happy to be in on anything that tweaks my big bro, even if I didn't entirely understand what was going on.)

"Par for your course. Or maybe bogie. Can you be reverent about anything?"

(Believe me, it happens on occasion. One day I'll surprise you.)

(On that topic of surprising people, we'll admit, we're curious. What were you going to do? There also may have been a side bet or two along the way. Were you going to spin the tapes or risk blowing the cover?)

"Tommy, what did you say?"

(I said you're a man of integrity.)

"Appreciated… So what exactly does that mean?"

(To be honest, I'm not sure, the whole thing seemed a bit complicated. I just said you're a man of integrity because I wanted you to feel good about yourself, big bro.)

"You're sweet. But seriously…Rez?"

(Ted, it's like I explained to your brother a couple years ago when we brought our first cat into the house even though I'm allergic. Tommy said to me, 'I can't believe you got that cat for your husband,' and I told him, 'Seems like a good trade to me.')

"Lovely!"

(Sorry, I'm feeling giddy, I can't believe I clinched the setlist tourney already!)

"Anyone? Pete? Mitch?"

(If I told you all that went down it would burn off both your ears.)

"Really?"

(Now I don't know but I been told in the heat of the sun a man died of cold.)

"Really?"

(Universal Dead lyric epigrams aside, the truth, hon, is that there were no bets. We all figured that you'd be real uncomfortable when Pete turned up the heat under your stew pot but that you'd already made a promise and you'd honor that promise because that's the kind of guy you are…)

(Even if it meant that everyone out there would want your Deadhead on a platter.)

"Ha! Well you got me there. So the name Chuck from Norfolk, was there a reason you selected it? I have to admit there was something there I couldn't quite put my finger on."

(Well who is the most famous Chuck from Norfolk? Mr. Bobby Weir assumes his identity on occasion when he takes us to the…)

"'Promised Land.' Chuck Berry. And you selected that because of April first, nineteen-eighty?"

(Indeed.)

(What in tarnation is that, big bro?)

"April first, nineteen-eighty was the night when they opened the show at the Capitol Theatre in Passaic, New Jersey in true April Fool's style with a version of 'Promised Land' that had Jerry Garcia and Brent Mydland on drums, Bob Weir on keys, Phil Lesh on guitar, Bill Kreutzmann on bass and Mickey Hart on guitar and vocals."

(I thought we might be in trouble, though, when you brought up April 3, 1982 at The Scope.)

"Right, right. That's the year that the Dead's April Fool's prank took place on April second and not on April first."

(And what happened that night, big bro? Did they wear their underwear on their heads? Put toothpaste in the audience's Oreos? Did they cover all the toilet seats in the venue with plastic wrap?)

"Jerry and Phil switched sides."

(Switched sides? Switched sides on their softball teams? Switched sides on the nuclear debate? Switched sides in the Israeli–Palestinian conflict?"

"Switched sides on stage."

(Now that's a subtle joke.)

"I might have made the connection but I never had time to give it much thought with all else that was going on. Mitch, were your deck problems part of this, maybe to distract me?"

(Sadly, no. I really was kneeling over a borrowed Sony D-6, so a kid wouldn't lose his signal.)

"What about those girls who came down to the tapers' section at set break? Were they in on it somehow?"

(Equally sadly no. Your discomfort was sincerely earned.)

(As was theirs.)

"Heaven help the fool."

STELLA BLUE

(This way, you two.)

(Are sure, Jen, I thought we parked over—)

(What do you take me for? I haven't been to a show for a little while I grant you, as the great state of New York had other plans for me but I have never made a tactical error when it comes to finding my vehicle after a show.)

(Two words: Buckeye Lake.)

(Well, okay once. That was the night I learned my lesson. Remember when we finally found our car in that corner lot across the street…)

(And we were so hemmed in that you literally fell asleep behind the wheel, woke up and we had moved one car length.)

(If that. Those were the days… A mistake I will not make again. So please trust me, it's this way. And not to be too heavy-handed with the word mistake but what the hell happened to the two of you?)

"Aunt Jennneeee!"

(Nice to see you're still with us, Stella.)

(It was an epic catastrophe with a happy ending. Let's just say that tomorrow night I'm keeping Stell on a short leash.)

"Mommeeee!"

(Not literally. Although I have seen it done.)

(Well, Alison, you deserve a beverage for your troubles.)

"Meeee tooooo?"

(Up to your mom. Here's a guy. How much?)

"Domestics a buck, nice cold tasty imports a deuce. Soda too. How about a Mountain Dew to go with that 'Morning Dew.' Just Dew it."

(Two Dews for the 'Dew.')

(Can do.)

(Here you go, Al, sorry you missed the song. I do have a consolation prize though, this lovely soda.)

(I don't need a consolidation prize. I may have missed the 'Dew' but I found myself an angel. A Stell Belle of my very own.)

(Where was she?)

(Some security office. Indoor arena staff, not yellow jackets. Can we talk about something more pleasant? Are there other groups you've been aching to see?)

(I've been hearing a bit about the Allman Brothers Band. They've just started touring again with this young guitarist who's apparently on fire. He was in the Dickey Betts Band for a while. The guy next to me was talking them up during set break. Apparently they have a new album coming out, so that's a good sign.)

(I like it. The Brothers. See, you're not the only one making a comeback.)

(What do you say, Stella, do you want to come with us and see the Brothers?"

"The brothers?"

(Yes, my darling daughter, what do you think of the brothers?)

"The brothers? Why are they in bread?"

(What?)

"Why are the brothers in bread?"

(Why are the brothers inbred?)

(Why do you say that?)

"Ernie and Berp on Sesame Street. Why are they in bread?"

(Jenny, tomorrow night we're heading in early. I am suddenly eager to have a conversation with arena management. Plus that way I'm hoping we'll make it inside with a little less congestion and simulated overpopulation. What you do say to that, Stella?)

"A Dew for the 'Dew'?"

(Well played, little girl.)

RANDY

"CLEAR OUT OF MY WAY! CLEAR OUT OF MY WAY!

"I NEED A DEAD MED! I NEED A DEAD MED!

"I HAVE A SEVERELY INJURED PERSON WITH ME IN THIS CART!

"I NEED A DEAD MED, I NEED A DEAD MED!"

(Hold on, hold on I'm Dead Med. Well, I'm a Deadhead and a doctor. How can I help?)

(*You're* a Deadhead?)

(No time, big bro. Let me take a look at him. Ted, can you run to the car and grab my bag. Hustle! What happened to him?)

"He was hit from behind. I saw it go down, I saw *him* go down. He hit his head on the edge of a car before he landed. I wasn't so sure about moving him because of the way he fell. He just didn't look right. But I didn't want to leave him there."

(How long ago would you say this happened?)

"About a half hour, maybe a little less."

(Okay let's gently raise his legs in the air. What's your name?)

"Randy."

(Can you hold his legs like that for a little while, Randy? It appears he's gone into a mild shock, he feels a bit clammy.)

"Can do."

(I'm going to take off his shoes and we'll see how responsive he is. Over here, Ted! Come on!… Well, there doesn't appear to be a major spinal injury which is obviously a great sign. Once my brother gets over here with my bag, we'll be able to learn a little more, but I have a feeling that this guy going is going to owe you a debt of gratitude.)

STEVEN

Uhhhh…

(Who are you? What your name? What happened?)

"Su-St-Steven."

(Saint Stephen, huh?)

"Su-Spelled different."

(Okay, well at least you can still spell. That's a good sign even though someone did a number on you and then it sounds like you clipped your head on a car. Ted, can you help me, keep a compress right here?)

(Will do.)

(He doesn't look so good and certainly doesn't smell so good but I think he's going to be fine. You're going to be fine. Some scars and a rager of a headache but you'll be okay.)

"Suhloney"

(What's that?)

"Solonely."

(Nah that's a Police song. No police here, just the Grateful Dead. And us Deadheads. You should be glad we've met because my big bro here, Taper Ted, is going to hook you up with tapes of tonight's show, tomorrow night's show, maybe all the shows. Right, Taper Ted?)

(Well—)

"Th-thanks."

(Yeah, Steven, he's got you covered. We've got you covered. We're family here. All of us. Remember that. We're Deadheads. We are everywhere.)

ZEB

The foot traffic's really picking up.

"Nice cold tasty imports. Domestics a buck, imports two. Nothing better than washing down that 'Sugar Magnolia' with a nice cold tasty import. Kind Beck's. I've got your kind Beck's.

Soda too. How about a Mountain Dew to go with that 'Morning Dew'? Just Dew it."

Another show. With the "Dew." There should be a star after all the shows I've seen with a "Dew."

"Nice cold tasty imports. Domestics a buck, imports two. Kind Bud-weiser. Kind Beck's… Yeah, just reach in there and take one yourself. Whichever one calls out to you. There you go."

There's another sale, something to put towards tomorrow's ticket. Tough ticket too. One More Saturday Night.

They're gonna be scarce. Gotta get started early.

Seventh row, Craig side would be right on for sure but nothing's ever guaranteed, especially out here with the Jersey devils.

"Kind Bud-weiser. Kind Beck's. Domestics a buck, nice cold tasty imports a deuce. And I need one. I need one ticket for tomorrow."

Making my move, could get lucky while I'm earning my tour. Then I gotta find somewhere to crash and something to eat.

Because tomorrow's another dawn.

Another day of the Dead.

I'll be out here.

Might as well.

Acknowledgments

The inspiration for this book was the announcement of the summer 2015 Fare Thee Well shows. The pairing of Trey Anastasio with the Grateful Dead Core Four brought things full circle, as I thought back to the late eighties and a period of time when I would catch my fair share of Grateful Dead and Phish shows (even if at that time each fanbase could be somewhat contemptuous of the other). As I reflected on that era, I recalled not only that dark night at the Brendan Byrne Arena on October 14, 1989 when Adam Katz lost his life, but the totality of my experience on tour reveling in the music and experiencing America during a singular moment of social and cultural history.

I wish to thank agent Paul Lucas (who I later met in Chicago at Fare Thee Well) for suggesting Tyson Cornell and Rare Bird as the ideal home for *Might As Well.* Alice Marsh-Elmer, Julia Callahan, and Winona Leon were supportive throughout the process, as were my dandy and delightful wife and kids, Leanne, Caroline, and Quinn. *Relix* was important to me during the era in which this book takes place, just as it is now. Above all else, a special thanks to everyone who shared a show with me and offered help on the way, in particular my late sister Stacy. *Sometimes the songs that we hear are just songs of our own...*

Dean Budnick is the editor-in-chief of *Relix* magazine and the coauthor of John Popper's autobiography *Suck and Blow: And other Stories I'm Not Supposed to Tell.* Budnick is the founder of jambands.com, cocreator of the Jammy Awards, and director of the documentary *Wetlands Preserved: The Story of an Activist Rock Club*, which earned film festival laurels, opened nationally via First Run Features, and then aired on the Sundance Channel. His previous books include *Ticket Masters: The Rise of the Concert Industry and How the Public Got Scalped*, *Jambands,* and *The Phishing Manual.* He has written for *The Hollywood Reporter* and *Billboard* and for many years cohosted *Jam Nation*, a radio show that aired weekly on SiriusXM. Budnick, who holds a PhD from Harvard's History of American Civilization program and a JD from Columbia Law School, also teaches in the history department at the University of Rhode Island.

CPSIA information can be obtained
at www.ICGtesting.com
Printed in the USA
FSOW02n0231030316
17554FS